*Dear Anna,*

*A novel by Mia Mandala*

*A note to the reader...*

*Dear Anna,* is a book that deals with lots of important, yet difficult topics. Some of these trigger warnings include: self harm, suicide, and sexual assault.

Copyright © 2025 Mia Mandala
All rights reserved.

Published in the United States by Kindle Direct Publishing

Cover design by: Makaela Johansen

ISBN: 979-8-9988126-0-6

This book is a work of fiction. Names, characters, places, events, and businesses are either products of the author's imagination or are used fictitiously. Any resemblance to actual persons, places or events is purely coincidental.

No part of this book may be reproduced, or stored in a retrieval system, or transmitted in any form or by any means, electronic, mechanical, photocopying, recording, or otherwise, without express written permission of the publisher.

*To my best friend*, Paloma, without you I wouldn't have known how to write about true friendships.

*And to my mom,* for creating my love of books, without you this book wouldn't have been a possibility.

# PART ONE

# 1

## September 2017

*L*ife is so bland.

I'm sitting in math class, mindlessly staring outside through a sliver of a window when it dawns on me.

*This is why so many teenagers hate their lives.*

When I really take a step back and look at my life from a distance, everything just seems so painfully dull. I wake up, go to school, sit in the same freezing classrooms for hours on end with teachers who look almost as miserable as their students, and with kids who hate mostly everyone, till summer comes around.

But by then no one has any motivation to even *try* to have fun. It's way too hot to go outside, and like clockwork school starts back up again before you even realize it. Once you finish with that *exhausting* cycle you eventually have to live like an actual person. Get a job and a car, deal with taxes and all that shit. The whole thought of it is enough to put me to sleep.

I know that's a bit of a dark way to look at life.

But, it's hard to stay positive when my whole life feels like a black and white photo I could toss in the trash without another thought.

*Tick*

    *Tick*

*Tick*

The large clock on the wall ticks away the seconds, the minutes, till we can leave this mind melting class. My teacher's voice has slowly become a blur of static sound in the background, and I've found that rhythmically tapping my pencil along the side of my desk has become far more entertaining than learning algebra.

*Scratch*

    *Scratch*

*Scratch*

The girl a few desks to the right of me, Isabelle, furiously fills her notebook with as many notes as possible. I can hear the scratches of her pencil against the paper from way over here. Honestly, I feel pretty bad for her. Everyone loves to make fun of her because she's the "teacher's pet." I don't even think she's a teacher's pet, she just *actually* turns her work in on time and manages to get decent grades.

It's not her fault we're all so stupid.

*Tap*

MIA MANDALA | *Dear Anna,*

*Tap*
*Tap*

Anxious teens tap their feet up and down on the ground, eventually sounding like tiny drums in the back of my mind. One girl is tapping her fingers along the desk, while the boy next to her taps his leg up and down. When I listen close enough their taps start sounding like a song of its own.

*Talk*
*Talk*
*Talk*

Alex and Dylan, the class clowns, are hiding in the back of the class blabbering away about things only they find funny. Our teacher has now threatened to separate them twice if they keep talking, and I can feel a third and *final* warning coming soon.

My eyes dart back to the clock.

*Tick*

Two minutes left. The teacher makes her final statements about the lesson.

*Tick*

One minute. Everyone quickly and noisily packs up their bags, the sound of zippers filling up the room.

*Tick*

The bell sounds its alarm, and in a matter of seconds everyone has piled out of class barely leaving our teacher with enough time to say goodbye.

MIA MANDALA | *Dear Anna,*

I hurry out of my class, and am greeted by my friend Emma, hovering outside the door. We both share the same second period so Emma has gotten into the habit of walking with me to class everyday.

Although, she's managed to make it seem more like a chore than a nice gesture.

We both smile at each other, not bothering to take the energy to say "*Hi.*" Emma starts walking down the hall, and I follow quietly behind. "How was science? Did Mrs. B. assign anything new?" I ask her, trying to spark up a conversation.

She looks at me for a second, "It was fine," then continues walking. She spends the rest of the walk to class not speaking, not even looking at me.

*I wonder if I just stopped walking if she would turn around to see where I had gone.*

I have to practically push past people just to walk forward a few feet. Large groups of girls crowd the halls, whispering and laughing obnoxiously, oblivious to anyone but themselves. A couple boys stand around my classroom's door, and it takes everything in me not to roll my eyes at them. Even when I attempt to open the door, they barely move an inch out of the way, making me squeeze past them.

When I finally get to class, I take a seat at my desk across from Emma. We make meaningless conversation until her new best friend, Nicolle, walks in. And, like always, all the attention shifts over to her.

"Oh my god, Em! Did you see the new kid Rayan? He's literally *SO* hot, I've been trying to get his number from someone all day!" Nicolle exclaims, with her over-the-top valley girl accent that seems to only come out when she talks about something exciting.

Emma laughs, "What happened to the last guy you thought was *SO* hot?" a hint of teasing in her tone.

Nicolle laughs at Emma's comment. Since I'm sitting right next to them, I take it as my chance to be involved in their conversation. "Do you have a photo of him?" I ask Nicolle excitedly.

Before she has a chance to reply, Emma turns around to face me. "No, she doesn't," she replies bluntly, immediately turning her back to me again. Nicolle and Emma giggle, and I turn as far away from them as possible.

Not long after, our teacher walks in and begins explaining our upcoming assigned reading for the week. I try paying attention, but by the end my eyes have glazed over the whiteboard and I'm totally zoned out.

I glance back to Emma and Nicolle who are both nodding along to the teacher, taking notes with their perfectly neat handwriting. Everyone around me seems so perfectly tuned into what they are learning. I wonder what would happen if I just stood up and walked out of class.

*Would anyone chase after me?*
*Would anyone even notice?*
*Would anyone even care?*

MIA MANDALA | *Dear Anna,*

  I love spending my time in class fantasizing about what it would be like to *actually* run away, even if for just a day. I think it would be quite fun.

  The rest of the period continues on mundanely, and nothing particularly interesting stands out to me. Things rarely do.

  I wish I could pinpoint when I stopped looking forward to going to school, although I guess from the start I was never its biggest fan.

# 2
## September 2nd, 2014
*Three years ago*

*I*t was my first day of middle school and I was absolutely terrified. My hands were shaking from nervousness as I walked into my first class of the day, following closely behind Anna.

A tall, red-headed teacher in a flowy sundress greeted us as we walked in, and asked for our names. She seemed fairly friendly, and had a warm smile that helped ease my nerves. "I'm Anna and ..." Anna said as she turned around, pointing to me while I stood quietly behind her, "... her name is Missy."

The teacher nodded, "Perfect. I'm Mrs. Towers, I'll be your English teacher for the school year. You girls can go sit at that table back there."

She pointed to a table in the back corner of the room, where a meek little girl with long dark hair sat by herself. Her head was down on the table, and if I didn't know better I would have thought she was asleep. "That's Emma, she just moved here. I think you guys will be very good friends," she said with a wink. We nodded our heads and smiled, walking over to the table.

Anna and I took seats on either side of Emma, placing our bags down under us. The girl slowly put her head up, allowing me to get a better view of what she looked like. She was much paler than Anna and me, and had pin straight black hair. Deep green eyes popped out from behind her thick eyelashes, and a couple small freckles ran along her face.

Anna took the lead in introducing herself, and I followed.

"I'm Emma," the girl told us, her voice so quiet I wouldn't have understood if Mrs. Towers hadn't already told us her name.

Class started, and the three of us sat there in an awkward silence as our teacher started explaining what the class curriculum would be like. "I will be your first class every day, so you will always report here in the morning. Then I will take attendance ..." Hearing her explain everything brought back my previous nerves and I got the sudden urge to just run out of the classroom as quickly as I could. I scanned the class, and noticed one thing that helped calm my nerves.

*Everyone* looked nervous.

At least I wasn't the only one looking scared out of my mind.

"I know starting middle school can seem intimidating at first, but it is important you take advantage of the time you have before high school. Right now your fellow students may not seem like anything more than unfamiliar faces ... but who knows? Maybe one day they will be your lifelong friends! Personally, many of my closest friends are people I met in middle school," our teacher happily explained.

I looked around the room, observing the different kids around me. Many of them I couldn't ever imagine being good friends with, let alone "lifelong" friends.

My head turned back to Anna.

Anna, of course, was different.

We *would* be best friends forever, I was sure of it.

I didn't feel the need for any more friends when I had someone as amazing as Anna as my best friend.

Mrs. Towers began explaining further on, "For the remainder of class, I want you all to take some time to get to know each other better. Branch out, talk to the people at your table, introduce yourselves, whatever you feel comfortable with."

Emma, Anna, and I all turned to each other, not quite sure what to say. I looked to Anna for help. Anna was typically the social butterfly when it came to new people, so I sat beside her quietly till I got more comfortable. She just shrugged at me, and stayed silent.

"Not helpful," I playfully mouthed back to her. She rolled her eyes exaggeratedly in response.

"So Emma—" Anna started, quickly getting cut off mid-sentence.

"Call me Em," Emma said sharply. Anna gave me a funny smile, and I had to stifle back a laugh.

"Okay. So, Em ... how do you like living here?"

Emma looked up from the table. "It's nice, I guess," she said quietly then immediately looked back down. She reached down into her bag, and took out a pen and pencil. She started drawing little doodles of stars, flowers, and swirls in the margins of a notebook. Never looking up at us, or even acknowledging our presence.

Anna looked at me with a shrug as if to say, *I tried.* I sighed, laying my head down on top of the table. Anna drew little hearts all over her hands, and Emma continued doodling on.

I looked up to the clock, wishing it would tick faster. If today was this awkward I couldn't begin to imagine how the rest of the year would go. I closed my eyes and tried to figure out the nicest way I could ask Emma to switch seats with me so I'd be next to Anna.

"Do you guys want to come over to my house this weekend?" Emma abruptly asked, breaking the silence.

*No,* I thought to myself. *No. I definitely do not want to go to your house this weekend, I want to stay in, sleep, and watch movies with Anna this weekend.*

"Yeah sure! That sounds fun," Anna exclaimed. Anna's enthusiastic personality was always something I admired about her, but right now I wished she would have just stayed quiet.

I gave her a quick look from across the table, but she didn't seem to notice.

The bell rang not long after, and Mrs. Towers made sure we were all okay with finding our way to our next class.

"Bye!" Anna yelled to Emma, as we parted ways with her in the hall.

Once I knew we were out of earshot from Emma, I turned to Anna, "Why did you agree to go to her house? We barely know her."

Anna shrugged. "I don't know. I didn't want to be rude," she explained. I'm about to say more but Anna continued, "And anyway, I like Em. She seems cool."

I laughed, "How could you tell? She barely spoke more than a sentence!"

"Not sure. I just could," Anna said mysteriously before turning around and walking into her class.

I walked a few rooms down, still not understanding what Anna saw in her. But if Anna liked her, I was sure I would too.

# 3
# September 2017

*I* get home from school a few hours later. I kick my shoes off into the bin and make my way to my room, fully ready to nap till dinner. My mom stands in front of my door, blocking my way. "Hi Mom," I say, reaching for my doorknob. She lifts my hand up, and starts leading me to the living room.

"What?" I ask. She doesn't reply till I'm sitting down on the couch while she and my dad remain standing, hovering over me.

"So Missy ..." my dad begins, "Anna's parents invited us over for dinner tonight and—"

"What?" I felt *frozen*.

It was all I could say.

"Why were you talking to them?" I ask with my heart in my throat.

MIA MANDALA | *Dear Anna,*

My mom looks taken aback. "Well, they've always been our good friends," she says defensively. "And anyway, I think it would be good for you. I mean you haven't even mentioned Anna since ..."

Suddenly, as if the name of someone was enough to drown you, *Anna* was currently suffocating me.

"Stop talking about her. I'm not going to any dinner," I tell them and start to walk away, not wanting to say anymore.

My decision is final.

My mom follows behind me and turns me around. "Really Missy? C'mon, it can't hurt to at least go over for a little. Say hi, we can all catch up."

"Stop talking about her."

*I can't breathe.*

*I'm drowning.*

My dad starts again, "Missy please, you know your mother and I have been talking about this and ever since—"

*I won't let him finish that sentence.*

"Stop *fucking* talking about Anna!"

*I need to get out of this house.*

*Right. Now.*

"Missy!" my mother screams. "You have no right to talk to us like that!" They both walk closer to me, continuing to scold me.

"I'll stop talking like this when you stop talking about her," I tell them, getting right up in their faces.

My dad scoffs, rolling his eyes. "Missy, this has gone way too far—"

"I'm not going to the dinner!" I scream it right in their faces, and I don't regret it for a second.

*I'm suffocating.*

*I'm drowning.*

*I. Need. To. Get. Out. Of. This. House.*

"Missy!" they scream, both inching closer to my face.

"I'M GETTING OUT OF THIS HOUSE!" I scream as loud as I can in their faces, pushing past them to get to the front door.

The next moments feel as if someone has taken over my body. I'm not sure what I'm doing until I find myself biking down the road as fast as my body lets me. I have no real destination in mind, but I know I can't bear being in that house any longer.

I keep biking, turning, going faster, farther and farther away from my house till it is nothing more than a speck in the distance.

I come to a sudden halt in front of the local park. The park is full of different kinds of trees, with a giant lake right in the center of it all. I want to keep biking, but my body feels like it will collapse if I go any further. I go to wipe my hair out of my face when I realize how hard I have been crying. I can only imagine the amount of mascara that now lays smudged across my face.

# MIA MANDALA | *Dear Anna,*

I walk down toward the lake and sit by the edge of it. The ground around me is filled with small pebbles and I run my hand through them. One by one I pick them up, throwing them into the lake with as much force as possible.

My mind is racing, but I am *completely* still.

It's like being in the middle of a crowded carnival. Bright lights and loud noises coming from everywhere, but you are there standing quiet and alone. Thousands of people surrounding you, screaming, crying, laughing.

*But you are completely still.*

You are in the eye of the hurricane.

# 4

## April 2nd, 2012

*Five years and five months ago*

*T*he first time I met Anna I *hated* her. It was early spring break, and my parents had invited a few close friends over for dinner. I was especially excited to meet the new family my dad kept telling me about. He met the dad during a work trip, and they became close not long after, and when he told me he had a daughter around my age, I couldn't contain my excitement.

 I ran out of my room the second I heard the doorbell ring. I wore my newest dress and had my hair braided into messy pigtails.

 My parents were busy setting up the table, but turned to give me their nod of approval to unlock the door.

I opened the door and was greeted by Miles and Laurie Williams. Behind them, a small girl hid quietly behind her mom's legs. Our parents said their "hellos" and hugged each other as they walked inside.

Laurie nudged her daughter slightly in my direction, and I got a better look at her. She had on a cute yellow dress, similar to mine, and her long blonde locks were brushed out neatly, shining in the sun.

I ran up to the little girl, and greeted her just like my parents had taught me to. "Hi! I'm Mi—"

"Okay," the girl said, cutting me off. I opened my mouth to ask her for her name, but before I was able to, she walked right past me.

*What was her problem?*

We followed our families into the kitchen and I watched as she once again tried hiding behind her mom. Laurie grabbed Anna's hand, and pushed her toward me slightly, taking the lead in her introduction.

"Missy, this is Anna. Your parents tell me you two are in the same grade!" I nodded my head excitingly, but Anna didn't have much of a reaction.

More and more of my parents' friends arrived, as my mom began setting the table full of food. The adults all sat down, and Anna and I sat all the way at the end, across from each other.

"I like your dress!" I told Anna, and for a second I thought she smiled. The rest of the dinner was spent in complete silence between me and Anna. If there hadn't been a bunch of adults at the table with us, the room would have been dead silent. Occasionally I looked up at Anna, trying to think of things to say but her eyes were always down, her expression never changing.

*I couldn't wait for this dinner to be over with.*

"Missy, why don't you go and show Anna your room?" That was code for "*Give us adults some alone time,*" in my dad's words. I knew it would be rude to do otherwise, but I really did not want Anna coming into my room. Nevertheless, I nodded to my dad and showed Anna where my room was.

I walked right in, flopping onto my bed. Anna walked in slowly after me, looking around carefully. I saw her face light up when she spotted the record player on my desk. It was nothing fancy, and was in desperate need of a new needle, but my parents had gotten it for me a few Christmases ago. "This is so cool!" she said, tracing her fingers over the side of it.

"Thanks," I said, not knowing what more to say.

"Do you have a lot of records?" she asked, and I nodded my head.

"Yeah, right over there is where I keep them all." I stood up slowly, showing her the case with all the records I had collected over the past years. I moved hesitantly, still unsure of what she thought of me.

Her smile continued to grow bigger and brighter as I showed her the different records I owned.

"Can I play one?" I nodded my head, and she smiled wide in excitement. Anna shuffled quietly through my collection of vinyls, silently reading the album names to herself, and smiling when she recognized one. "This one looks fun," she decided, pulling out the last one in the box. The record was almost completely dark blue, and I didn't realize what it was till she set it on the record player and the music started playing. It was mainly an acoustic song, with a woman singing something about the ocean. It wasn't from any band I recognized in particular, but the memory of when I bought it was so distinct in my mind, it felt like it just happened yesterday.

My dad had just picked me up from school when we drove by one of our neighbors having a huge garage sale. It intrigued me, so my dad let us stop and look at it for a few minutes. When we actually started looking at stuff, I realized it wasn't all that interesting, and the most I found were old picture frames or dusty vases. But just as we were getting in the car my dad told me, "Hold out your hands, and close your eyes." I did as he said, and when I opened them I was holding a deep blue record by some band I didn't know.

Nevertheless, I *loved* it.

Anna seemed to also.

She sat cross-legged on my floor, swaying side to side to the sound of the music. For a moment I just watched her, wondering how someone could look as utterly peaceful as she did. Her eyes were closed, and her hand laid softly by her side.

I just had to ask.

"Anna?"

"Hmm?" she asked, her eyes slowly opening back up.

"Uhh ..." I started to regret even asking, realizing now how silly the question will seem. "Do you not like me?" I finally asked.

Her eyes widened, and her jaw dropped. "What?!" she exclaimed. "You thought I didn't like you?"

I laughed, seeing how poor my judgment was. "I don't know! It seemed like all night you didn't want to talk to me," I admitted.

Anna looked to the floor and laughed. "Want me to be honest?" I nodded my head.

"I was scared of you."

Now it was my turn to laugh.

"What! Why?" We both laughed.

"Honestly you just seemed really cool and I wanted you to like me," Anna explained, and I don't think either of our smiles could have grown any bigger then.

"You thought I was cool?"

"Yes!" Anna said, her cheeks turning red from embarrassment.

"I thought *you* were cool!" I admitted.

"Well I guess this just means we are *both* very cool!" Anna said, dramatically flipping her hair behind her. We fell into a fit of giggles, all of the previous tension and nervousness nowhere to be seen.

*I could really imagine being good friends with her.*

I searched my room for things we could do together, now that I knew she didn't despise me. I spotted an old friendship bracelet kit tucked in the back of my closet. "Do you know how to make friendship bracelets?" I asked her. As if on cue, she raised up her arm to reveal three intricately designed friendship bracelets, all different colors and patterns. I laughed, "Did you make all of those yourself?"

She nodded her head, "Yep! I can teach you if you want!" she offered, and I nodded my head.

We spent the next few hours laughing, talking, and sitting on my bedroom floor making as many bracelets as we possibly could. We realized how much we had in common, and talking with her felt like I was talking to someone I had known my whole life. Eventually her parents had to come up to take her home. We both begged and begged until they caved in and let her stay the night.

My parents let us sleep in the living room, and we built a giant pillow fort to sleep in. I brought flashlights in from the garage, and we filled the fort full of pillows and snacks. We stayed up till 11 playing card games, and when we started feeling sleepy we binge-watched one of our favorite tv shows.

"Missy." Anna and I were tucked away into our sleeping bags, our eyes getting droopy, both on the verge of falling asleep.

I was facing away from her, but rolled over when I heard her whisper my name. "Yeah?"

"I think we're going to be best friends," she said with a smile.

I returned the smile and nodded. "I think so too," I answered sleepily, and then we both drifted off to sleep.

# 5
## September 2017

"*H*elloooo! Are you dead?" I feel something kicking my side, and I rub my eyes open. Almost screaming from shock, I am greeted by a teenage boy towering over me. "Oh. You're alive," he says, stretching out his hand to me.

"Wha—?" It takes me a moment to regain consciousness and remember what I am doing here. I look up to the boy, taking his hand. "What time is it?" I ask, standing up with his help.

He looks down at his phone, then to me. "A little past 7."

*How long had I been asleep for?*

The boy can clearly tell how disoriented I am right now, and leads me over to a park bench. We sit down on either side, a lamp post illuminating us as the sun slowly moves down. I'm able to get a better look at him, and realize I have definitely seen him before. "I think we go to the same school."

He nods and laughs, "Yeah, I think I've seen you around before. You're a sophomore, right?" he asks.

I shake my head. "No, I'm a freshman." He stays silent but continues nodding. "You?" I ask.

"Senior. Last year in that hell hole!" We both laugh.

*He has a nice smile.*

"What are you doing out here anyway?" he asks, inching closer to me. I don't quite know how to answer that. Flashbacks to the fight with my parents rush through my mind. I wish I could make sense of why I got so angry, but everything feels like a blur.

I look at him and shrug. "I needed to get out of my house for a little while. I got into a stupid argument with my parents." The boy doesn't reply, instead he reaches into his pocket to grab something. For a split second, I begin to panic and wonder if I should just go back home now. Instead, I stay, and watch as he pulls out a cigarette box and a lighter.

He takes a second to light one, and brings it to his lips. He leans in closer to me, blowing the smoke just over my head. "I'm Logan by the way." He passes a cigarette to me, and I decline.

"Oh no, I'm fine. I don't smoke." He rolls his eyes, lights it for me regardless, and hands it back to me. I nervously put the cigarette to my lips, inhale, then immediately cough out the smoke in his direction. "I'm Missy," I manage to say when the coughing subsides.

He smirks and comes even closer to me.

"So ..." he says, while lightly draping his arm across the back of the bench. I'm not sure how to feel about this, but I go along with it anyway. "You got into a fight with your parents, and decided to fall asleep in a park?" he asks, laughing a bit too hard.

"Well, of course I didn't *mean* to doze off, I just had a lot going on and—I don't know. I just had to get out of my house."

He boldly pats me on my back. "*Trust me*, I understand a lot about wanting to get away," he says.

"So ... why are *you* out here Logan?" I ask, looking into his eyes. He looks back at me like he's searching for an answer. He puts the cigarette to his lips and exhales long breaths of smoke into the early evening air.

He looks back into my eyes, and I do the same.

"Why are you out here Logan?" I ask again as he gets closer and closer to me.

*Suddenly there is no space between us at all.*

He brushes my hair behind my ears, and gently wraps his hand around my neck.

I don't fully realize what is happening till his lips are on mine.

I touch his face with my right hand, and keep my lips on his. He kisses with passion, and every touch of his lips is deep and full of emotion. Time seems to stop, and I can't tell if we have been kissing for a few seconds or minutes. I find myself hovering on a fine line between eagerly kissing him back and thinking that I should just get out of here. My mind is screaming at me.

*I just met him.*
*I don't know him.*
*He tastes like cigarettes.*
*What am I doing here? I should leave.*
But my lips seem to feel otherwise.

Eventually he stops, and I let myself catch my breath. He stares at me, and I feel at a complete loss for words. Suddenly this all starts to seem very, very wrong. He goes to put his hands back on my face, but I stand up before he can.

In an instant I am running to my bike, and pedaling as fast as I possibly can toward home. From far away I can hear a faint whisper of him calling my name, but I'm already gone.

By the time I get home, my face is wet with tears. I open the door to find my parents screaming at me for running out. I am so lost in my thoughts, their voices sound like dead air in the background. I lock my bedroom door behind me until they stop screaming and eventually go to sleep. Not having the energy to change, I slip off my shoes and fall right to sleep.

# 6

## September 6th, 2014
### *Three years ago*

After a long week of school, there was nothing I craved more than some well earned sleep. Instead, I was on my way to sleep at someone's house that I neither liked nor knew anything about.

I got into Anna's car and stared out the window, wordlessly admiring houses we passed on the drive. "Oh c'mon Missy, it will be fun! Stop moping around."

"I'm not moping," I said defensively. Anna gave me a knowing look. "What?" I asked.

"I think it will be fun," she said.

I shook my head. "We barely talked to her, it's going to be so awkward!" I exclaimed, falling back dramatically into my seat.

Anna shook her head and pursed her lips. "Well, I think you're wrong. I think she seems fun."

I truly wished I could understand what Anna saw in her from the two sentences they shared, but I didn't ask, not wanting to argue. I looked back out to the houses, facing away from Anna. She hummed along to the music that played on the radio. After what felt like an hour, we finally arrived at Emma's house. As Anna and I stepped out of the car, we both uttered the same words under our breath.

"Oh. My. God."

Emma's house was *gorgeous*. It was in a beautiful, cookie-cutter type neighborhood, where every house looked like some variation of the other. Her house was very modern, two stories, all white, with huge windows that went from the floor to the ceilings. My eyes widened as I looked at Anna, and hers did the same.

We strolled up to the front door, duffel bags in hand, waved goodbye to Anna's dad, and hesitantly went up to ring the doorbell. Within a second, the door swung open to reveal Emma standing in the doorway. Her hair was in a long ponytail and she wore gray sweatpants paired with a small pink tank top. Compared to how dismissive she was at school, she now seemed totally relaxed and excited to see us. She motioned for us to come inside, and gave us both hugs.

Her parents stood off to the side, and I could see them carefully watching us walk into the house as if they were evaluating us. "Um, I guess we should go to my room ..."

Emma said, which sounded more like a question than a statement. Anna could see right through to her nervousness, and nodded, smiling big.

She stopped at the room all the way at the end of the hall, and pushed open the door. My jaw dropped as we walked inside. In the center of her room was a giant bed with a pink canopy over it, and the whole room was filled with small succulents and movie posters.

The three of us walked in awkwardly, unsure of what to say or do. I wished I could tell Anna, "*I told you so,*" but it didn't seem like the appropriate time. Emma sat on the edge of her bed, and Anna and I sat next to her, the three of us making a line along the edge of her bed. Emma looked around anxiously, then back to us.

"Sorry, this is probably boring. I've never had people stay the night before," she started explaining. "My parents don't really let me have people over a lot. So ... what do you guys want to do?" Emma asked, and I stayed quiet.

"We could bake something?" Anna suggested. "I think I saw some ingredients on your kitchen counter when we walked in.

Emma's eyes lit up. "Yeah! I have a ton of ingredients in my kitchen, we can make cupcakes, cookies, a cake, brownies, muffins, whatever you guys want!" Anna looked at me and I shrugged.

"I don't care, whatever you guys want is fine," I said.

Emma and I both looked at Anna. "Cupcakes sound good," Anna said, and we all nodded our heads.

Emma helped us put our bags away and led us into her kitchen. She started pulling out all the ingredients we needed from various cupboards around the room. I had no idea the most basic thing about baking so I just sat back and watched as she and Anna got started, waiting for when they needed my help.

Last time I tried baking something, it was months ago for Mother's Day breakfast-in-bed pancakes. They ended up so burnt my mom wouldn't even try them.

Anna and Emma seemed to know what they were doing though, so I had faith this wouldn't end so badly.

# 7
## September 2017

*W*hen I wake up the next morning my parents don't mention anything about yesterday.

Neither do I.

None of us say much that morning, but the quiet is better than another argument. I leave the house with nothing more than a short "Bye" from my mom.

*That's* how my family likes to deal with its problems. We avoid them until we forget them.

I walk to the bus slowly, trying my best to grasp what happened last night. It all still feels unreal, and I have so many questions. When the bus pulls up to my stop, I take a seat in the first row against the window. I do this, because I know that typically no one likes sitting in the front of the bus, and this way I'm not forced into any more social interactions than necessary.

Freshman year is the first year I've had to take the bus to school. Before that I used to carpool with Anna *every* day. We would roll the windows down and scream songs all the way to school. After school, we'd spend hours at each other's houses, completely lost in all sorts of conversations.

I'm not really friends with anyone in my neighborhood, and my parents have early morning work, so the bus is my only option now.

I've grown to like observing the people around me on the bus. Sometimes it feels far easier to just listen to people's conversations, than to actually be in one myself.

I've always found it interesting to see how people's relationships evolve over time—how you can watch someone's friendships grow as they get more comfortable with each other, then fade away when they get into a fight and one of them dares to sit with someone else.

I remember seeing how much happier this one girl Amelia got after she stopped talking to her former friend, Alana. From what I overheard, they had been friends since preschool, but it always seemed like Amelia was way too influenced by Alana.

When Alana dyed her hair purple one day randomly... The next day so did Amelia.

They were always getting into arguments, even in classes you could hear them bickering about the littlest things.

    I'd never talked to either of them, and had no desire to either. I just always found their friendship to be such an interesting dynamic.

    Most days I spend staring out the bus window, talking to myself in my head. Everything from random scenarios I make up to things I would have said if I were back in an argument with someone I had years ago. Sometimes I even pretend I'm giving a really deep TED Talk about the strangest topics.

    I think it makes me feel a little less alone in this world when I talk to myself.

    Some days I find myself getting so caught up in it, I have to remind myself that it's actually just me *alone* talking.

    I have a lot of deep thoughts staring out the window of this bus.

    *I wonder if other people think this much into things.*

***

I walk off the bus to find Emma, Nicolle, and Kaylee at their usual meetup spot outside the front door to school. They are deep in conversation and pay me no mind when I walk up to them. I stand there awkwardly, not wanting to even attempt to join their conversation. It always ends the same way, Emma ignoring me and me regretting it. I tap my foot impatiently, waiting for the bell to ring so we can go inside.

Before it does, I hear a familiar voice call out my name.

"Missy!"

I turn to find Logan waving me over, surrounded by a group of kids around his age. I look back and see Emma, Nicolle, and Kaylee, completely absorbed in conversation, not even noticing Logan in the slightest.

I walk up to him and say, *"Hi,"* so quietly I'm not sure he even hears me.

When I think back to what happened at the park with Logan, I can almost convince myself it was all a dream. But standing here next to him, his arm draped around me with all his friends watching, makes it clear it was all very, *very* real.

"What class do you have right now?"

"Uh ... math," I tell him.

"Perfect! Math is useless so ... you'll be coming with us," he says, looking at me then to his friends as they all laugh.

"What? Where are you going?"

Logan turns to me and looks me directly in the eyes.

"Just trust me," he smirks, and kisses me on the cheek.

He takes my hand in his, and we wait till the bell rings to flee the school. Hiding in plain sight, we let the crowd of students cover our tracks as we duck off behind the school, a few of his friends following close by. Once we are out of sight of the school I feel I can finally breathe.

*Oh my god.*
*I can't believe I just did that.*

We end up in a parking lot that is almost entirely empty. At most there are half a dozen cars parked in it. Otherwise, we are completely alone.

At first I stay completely quiet, silently observing Logan and his friends. I stay put against a brick wall, almost too scared to move. One of Logan's friends must have seen how terrified I look, and she makes her way over to me. She introduces herself and tells me her name is *Harper*.

She has long, thick, dark brown hair worn in two braids and wears baggy jeans with a small tank top. "Here, come. I'll introduce you to my friends."

I follow behind, as she leads me to where Logan is sitting on the ground, surrounded by a few more seniors. To his right, a girl lounges comfortably between a guy's legs. Her hair is long and blonde, similar to Anna's, but a bit longer, and she is dressed entirely in pink like a living *Barbie* doll. The guy behind her is much larger than she is but touches her hair with such gentleness, as if he worries he might break her.

Of course, there's Logan, and next to him another boy. From afar I would have mistaken them for brothers, but up close I can see the other boy has slightly lighter hair and a lighter complexion than Logan.

Harper points out to me who's who, and I learn that the *Barbie* doll is Morgan, her boyfriend is Mark, and Logan's lookalike is Sam. They invite me to sit down with them and I kneel slowly next to Logan, who sneaks a small kiss on my lips.

Harper starts rummaging through her bag, and Logan whispers in my ear, "Harp's dad owns a smoke shop, and Harper *loves* to 'borrow' from it." Harper pulls out a joint and passes it around, as Logan and his friends take turns taking hits. Harper hands it to me, but I decline the offer, not wanting to embarrass myself.

I look over to see Logan rolling his eyes. "C'mon Missy ..." he begs, and I quickly take it back from Harper, smoking it a little and handing it over to Logan. He looks at me and smiles, kissing me on the cheek.

We stay like this for hours. At one point Harper, Morgan, and I walk over to a small concrete wall and walk along the narrow top of it. Careful not to fall over, we laugh and help each other stay balanced. Logan notices us, and makes his way over to me. Offering his hand to me, he helps me as I walk across. He stands up tall and picks me up bridal style, making me yelp in surprise.

He starts to run around with me, still in his arms, and I laugh so hard almost no sound comes out. He stops near the back of the lot, and puts me down against a wall. I laugh, and turn to walk back to Harper and Morgan, but he places his hand around my waist, and pushes my back against the wall.

"Having fun?" he whispers in my ear, pulling back a strand of hair from my face. I just smile and nod.

He puts one hand around my neck, and pulls me in for a kiss as I wrap my arms around him. His other hand keeps a firm grip on my waist, and we kiss till Harper walks by and says teasingly, "Ew guys, get a room!" I instantly back away from Logan, my cheeks flushed with embarrassment. Logan keeps his hands on me, and I have to squirm a little to loosen his grasp.

"I should be heading home soon," I tell them. I grab my school bag, and begin saying goodbye to everyone. I go to give Logan a final kiss, but he protests and tells me, "I'll drive you back, c'mon."

We grab his car from the school parking lot and the ride home is exhilarating. Every window is rolled down so the wind hits my face and my hair flies in every direction. Logan recklessly speeds through what feels like a hundred red lights, and it takes everything in me not to scream like I'm on a roller coaster.

Logan drops me off a few houses down from my own, leaving me with one last passionate kiss, and a feeling of disappointment that I have to go home. When I make my way inside, I'm happy to find my parents don't question why I'm back so late.

I begin to head in my room, but am stopped by my mom before I can.

"Put your school bag down, then come to the dining room. I made dinner!"

## MIA MANDALA | *Dear Anna,*

My mom attempts to have a "proper family dinner" every other week, but it never goes well in the end.

*She should have learned that by now.*

And tonight is nothing different.

"Guess who I saw at yoga today!" We all sit at the dinner table, eating in complete silence. The only sound to be heard is the occasional clinking of forks on plates.

"Hm?" my dad asks, not bothering to look up from his phone.

My mom rolls her eyes aggressively. "Whatever, you're clearly not interested in what I have to say." She stands up from the table, taking her plate with her, and walks angrily into the kitchen.

My dad looks up to me confused and I just shrug. "Michelle..." my dad says, trying to get my mom to sit back down. "C'mon, don't be like this. Just sit down and tell me whoever it was you saw at yoga today." My mom pouts and crosses her arms, but sits back down, glaring pointedly at my father.

"It's not important. It's fine."

"*I tried,*" my dad mouths to me. I just look at him blankly. At this point they should be used to it. Family dinners always seem to end like this. I think it makes us all realize how little we have in common with each other. My dad is a lawyer and on his phone 24/7, but at least he'll binge-watch old movies with me on the weekends. My mom, on the other hand, is the complete opposite. She is obsessed with anything and everything health and fitness. Ironically, she also takes far too many pain medications she doesn't need, and smokes like a chimney. But *god forbid* her yoga clients ever find out about that.

She's all about promoting a "healthy, clean lifestyle," but when it comes to her own life, she is nowhere near.

We spend the rest of dinner in silence, and once we finish cleaning up our plates my dad offers to watch a movie with me. I'm so tired by the time we turn one on that I barely remember what we picked. My dad falls asleep within the first few minutes, and I'm pretty sure I close my eyes soon after he does.

I do have a vague memory of my dad waking me up and telling me to go to bed.

\*\*\*

*Knock*

    *Knock*

*Knock*

I'm suddenly woken up by the sound of light taps on my bedroom window. "What the—" I slowly whisper, making my way to my window. I pull open the blinds, and to my surprise, I find Logan standing below, throwing small pebbles in my direction. I crack the window slightly, just enough to be able to hear him. He goes to throw another rock but stops when he sees my face. "What are you doing here!?" I whisper-yell at him.

He shrugs and gives me a dopey grin. "What, aren't you happy to see me?" he teases, bending down to grab something.

I laugh. "No, I just wasn't expecting all this," I explain, motioning to him and the handful of pebbles now scattered across our back patio.

"Well ... I got you something." He pulls out a small bouquet of flowers from behind his back. To be fair, the majority of the flowers are either crushed or on the brink of death. But still, I can't get over how cute he looks, standing at my window with flowers in hand.

*All for me.*

I smile at him. "Very sweet. But seriously Logan, what are you doing here? I could get in so much trouble, if my parents find out—"

"Chill, they didn't see me and they won't know I'm here ..."

"Okay, but why did you come here anyw—"

"I came, because I'm meeting up with a few friends at the skate park near 15th street. Do you want to come?"

"I ..." I hesitate, unsure of what to do.

*Of course,* I want to go with him. I would go wherever he wants, but I'm already on thin ice with my parents, I can't imagine what they would do if they found out.

MIA MANDALA | *Dear Anna,*

    Instead I ask, "How can I get out without my parents hearing?"

    He then proceeds to help me pry the window open even further, just enough so I can squeeze through without being too noticeable. My whole body jumps when the window makes a loud squeaking sound. I slip on a pair of sneakers, grab a hoodie, and climb through the window, praying I won't get caught.

    He pulls me in for a kiss before I even have the chance to say "Hi". Without saying anything he takes my hand in his, and walks me quickly over to where his small car is parked outside of my neighbors' house. He opens the door for me and I step into the car as he climbs in on the driver's side.

    Now that we're not driving at what feels like a thousand miles an hour, I notice that the interior of his car is dark brown, and has Logan's signature scent of smoke and sweat. He leans over, turning the radio all the way up till my eardrums are bleeding from classic rock. He rolls down both our windows as he starts to drive away. I look back at my house longingly, and for a split second I wish I had just stayed home.

    Logan spends the ride singing along under his breath, with his hand on my thigh. I stare out the window and let my mind wander. His hand slowly makes its way further and further up my leg, sending tingles up and down my whole body.

We come to a stop just outside the dimly lit skate park.

"Missy!" I see Harper as she runs up to us, and she wraps me in a tight hug. She sets me down, and walks with me to where Morgan is intensely watching Mark skate back and forth. Logan walks away from us, and Sam tags along behind him.

I sit next to Harper, our backs up against a wall covered in all types of designs and graffiti tags, our legs bent in front of us. I watch a few other people pathetically attempt to skateboard, and Harper and I look at each other and laugh quietly.

"Look what we got ..." I look over to find Sam and Logan making their way to us. The boys each have a plastic bag in hand, and are wearing stupidly giant sunglasses on their faces. Logan hands his bag to Sam and jumps on a skateboard. They get closer to Harper and me, and Logan goes to jump off his board, sending it flying in my direction. Luckily Harper reaches her hand in front of me and catches it before it has the chance to hit me in the head.

Harper gives Logan a look. "C'mon, dude. Be more careful, that almost hit her in the face." He just laughs and reaches his hand into the bags Sam is holding.

They pull out two bottles of vodka and a few shot glasses and start passing them around. They raise their glasses with a clink, and swallow it down in an instant. Everyone pours themselves more, and Logan pours one for himself and one extra. He hands it to me and gives me an encouraging look. I freeze, unsure of what to do. Harper senses my hesitancy and scoots closer to me. "C'mon, let's do it on 3," she says, picking up hers and clinking her glass against mine.

"3,2,1!" I flip back the glass, and attempt to drink it in one gulp. My eyes widen at the burning feeling of it going down my throat, and I would have done anything to get rid of that taste. I try to hide my reaction, but everyone can see right through me and laughs as I try my best not to gag.

"First time?" Sam asks laughing, and Logan gives me a look of annoyance while taking another shot.

*"Sorry,"* I mouth to him.

# 8
## September 6th, 2014
*Three years ago*

The awkwardness of hanging out with Emma seemed to totally vanish once she and Anna started baking. They had gotten busy with making the cupcakes, and halfway through had stopped asking for my help entirely. I wasn't too upset. I grabbed a chair from Emma's kitchen, sat quietly, and watched as they mixed all the ingredients together.

    I started to feel a little cold, and told them I'd be right back. I made my way back to Emma's room and reached into my bag for a sweater. I pulled an oversized, gray hoodie over my tank top, and started walking back to the kitchen. From the hallway I could hear Anna and Emma laughing, and they got significantly louder as they started singing along to something. I walked in to find them blasting music, and spinning each other around as they threw little pinches of flour at each other.

"Em!" Anna exclaimed, as some flour almost hit her right in the eye.

"Oh my god, I'm so sorry!" They both burst into a fit of laughter on the floor.

They helped each other stand back up, and started adding spoonfuls of batter into the muffin tins. I sat down, and watched as Emma put on a red and green oven mitt, helping Anna push the tins into the oven.

"Missy, set a timer for fifteen minutes," Emma said sharply. I opened my phone, and set the timer as Emma pulled Anna into the living room with her. I followed behind, kneeling on a small chair next to the couch Emma and Anna were sharing.

"Anna, I have this show I just started watching, I think you would just love it!" Emma reached for the remote and started clicking through the channels till she stopped on one that showed a boy with dark brown hair, on his knees, professing his love for the girl standing above him.

Anna gasped, "I *love* this show! I watch it like every night! Oh my god, isn't Brayden just *the cutest!* He and Paloma would make *the best* couple!"

I tried my best to follow along, despite not having the slightest clue as to what was happening, or even knowing the name of the show.

They settled into the couch, wrapping themselves in huge, white, fluffy blankets that covered their entire bodies.

A few minutes later my phone started to beep. "Missy, can you take the cupcakes out of the oven?" Emma asked, not looking away from the TV.

Anna stood up after me. "I'll help you."

Emma pulled on Anna's arm. "But we're just getting to the best part of this episode!" she complained, trying to get Anna to sit back down.

Anna pulled her arm back. "It's fine, just pause it Em." Emma frowned, clicking pause.

Anna and I walked into the kitchen silently. I opened the oven, and was foolishly about to grab the hot tins when Anna stopped me. "Here, let me. I don't want you to burn yourself." She pulled on an oven mitt and stuck her hand in the oven.

"Thanks." I gave her a small smile that she returned.

Anna placed the tins on top of the stove, and leaned against the small kitchen island. "So... what do you think of Em?" she asked, propping her head in her hands. I took a moment to reply, not really knowing what my answer should or would be. I truly didn't have a problem with Emma, I just wished Anna didn't seem so enamoured by her, but I immediately felt selfish for even thinking I shouldn't be happy for her.

I *was* happy for her.

"She's really nice," I told her.

Anna smiled, "Okay good, I couldn't tell what you thought. I'm trying really hard for it not to be awkward, I really want us all to be friends."

I shook my head. "Don't worry Anna, we all will be." She smiled at me and a look of relief washed over her face.

"Anna, c'mon!" we heard Emma yell from the next room, and Anna told her we'd be back in a second. We took the cupcakes out of their tins, and let them cool down a little before covering them in icing and bringing them into the living room.

The rest of the night went smoothly. We burnt the cupcakes a little but they still tasted great. Anna and Emma watched their TV show till we were practically asleep. Eventually, even I found the show entertaining, but that may just have been because of the hilarious commentary Anna and Emma made on every single thing that the characters did.

"WHAT!?" They both shrieked when their favorite character was suddenly killed off. "Elisa is so hot!" "No way!" "OMG!" were just a few of the many reactions they yelled while we were watching.

A few minutes had gone by when I realized things had been unusually quiet. I looked over to find them both fast asleep on opposite ends of the couch. I crawled out of my chair, carefully grabbing the remote out of Emma's hand, and turned off the TV. I found a small black blanket by the couch, and bundled myself into it before falling fast asleep on the floor.

# 9

## September 2017

*B*y now, I'm on my third or fourth shot. I stopped keeping track a few minutes ago.

Logan stands up in front of me, and extends his hands out to me. I grab them and he helps me up, my eyes blurring for a second. I take a step, and without realizing it, step right onto Sam's skateboard, sending myself falling over the front of it. My hands and knees get all scraped up, and it takes me a moment till I can stand back up. I look around for Logan, expecting him to help me up, but instead see him hiding a laugh at me with Sam. I push my hands underneath myself and manage to stand back up. Everything in my body feels like it's spinning, and I barely know where my feet are going till I end up almost falling onto Logan.

"Come with me," he whispers in my ear, and I enclose my hand in his. He leads me past Harper, past Sam, past Mark and Morgan, past the skate park. He walks so fast, I trip over my feet multiple times trying to keep up. I stop for a second, thinking I might be sick, but he tugs on my arm so I keep following.

He pulls me into the public bathroom, quickly closing the door behind us. He pushes me up against a wall, and I feel my body go limp under his hands. My whole body feels numb and tingly, like I barely have any control over my movements.

We start kissing, and his hands move up and down my body. I start feeling like I'm about to collapse onto him but he securely grips my waist, preventing me from doing so. He keeps one hand on the front of my jeans, his fingers slowly playing with the button. I open my eyes, trying to see what he is doing. Everything seems so blurry and I start to panic, unsure if he has started to take off my jeans or not.

A few seconds later he stops, and moves his hand to the bottom of my shirt. He pulls my shirt over my head, and I really start to feel like I might fall right onto him if he doesn't keep holding me up.

Suddenly the bathroom door is swung open by someone I don't recognize.

"Fuck!" Logan jumps and pushes me off him, and I have to steady my feet to stop myself from stumbling over. I grab my shirt and put it on as quickly as possible, doing my best to run out of the bathroom as quickly as I can.

I find Harper and Morgan deep in conversation, a bottle of vodka left half empty between them.

"Woah Missy ..." Harper says. I laugh, my feet tripping underneath me. Harper takes my arm to prop me up and starts walking me away from everyone.

"What, where are we going?" I ask, looking back toward Logan longingly.

Harper looks me up and down. "I think it's time for you to go home."

"Ugh Harper! I wanna stay with Logan ..." She doesn't acknowledge my whining, and instead opens the door to her car, motioning for me to get in. I roll my eyes at her and push myself into the car.

Harper starts driving, and I tell her my address. I watch her roll down her window and spend a minute just staring at the way her hair flies behind her.

It's a little past 1 a.m. by the time I get home.

I stumble out of Harper's car, blowing her a kiss as I walk up to my front door. I open the door slowly, knowing my parents must be fast asleep by now. I tiptoe inside, shutting the door behind me.

\*\*\*

"Where the hell were you?!"

*Oh shit.*

My eyes slowly adjust to the dim light and I see both of my parents sitting on the couch, the entire room lit by just a small lamp.

"I—" I rack my brain for what could possibly make sense as an excuse, but nothing comes to me.

My mom stands up, getting so close to me I can feel her breath as she speaks. "No. I'm not going to listen to whatever *bullshit* answer you're about to give me," she says, crossing her arms.

"But look, I was just—" I start, but she cuts me off again.

"No,s Missy. I want you to imagine what it was like for me to go into my daughter's room, and find that she is *nowhere* to be found." I open my mouth to reply, but my brain is so foggy her words get all jumbled up in my mind.

Now it's my father's turn to stand up and yell, "Please! Tell us! Where were you at 1 in the morning? Please, we would love to know." They are both inches away from my face, and my breaths start to feel harder and harder to catch.

I wish the floor could just consume me, and I could disappear into an endless pit forever. Like being eaten alive by a black hole.

*You're there for a second. Then you're gone.*

In stressful times like these, I try reminding myself that a few years from now none of this will matter. That this moment is simply just one moment in my life. I detach myself from my reality so much that bad things seem to not be all that bad anymore.

"Missy! Answer your father right now! What has gotten into you?" I try composing myself, blinking back the hot tears forming in my eyes.

"I didn't feel well, so I went to take a walk to get some fresh air." I knew even as I was saying it that it was a lame excuse.

I look up to find my mom literally laughing in my face.

"Missy, we"— she motions to herself and my father—"we were teenagers once." She laughs about it in a way that makes my blood boil. "Don't give us some lame excuse, and just tell us where you went. You're grounded either way, so really it doesn't ma—"

Now it is my turn to cut her off, "You really think I would lie to you guys like that?"

"Missy seriously—" my dad starts.

"No. I mean, really? I have done nothing but always been truthful with you both. You *really* think I would lie about something like this?" I cross my fingers behind my back, praying they believe my absolute gaslighting. A sudden urge to throw up grows in me, and I really wish they would just let me go to my room. "I thought you guys trusted me. But I guess not," I sigh dramatically, walking past them and toward my room.

"Don't you DARE walk away from me!" I hear my mom yell as she storms after me. I quickly open the door to my room, locking it behind me before she even has a chance to touch the doorknob.

"Let me guess. You were out with some boy?!" she says mockingly, as if she didn't go out with practically every guy in her high school. She starts banging on the door, and I grab a pair of headphones off my desk. I slide myself down against the door and sit at the bottom of it, my legs curled tightly under me. I start blasting music, until all I can hear from outside are faint knocks coming from my parents.

Knocks I *will* be ignoring.

When I think she has finally given up on trying, I slip my headphones off, just in time to hear her scream one last thing, "Is this because of Anna? Because you have been *completely* impossible since—"

I feel like I am going to be sick. "STOP TALKING ABOUT ANNA!" I stand up and hit the door with my fists as hard as I possibly can.

I see the shadows of my mom's shoes jump back. "Missy!" she yells, just as loudly as I had screamed before.

"Mom, just stop!" my voice breaks into sobs, but I can't let her know that. I feel my brain start to spiral.

Like I am falling into a deep hole that I can't climb out of.

I kick the door with full force, and when I don't hear my mom scream back, I know she is finally gone.

MIA MANDALA | *Dear Anna,*

I fall back down to the floor as I start completely hyperventilating. Everything inside and out is so foggy. My hands travel to my face and I can feel heavy, wet tears, but I'm so numb that it doesn't even register that I'm crying.

*Nothing* feels real. My mind feels like a whirlpool of thoughts, and I can't get it to stop.

*Sneaking out.*

*Getting caught.*

*Logan.*

*I'm so unhappy.*

*Why are you so unhappy Missy? You have a great life.*

But...

*Anna.*

*Anna.*

*Anna.*

*I just want to disappear.*

I want to kick and scream and destroy anything and everyone I possibly can. It feels like there is fire in my brain, and all I can do is try to stop my hands from shaking.

There's a small, glass vase sitting on top of my dresser that holds a single, half-dead white lily. I throw it off the dresser, and watch as it smashes against the wall into tiny bits and pieces. Little shards of glass fly all over my room. My breath quickens as I realize what I just did.

I kneel down and pick up a few shards in my hands. I rub them along my fingers and look at them through the light. My hands stop shaking, and for a moment I feel like I can finally catch my breath, but the tears are still coming full force.

Then, the most sudden urge comes over me. It happens so fast, *I don't realize what I have done till my leg is bleeding.*

It's as if someone has taken over my body, and suddenly I'm rolling up my pants as far as I can.

Even as I do it, I know it's wrong. I know it isn't the way to deal with what is going on.

But at the moment, it feels like the only option. I want to physically feel the pain that I feel so strongly from everyone else.

To gain back a little control over my life, instead of feeling like it's flying out of my grasp.

I don't want to stop, but when I see the blood, I start to freak out and throw the glass quickly away from me.

*Oh my god, Missy.*

I keep looking over and over again at what I have done. I don't know how long I have spent just sitting there, staring.

Everything around me seems to freeze and I can finally breathe. My mind is still spinning as I lay down and wrap a blanket around me, but I finally get some sleep.

## 10

## September 2017

*T*he morning after. After what I did to myself.

It is a weird sensation to have, to wake up like every other day but to have *everything* feel so entirely different. The moment I open my eyes, I am hit with sudden flashbacks of the night before.

I go into the bathroom to carry out my usual routine, but am scared to change and have to see what I did to myself. Eventually I muster up the courage, and slowly slip off my sweatpants. For a moment I just stare, then I feel like I am going to be sick and quickly put on a new pair of pants. I step toward the mirror to put on makeup and think: *my god I look rough.*

I open the bathroom drawer to grab my toothbrush and take notice of the many bottles of random pills and pain meds my mom takes on the daily. I pick one of them up, curious as to what they are for. The prescription is difficult to read, but I think it has something to do with headaches. I read a few more, taking note of the doses and refill dates, and the hefty lists of *just slightly* concerning side effects.

After some rummaging, I find my toothbrush and a hairbrush. I look in the mirror, noticing how bad my hair looks. Where it's not greasy, it's dry and knotted, but I don't have the energy to try to brush through it right now. I apply a small amount of toothpaste to my toothbrush, and hold it up to my mouth.

I spend a few minutes just staring at myself in the mirror, examining all my facial features. Slowly, the image I see starts to feel less like a reflection of myself, and more a reflection of someone I've never met.

*And suddenly I'm the biggest stranger to myself.*

I pull on the skin under my right eye, and then again on the left, getting a full view of my eyes.

*Eyes staring at eyes, staring at their own eyes, staring back at eyes, staring back at their own eyes,* and on and on again into a never-ending cycle.

Pulling on my bottom lip, and then my top, my own touch doesn't feel like my touch. *It's the girl in the mirror's touch* of course.

I'm the girl in the mirror, *of course.*

I don't know how long I spend staring, I could have stayed there for hours if I really let myself zone out. There is something so eerie about really staring at one's own reflection, it makes you step back and think about your life.

*Snap out of it, Missy.*

Like a sudden switch that goes off in my brain, everything goes back into focus and I'm able to finish brushing my teeth. I get ready and walk out my front door quietly, both of my parents are still fast asleep.

The bus ride to school feels so different, despite being part of my everyday life for the past few weeks.

*Everyone carries on as usual.*

Not that I actually think something *I* did to *myself* in private should affect others too much. Especially when they don't even know it happened.

But it still makes me so, *so* angry for some reason.

Seeing everyone laughing, and talking, and gossiping with their friends as they do every other day makes a big part of me want to get up and scream, *"Hey look at me! Look at what I did to myself last night!"* But I know I can't do that.

The other part of me is absolutely terrified of anyone finding out.

I don't understand my mind sometimes.

School isn't any different. I spend my classes just trying to focus on something, *anything* besides the gnawing feeling coming from the back of my brain. Everything reminds me of last night, and everything makes me want to relive it again. I can't escape it, the feeling of the glass, the panic, tha pain, the relief, the guilt, and then even more panic.

It won't leave my thoughts. I almost don't even notice when the dismissal bell rings for my first class. I gather my stuff together and walk to my next class, trying to free myself from my thoughts.

Emma brushes past me in the hall, and doesn't so much as look in my direction.

I *really* hate it when she completely ignores me. When she acts like we were never even friends. I've racked my brain over and over again trying to understand what I possibly could have done for her to be such a bitch to me.

I still have no idea.

Any time I even *try* having a conversation alone with her, she manages to find someone else to have an even more exciting, even more interesting, and even better conversation with *by far*.

At a certain point I just gave up, but I think she gave up way before I did.

I still sit with her when I can, and to anyone who asks, we *are* still friends. Just definitely not best friends.

I watch her walk past me, her black hair bobbing in a tight ponytail. Her smile brightens as she spots a group of friends. They pull each other in for affectionate hugs, and laugh as they spin each other around. Without noticing, my mouth has grown into a small grin just by seeing her look so happy. Even if we don't talk anymore like we used to, I still want to see her as happy as she used to be with Anna and me.

***

"Hey, did you guys meet the new girl yet?" We are now all at lunch—Emma, Nicolle, Kaylee and me.

"What new girl?" I ask Kaylee.

"She's in my drama class. Her name is uh ... Hailey, I think." Emma's eyes widen, and she turns around to face us.

"Yeah, I have like two classes with her. I feel *so* bad for her though," Emma says, making a pouty face to me and Kaylee.

"What? Why? What happened to her?" Kaylee asks, excitement lingering in her tone.

"I heard at her old school she was bullied *so badly* that she started cutting herself. That's why her parents made her change schools."

"Oh my god, that's awful," Nicolle says, and I just nod my head.

"Don't mention this to anyone, but when I was in math class yesterday, I could see the scars of cuts along her arms. It was *awful*, and she seemed so sad," Emma tells us, and we all go quiet.

"I feel so bad ..." Kaylee adds.

"That's horrible."

"Yeah, it is.'

*I agree in almost a whisper.*

Flashbacks from last night start flooding my mind. I feel like I'm reliving the feeling of the glass over and over, so I have to shake my leg a little to remind myself it's not actually happening again, and I end up kicking Nicolle a little by accident.

"What was that for?" she asks, glaring in my direction.

"*Sorry.*" She ignores me and goes back to her previous conversation.

*She's such a bitch sometimes.*

*Most of the time.*

*No.*

*All the time.* I can feel the same feeling I felt while on the bus start to rise up again.

*Anger?*

*Frustration?*

*Jealousy?* Not necessarily. Just the longing hope that *someone* would notice. *Like they noticed her.*

I don't feel like engaging in any more conversations during lunch right now. I put my head on the table, letting myself get close to drifting off to sleep but not fully.

I don't remember much of what happened the rest of the day. I tried to ignore everything as best as I could.

*I just want to disappear.*

I count down the minutes till school ends. I don't even want go home. Home is the last place I want to be right

MIA MANDALA | *Dear Anna,*

now. I just can't take another second of having to carry on with my day as if everything is normal.

Because it's not.

*I've changed.*

I just wish everyone could see that too.

The bell *finally* rings and I don't think I've ever run out of class so fast.

# 11

## July 4th, 2016
*One year and two months ago*

"You girls almost ready?"

"Almost Mom!"

Anna and I finished smearing glitter all over each other's cheeks and ran downstairs to her mom.

"Well, don't you two look festive?" We laughed as Anna's mom checked out our outfits. Anna and I had decided to go all out for this 4th of July, and fully decked ourselves out in our most patriotic clothing. We both wore little jean skirts, with Anna in a red shirt and me in a bright blue one. A few weeks ago we bought matching American flag headbands, and couldn't stop laughing whenever we looked at them. We even bought an extra one to give to Emma.

"Get in the car, I'll be right behind you two." We hopped into Laurie's car and strapped in.

Anna jumped up and down, "I'm so excited!"

"Same!" We had the biggest smiles pasted across our faces, and our cheeks hurt from smiling so much. Anna texted Emma quickly that we were on the way, then plugged in her phone to play music.

"What do you want to listen to?" she asked. I thought for a second, then scrolled through her playlist till I found the one titled: Anna + Missy 2015. "Oh my god! I forgot about this!" Anna exclaimed, while scrolling and looking at all the different songs. It was full of all our favorite songs that we listened to on repeat last summer. We knew every lyric front and back, and must have played each song a thousand times. Anna pressed play, and every song that came on felt like a flashback to the previous summer.

Anna's mom pulled into the driveway of Emma's house just a short while later, and we called her to come out. In a matter of seconds, Emma was out of her house and ready to go.

"Oh my god, I *love* this song!" Emma hugged us and joined in singing along for the rest of the car ride.

We drove up to what looked from afar like an explosion of color. The fair was lit up by its huge mix of games and rides, with more people than we could possibly imagine in one place. Laurie handed us some money, and made sure all our phones were charged. "Okay girls, please stay safe! Text me if you need *absolutely* anything! Are you sure you don't want me to come with you?"

"Mom! We'll be fine, I promise. I'll text you when it's time to pick us up, okay?"

Laurie sighed, "Okay, love you all! Bye girls!" We waved back as she began to drive away.

"Bye!" we all yelled back. We craned our necks, watching as Laurie drove away. We waited until she was fully out of view. Once she was, we all started screaming in excitement. "C'mon, let's go!" We interlocked our fingers with one another, and took off running.

For us it felt like the first real glimpse into what life would soon be like. Going out by ourselves, our parents trusting us to be responsible enough to be on our own, and spending *every* single second with each other having all the fun in the world.

The three of us strolled along inside, taking in the view. We pointed out everything and anything that caught our eye. Crowds of people passed by us, and I even recognized a few of them from school.

"Woah! Look at that!" Emma exclaimed while pointing up.

We looked to the sky in amazement to find the biggest mess of loops and all the twists and turns you could possibly imagine, all clumped together in a giant cotton candy pink-colored roller coaster. I looked at Emma, her eyes widening. "Oh my god, let's go!"

Anna shook her head, slowly backing away. "No way am I going on that!" she said, quickly turning away from us. Emma and I each grabbed one of her arms and spun her back around to face us.

"Please! It looks so fun!" I argued, motioning to the roller coaster behind me. She looked at me like I was crazy, and I thought her eyes even started to water just looking at the ride. I quickly changed gears and tried to reassure her,

"If you guys want to do it, you guys should go. I can wait for you down here," she told us, sitting down on a park bench. Emma and I glanced at each other. "Go! I'll be fine," Anna said, jokingly pushing us toward the ride.

Emma looked at me and smiled, "Okay! We'll be right back." Emma and I took off running, arms linked and laughing the whole way there.

We stopped at the entrance, a tall gated entryway painted entirely black, and at the top was a huge sign with the words: "*The Thrill Coaster!*" drawn in fancy calligraphy. Emma turned away from the entrance to look at me, and I did the same. We stood there frozen, the fear slowly starting to seep in. Emma looked like she might faint, and I looked her in the eyes and said, "We don't have to go if you don't want to."

She grabbed me by the shoulders, spinning me back around, "No. Let's go."

We pushed our way through the gates, and entered a long line of people waiting to get on the ride. A couple feet above us stood a sign flashing the words: "*15-minute wait*" over and over again. We looked at each other, sighing, watching as the line grew even longer behind us, while the line ahead didn't seem to move at all.

The first few minutes of waiting felt like torture. We stood there in silence, occasionally commenting on how long the line was taking.

I really didn't mean to be so quiet, I just couldn't find anything to talk to her about.

It dawned on me then that Emma and I hadn't actually spent that much time together, *alone* that is. I hadn't realized how hard it would be to talk to her when we didn't have Anna to lead the conversation. An idea sparked, and I hoped she would like it. "Em," I said, catching her attention.

"Yeah?"

"Wanna play *Never Have I Ever*, to pass the time?"

"Please! This is so boring!" I laughed, agreeing with her. "Okay, you go first," she said, as we put both our hands up as if counting to the number 10 on our fingers.

"Hmm. *Never Have I Ever* kissed a boy?" Emma giggled and put a finger down, while I left mine up. "Em! Who?" She pretended to zip her lips, and shook her head no.

"This isn't truth or dare, we don't have to say."

"Wow! Okay ... your turn now."

She cocked her head to the side as she thought. "*Never Have I Ever* ... snuck out of the house." Neither of us moved any fingers down.

MIA MANDALA | *Dear Anna,*

We continued playing till we were almost at the front of the line, and the sign had gone from flashing: "*15-minute wait*" to "*5-minute wait*". The time flew by quickly, as we each laughed at the stupid things each other had done, or hadn't. I got to know more about Emma during that short time waiting than I had known about her in the entire two years we had been friends.

Finally we made it to the front of the line. We waited as the group ahead of us took their turn, and pulled out our money to pay. Two boys working there helped us into the ride's seats, and made sure we were securely fastened in. They seated us next to each other, and we each had a small rail on either side of us to hold onto. Emma and I looked at each other, excitement and nervousness all at once painted on our faces. In a matter of minutes the ride started, and we took off.

The ride sped ahead, and everything around me turned into a blur. The ride went over a bump, and Emma and I both yelped. We gripped onto the handles till our knuckles turned white. Everyone screamed excitedly as we reached the top of a steep drop. The ride swooped down in an instant, and Emma threw her hands up in the air. It made its way upside down and spun around in more circles.

The roller coaster came to a stop after a few minutes, and we both wished it hadn't.

We hopped off the ride, and laughed as we tried walking without swaying side to side, still dizzy from all the twists and turns. We ran back to Anna and found her sitting on a park bench staring up at the sun, three giant puffs of cotton candy in her hands.

"So, how was it?!"

"It was so fun!" We both exclaimed at the same time.

"Anna, you *really* should go!" Emma begged.

"No, no, no. I'm good just watching you guys! Plus, I got us some *amazing* cotton candy!" We took the cotton candy from her, and sat alongside the bench.

I took a bite. "Wow! This *is* good!" Emma and Anna nodded agreeably, each taking bites of their own. We all looked up to the sun, watching as it quickly got darker out. We sat in silence, enjoying the treat.

Once we were all done, we stood up and Anna suggested that we walk around.

We walked shoulder to shoulder, taking in the sights. Soon enough we came across a large patch of grass connected to a nearby park. What would usually be a popular picnicking place was now totally vacant as large sprinklers went off in every direction. Anna looked at us and smiled as wide as I've ever seen her smile.

Then she took off running into the grass, getting soaked almost instantly by the sprinklers. "Guys!" she motioned for us to follow, and we looked at each other hesitantly. "C'mon!" Anna spun around, waiting for us to join her. Emma and I took one last look at each other before speeding ahead into the grass. I felt the sprinklers shower over me, and we ran over to where Anna was standing, head to toe drenched in water.

"Anna, you're getting soaked!" I said.

She shrugged. "So are you!" and laughed.

Anna crept up behind Emma and tapped her on the shoulder. "Tag! You're it!" she yelled before taking off running. Emma took off after us, and we all ran around in circles trying not to slip as the ground grew increasingly more slippery. Emma popped up next to me and tagged me before I had a chance to run away. I chased after Anna, following her straight into a sprinkler.

The three of us spun around and around until we fell over so dizzy we couldn't see straight. We laughed till our cheeks hurt and our eyes grew teary-eyed. We fell onto the grass, sprawled out with our legs and arms splayed like starfish. Looking up at the sky, I could see more stars than I ever had before.

Emma pointed to the sky, naming all the stars and constellations she could see.

Laying there I felt I had never been as happy as I was right then, lying side by side with my two favorite people in the world.

I wanted to stay like that *forever*.

# 12
## October 2017

*I* send a quick text to my parents, before picking up my bag and walking out of school:

> *i'm gonna walk home today,*
> *i'll be back a little later than usual*

Instead of continuing down the side of the road toward home, I take a sharp right and walk through a small park.

I stop for a second and sit in the grass. Surrounding me is a brightly colored children's playground filled with a swing set, slides, and a rickety monkey bar set with its paint peeling off.

## MIA MANDALA | *Dear Anna,*

Looking around I get a sudden hit of nostalgia.

Memories of when I was little and would come here all the time with my parents. Almost every weekend my mom would take me, let me run around till I got tired out, and then get ice cream later. I can almost picture myself as if it were yesterday, eight years old and sliding down the same slide I sit next to now.

I wish I could go back to that time.

*Before everything went to shit.*

When my biggest problem was if my parents would let me get the large ice cream or just the small one that day.

I remember there was a game I made up with my mom, and I made her play it with me for a full year. "Fairy Hunting" is what we called it. We would decorate fairy houses, and leave food and jewels out for them. The next day, we would check to see if it was still there, and try to see if a fairy was in it. I was always so fascinated by the idea of them. Little creatures filled with magic that could fly, and they were always depicted in books and movies as being so beautiful.

*I wish I could fly.*

I would fly away from everything, go up as high as I possibly could, then fly away from here. Wherever, I wouldn't care.

Just far, far away from here.

This park used to be my favorite place. Now it just seems dull and lifeless. Filled with dead memories I so badly long for. I hate looking back on what used to be.

I hate rotting my brain over something I can never get back.

I feel like everything I do is wrong.

I keep messing up.

And I *can't* seem to stop.

I don't realize till I look down that my hands are shaking in my lap and I have started hyperventilating. My anxiety rises, and tears form. My brain feels like it's screaming at me, and I know what it wants me to do.

I take a look around, and find that the only person around is an old woman slowly making her way through the park. I wait until she's almost out of sight, then slowly open my school bag. I take in a deep breath before reaching my hand into the inside pocket. I find the small piece of glass I put in my bag this morning. It's wrapped in a thick cloth, ripped off from an old blanket. I'm not quite sure what I was thinking when I put it in there.

I felt like I needed it with me.

*Just in case.*

I roll up my sweater sleeve, and start pushing down. My body is once again overcome with the same feeling of relief I got last night. A weird sensation that lands on that invisible line between calm and madness.

My mind is swimming and even the feeling of the glass doesn't make it stop. I don't know why I keep doing it, or for how long.

I can't stop.

MIA MANDALA | *Dear Anna,*

When I am done I pack everything up, and head home pulling my sleeve back down and barely wincing at the pain.

As if nothing happened.

But *everything* is different now.

\*\*\*

The rest of my day continues on as usual.

I eat dinner in my room, while my parents watch some show in the living room. It's past 11 p.m. and I'm still not even the slightest bit tired. I start to pace around my room, my hands shaking, and my breathing getting faster and faster. I sit back on the edge of my bed, closing my eyes. I try to calm myself down, reminding myself that this feeling will pass and tomorrow morning I'll be okay.

That's a lie though, and I know it is. I won't be okay tomorrow.

Or the next day. Or the day after that.

And so on.

One thought keeps ringing through my head, but I ignore it for as long as I can until it is pulsing through my brain.

*Anna.*

*Anna.*

*Anna.*

I miss her so goddamn much.

MIA MANDALA | *Dear Anna,*

I feel like I'm barely breathing at this point. I look around my room, and am flooded by memories of when Anna was in here. I look at my door, and can perfectly picture her walking through it. Looking at my floor, I remember exactly where she sat when we would play *Truth or Dare*.

My room is filled with her. Everywhere I look she's here. Her memory haunts this room. This whole house.

My whole life.

She is everywhere.

I try to ignore it, to push the feelings down as much as possible. I usually can, but tonight I just can't. She is all I can think about. I do everything to try to regain my composure. Taking deep breaths, and counting, focusing my thoughts on a single sense.

Nothing is working.

I look over and see the few pieces left from the broken vase that I still haven't cleaned up. Suddenly my brain is screaming again. Do it.

Do it Missy.

It seems like my only option to get relief.

But it isn't until I'm sitting back on my floor that my tears stop. And I realize that nothing has changed. The feeling is still there, and the pit in my chest has only grown. Even still, I want to do it again. I want to do it millions of times again.

I don't know how late it is when I finally fall asleep. I lay there clutching the teddy bear Anna and I won at the fair

MIA MANDALA | *Dear Anna,*

last summer, and by the time I finally doze off it is soaked in my tears.

# 13

## October 31st, 2016
*One year ago*

"*W*hy is there always some sort of an issue with you Emma?"

It was Halloween night, and I was spending it with my two best friends. It was supposed to be *perfect*. Maybe it could have been, until Emma said in her whiniest voice, "Guys, this is getting kind of boring. Let's go out and *do something*. I think Ava's having a little party, she said you guys could come with me." Anna and I threw each other nervous looks.

Ever since Anna and I have been friends, we've spent every Halloween in the same way. Together, in my room, watching as many horror movies as we could until we finally passed out.

It all started on our first Halloween together, when our parents took us out to go trick-or-treating. It started off fine. We were both dressed as witches, our hats so big they were about to slide off of our heads. We stepped up to a large white house with a bright blue door. The two of us held out our matching pumpkin bags and Anna stepped up to the door.

"Trick-or-treat!" we yelled gleefully. Slowly the door creaked open, an old woman answered while her friend stood next to her dressed head to toe as a deranged circus clown. She had blue and red triangles above and below her eyes, a red nose, and a wide overdrawn smile dripping in fake blood.

I listened as an ear piercing scream left Anna's mouth.

She dropped her bag in a panic, and ran as far from the house as she could. I quickly picked up her candy bag, and started to sprint after her. "Anna!" I finally caught up to her, panting as I tried to catch my breath. "Anna! What happened?" She turned around slowly, crying so hard she could barely get her words out. Unsure of what to do I wrapped her in a tight hug, and led her over to a patch of grass. Helping her sit down, I offered my sleeve for her to wipe away her tears. "Anna …" I started to say softly, shaken from seeing her cry so hard. "Are you okay?" She took in a shaky breath, her eyes not meeting mine just yet.

"I'm fine," she said in barely a whisper.

"But why did you take off like that?" I asked again. She laughed a little, "It's so stupid."

"Just tell me, please."

She looked up at me and confided, "It was the clown. I'm *terrified* of clowns." I felt my face turn into a small smile, and had to remind myself it wasn't the time to be laughing. "I know, it's really dumb. I don't know why I've always been so scared of them, they're just so creepy!" she said, less embarrassed this time.

"It's not dumb," I told her.

"You wanna know a secret?" I asked, motioning for her to come in closer. I leaned forward and whispered in her ear, "I have a *huge* fear of spiders! I even freak out when I see those fake spider decorations!" To my delight I heard her let out a faint laugh.

"I feel bad, let's keep walking around," she said, taking my hands and standing up. I could feel her hands still shaking underneath mine, and I knew she needed more time.

"Anna..." I pulled her back down to sit. "Are you sure? I think we have enough candy by now anyway, so why don't we go back to my house? I can ask if you can sleepover, we can watch scary movies and eat *all* of our candy!" I saw a look of relief cross Anna's face.

"Are you sure?" she asked, and I nodded my head reassuringly.

"I'm sure. C'mon, let's go."

We spent the rest of the night huddled together on my couch. We started off watching *Coraline*, then *Scream*, falling asleep just as the killer would have been revealed in the second movie. The next Halloween we didn't even bother to go trick-or-treating, and instead spent our night gorging out on store-bought candy and chocolates, and binge-watching a million movies.

Every Halloween stayed the same, and we knew the two of us would have a much better time staying inside than going out, the large crowds of people walking around being too stressful for our liking. We promised each other that from then on we would spend every Halloween the same way, and since then they had all been perfect.

***

This was the first time Emma would be spending Halloween with us. We had told her all about how we were going to spend the night, and even told her the now funny story about Anna's freak-out with the clown. We laughed and laughed about it, and Emma agreed to stay in with us, saying, "It's going to be so fun! Of course I'll hang out with you guys."

She came over to my house a few hours ago, along with Anna, who had brought bags and bags of candy. We changed into matching Halloween pajama pants and tank tops covered in black cats. Anna and I even let Emma choose what movie we would watch first.

Everything was fine, we all agreed on how much we enjoyed the movie and had just started the second one. That was when Emma decided she was too bored by our plans.

MIA MANDALA | *Dear Anna,*

Anna looked at me unsure of what to say, I knew what she was thinking though. Despite her fear of clowns being long gone by now, we both still preferred the comforts of staying home. Anna opened her mouth to reply, but I went ahead and said it for her. "Em, it's already pretty late. I think we would both rather just stay in."

Anna added, "Yeah, I don't think my parents would let us go anyway."

Emma rolled her eyes. "Ugh, that's so boring though!"

Anna looked around nervously, "I don't know Em, I would *really* like to just stay in. If that's okay?"

"Ugh, fine," she agreed, but not happily. She spent the rest of the movie with her arms crossed, and when I occasionally looked over at her I'd catch her rolling her eyes at everything I said. Instead of saying anything to us about it, she just kept huffing and puffing like an upset toddler. Finally, I had enough of her moping.

"Anna?" I asked, not wanting her to be around when I confronted Emma.

"Yeah?" she said, barely taking her eyes away from the screen.

"Could you get Em and me some water? Oh, and do you have any of those chocolate cookies left?"

She smiled at me, "Yeah! I'll be right back."

"Thanks!" I said, and returned her smile, watching as she disappeared into the kitchen. I leaned forward and paused the TV before turning around toward Emma.

"Emma."

"Hm?" she so much as whispered.

"Why is there always some sort of an issue with you? Why are you acting like this?"

"Like what?" She turned toward me, arms still crossed, lips pursed.

"Don't try to force Anna into something she doesn't want to do," I said.

"She can make her own decisions. Why do you care so much?" she asked aggressively.

"Because this is what we have *always* done," I explained. I didn't think any more reasons were needed.

"Okay, and ...?" she asked sarcastically.

"And, we have always had a *great* time doing it like this."

"Seriously? This is *so* boring."

"It's not boring. Anna and I are having a good time, like we always have, and quite frankly if you are truly having such an awful time with us then you should leave. Be my guest," I said with a small smirk.

As the words left my mouth I could barely believe I had just said something like that, but I've never felt more relieved. For a split second I saw her let her guard down, and her jaw dropped. She never expected anyone to stand up to her, *especially* not me.

"Really, Missy?"

"What?"

"I'm just trying to have us do something fun *for once.*"

"This is fun," I protested.

"No, it's boring. And you're too protective of Anna. Just chill out for once." She turned back to the TV, but I grabbed the remote before she could turn it back on.

I heard Anna making her way back to us. "Emma. Anna and I are staying here, this is what we want to do. It is what we have *always* done. If you want to leave, then go, have fun. But I will not have you ruining one of Anna's favorite holidays because you decided halfway through that spending time with us wasn't exciting enough for you. Go to Ava's party if that's what you really want to do; it's not like you constantly tell us how much you dislike her." I shot her a look during that last sentence, and I knew she felt it. She stayed silent after that, and to our luck Anna walked back in just as I had finished. She gave us each a glass of water, and set down a tray of warm cookies in front of us. For a moment there, she seemed uneasy, and I prayed she hadn't heard what either of us had said to each other. The tense look on her face quickly went away when Emma leaned forward and grabbed herself a cookie, smiling as she took her first bite. Anna sat herself back down in between us, and we resumed the movie.

MIA MANDALA | *Dear Anna,*

  I stretched out my blanket so Anna could get some of it too, while Emma leaned her head in the opposite direction. Her eyes started to close before the movie was done. Anna and I became more and more invested as the film went on, and made sure not to fall asleep before it ended. Our blanket was up to our chins, and we were practically glued together on the couch. I was watching the film so intently I didn't realize Anna had laid her head on my shoulder till I looked over to find her fast asleep, a small smile on her lips.
  Nothing could have made me happier.

## 14
## October 6th, 2017

"*M*issy! Come over here ..." School had just let out, and I began making my way over to where Harper was slouched against a wall. I feel my phone buzzing in my pocket, just as I'm about to sit down.

"One sec"—I answer the call, putting the phone to my ear—"Hello?"

"Missy, you can't stay late today, I'm picking you up from school right now. I'm about a minute away." My mom sounded firm in her words.

"What? Why?" I ask, my voice full of concern. My mom is never like this.

"Your father and I have to talk to you about something."

"What? About what?"

"Stop asking questions Missy, just come out to the car," she insists.

"Uh ... yeah sure." I hang up the call, having no clue what is happening.

I look back at Harper, sitting next to her now are Logan and Sam. Nearby, Morgan lounges in Mark's lap. Harper motions for me to come over, clearly having seen my weird reaction to the phone call.

"Hey, is everything okay?" Harper stands up.

"Yeah, I think. I don't know, my mom's being all weird. She says I have to go home. I'm sure it's all fine, just kind of random," I explain quickly. Harper gives me a worried look. "I gotta go, my mom should be here already."

"Okay, let me know if you need anything." Harper gives me a warm smile, and a quick hug. I lean down and hug Logan from behind, kissing his cheek.

"Bye," I whisper in his ear, and I see a smile creep up his face. He turns around, holding onto my arm before I can walk away.

"Why are you leaving in such a hurry?" he asks, kissing along my arm.

"I don't know. Something with my parents, they need to talk to me, I guess." I look down at my phone and see a missed call from my mom and a missed text asking where I am. "I really gotta go. Sorry." I give him another kiss on the cheek, and he immediately turns back to Sam, continuing their previous conversation.

I walk away from them, and give a final look back. I don't know exactly what I wanted Logan to do. I guess I was just hoping he would be more interested in what was going on.

Like Harper was.

Two thoughts ring through my mind.

It doesn't matter, it's not his job to worry about me.

But he didn't even seem to care at all.

*I wish he would care more.*

The ride to my house is spent in complete silence, and my mom keeps a death stare on the road. I try turning up the radio, but she turns it off without a word.

We walk inside awkwardly, as if my mom is trying to avoid my eyes as much as possible. Once we get inside and I see my dad sitting anxiously at the dinner table, I know something is up.

"Okay, what the hell is going on?"

My dad storms up from his seat, slamming his hand on the table. "Missy! Sit down. And when you talk to us, you will talk to us with respect."

I laugh a little on the inside and pull out a chair while my mom sits down across from me. "What's going on?" I ask once again.

"We know you've been skipping your classes."

"I—"

"No, Missy. This is *completely* unacceptable. What are you doing?!" My mom stands up out of anger, making her way toward me. "Seriously, we are done with the shit you have been pulling. You need to get your act together or I swear Missy—"

Now I stand up, "Or what Mom? What will you do?"

"Sit down!" my dad screams, and his booming voice takes me by such surprise that I do slowly sit down.

My mom towers over me, and I have to crane my neck to look all the way up at her. "If we find out you skip one more class—"

"Then what? You're not going to do anything," I scoff in her face.

"You are acting *completely* insane!" my dad screams, inching closer and closer to my face.

"Your dad is right Missy, you are acting crazy and I don't know what has gotten into you!"

My parents keep staring at me, and to be honest it's quite unnerving. It's like they are just waiting for some reaction. Like they want me to fall apart and sob into their arms, confessing how miserable my life has gotten.

But I won't give them that satisfaction.

I stand up from the table, tuning out their screams of protest. I slip out of the house as quickly as I can, loudly slamming the door in their faces. I leave them alone with their anger, and sprint away from my house till I'm a few houses down and out of their view.

I take out my phone and dial Logan's phone number. He answers after a few rings. "Huh?" His voice sounds all gravely, like he just woke up, even though it's still only just after 3 p.m.

"Can you come pick me up? I *need* to get out of this house."

It's like I can hear him smiling through the phone.

"Yeah sure, be there in a sec."

"Pick me up a few houses down. I don't want my parents seeing."

"Yeah, of course," he replies, then hangs up.

***

"Hey, Missy!" I look up to see Logan, with his head hanging out the window of someone's SUV. He's a few houses down, and I run to catch up to him. The person driving the car rolls down the windows.

"Come on, get in." Harper smiles at me from the driver's seat, and I catch a glimpse of Morgan sitting across from her. I open the door to the backseat, where Logan, Sam, and Mark are all squished up next to each other.

I guess Logan brought the whole group with him.

I look around, trying to figure out where I'm supposed to sit, because I know there is *no way* I can squeeze between the three boys who already barely fit. Sam and Mark look at each other laughing, then back to me. "Come on Missy, sit on your *boyfriend's* lap," Sam says to me, except it sounded more like, "Come onnn Missyyy, sit on your boyyyfriend's lapp," as his words were extremely slurred. I look at Logan, and he motions for me to sit on his lap.

I cautiously sit on his lap, and take a few seconds to find a way I can sit comfortably without totally squashing him. He wraps one arm around my waist, and uses the other to hold my face as he greets me with a kiss. Out of the corner of my eye, I see Sam and Mark "oohing" and "aahing" at us but I just ignore them and roll my eyes. I can't help but let Sam's words ring through my mind. Sit on your *boyfriend's* lap.

Your *boyfriend's* lap.

Your *boyfriend*.

*Boyfriend*.

Is that what we are? Is he my boyfriend? Am I his girlfriend? The thought of it almost sounds bizarre to me.

I'm not sure why it does though.

I mean it would make sense.

We are together almost all of the time. Most of that time is taken up by making out and it's not like my feelings for him aren't there.

But boyfriend?

*Does he call me his girlfriend?*

I should feel happy about this, but I can't help but have the same sinking feeling I had when we first met in the park.

*That this is all wrong.*

My mind is still wandering, so it takes me a second to realize Logan has tilted my face toward his and has begun kissing me all over.

*But everything feels so right.*

I kiss him back, and while it's a little hard to make out in a squished car that keeps bumping up and down, we make it work. Harper's eyes are locked on the road and doesn't seem to notice what me and Logan are doing. Morgan looks back, and winks at me. The sound of us kissing gets drowned out by the radio that Morgan turns up to full volume, as does the sound of Sam and Mark inanely blabbering on about something nonsensical.

I keep myself as close as I can to Logan, so that my whole body is pressed against his chest. The car goes over a speed bump, but Logan holds me against him. His fingertips trail up and down my thighs, and we don't take a second to breathe. Harper rolls down everyone's windows, and I feel a rush of wind come over me. My hair is going wild and is all in my face, but I quickly tie it into a ponytail, not letting my lips leave his.

We pull our faces away from each other's for a moment, both catching our breath. "Hey," he says, pushing a strand of hair out of my face.

I practically want to die at the sight of him.

*Oh god, what his smile does to me.*

It takes everything in me to not start blushing and giggling like a little girl. "Hi," I say, and give him a quick peck on his lips. He goes to grab my face again, wanting a repeat of what just happened, but I lift my head up, needing a second to breathe. I'm sitting with my legs slightly to the right of him, so I swing them up and let them lay on top of Sam and Mark.

"Finally you two are done," Sam remarks, trying to push my legs off him. I just laugh and playfully kick the air near his face.

"Thought you two were about to have a quickie in the back of Harp's car," Mark adds.

"Ew! *Please* do not!" yells Harper from the driver's seat.

Logan flips Mark off, "It's not like you and Morgan are any better." Morgan throws her head back, giving both boys a look.

Logan brushes my hair out of my face, and I think he's going to go in for another kiss. Instead, he moves toward my neck, and starts kissing me from my collarbone up to my chin.

By the time he's done, Harper is pulling the car to a stop.

I awkwardly crawl off Logan's lap and hop out of the car. Everyone else is busy getting out of the car, and I look around at where we are. While it looks like we are just in an empty parking lot, I look past it and can see waves crashing against the sand.

*I haven't been to the beach in so long.*

Logan runs up behind me, grabbing my waist. I giggle as he squeezes his arms tight around me. He kisses my cheek softly, which tickles a little.

Sam and Mark take off running into the water, and Morgan follows behind. Logan starts running after them, and grabs my hand, pulling me along with him. I laugh as we run down the sand, not caring about the loads of sand getting in my shoes. Logan throws off his shirt, and unbuttons his pants so he's just in boxers. He starts to drag us both into the water, but I pull back and quickly take off my sweater, so all I'm wearing is my bra and shorts. Logan gives a quick look at me, and smirks.

"Come on!" Sam yells, who is already far out in the water and standing where the sand bar is. Logan runs into the water, and I follow behind. Mark splashes Morgan, causing her makeup to slowly run down her face.

"Mark!" she pushes his shoulders, and he dramatically falls back into the small waves, getting completely soaked. They both laugh as Mark pulls Morgan down into the water with him.

The water is freezing but I don't care. I jump on Logan's back, and he spins me around before letting us both fall back into the water.

I stay in the water for a little longer with Harper and Morgan. We splash each other till not an ounce of makeup remains on our faces, and we are completely drenched. Mark and Sam throw a football back and forth in the sand, and we laugh as Mark falls over trying to catch the ball. He stands back up, all the sand sticking to his hair and his shorts.

Logan walks back over to us, bringing towels and a few bottles and cups from the car. We get out of the ocean, and sit around Logan. He starts passing around cups full of some alcohol I don't even know the name of. I hesitate as he hands one to me, remembering what happened the last time. I lower my nose into the cup, and get a whiff of what smells like a mix of hand sanitizer and cleaning supplies. I look around and see Logan and all his friends drinking without hesitation, barely taking a second to put their cups down.

*Screw it,* I decide.

Today has been such a shitshow already, and I need a break from it all.

I put the cup to my lips, and start chugging the drink till the taste in my mouth is burning and sickly.

I pour myself more and more, passing it back and forth to Sam and Logan who seem to be drinking with the same speed and necessity as I am.

"Woah Missy, leave some for the rest of us!" Morgan jokes as I pour more, filling up the entirety of my cup.

I look at her and pout, before tilting back the whole bottle and drinking a few sips straight from it. Logan and Sam holler and cheer me on. I hand the bottle back to Morgan, leaving her with just barely two sips left. She gives me a weird look, then looks over to Harper. I ignore them, and crawl over to Logan.

"Dance with me."

He laughs, "What?"

"Dance with me," I repeat.

Sam nudges Logan in the side, cracking up, "Yeah Logan, go dance with your girl." I look at him wistfully, grabbing his hands.

"Come on! You're so boring! Let's dance!" I pull him up awkwardly from the sand till he gives in and follows me.

I lead him closer to the ocean, and wrap my arms around his neck, having to go on my tiptoes to reach all the way around him. I sway in a drunken fashion against his chest. He stands there stiff, completely uncomfortable and unsure of what to do. I grab his arms and pull them around my waist till he's supporting most of my weight and keeping me from collapsing against him. Logan grabs my hand and twirls me around till everything in my sight is a complete blur. I spin into his arms, trying to let my vision refocus itself.

I lean my head against his chest and close my eyes, listening to the sound of the ocean waves crash against the shore.

Memories flood through my mind, flashbacks to a *different* time, when I was a *different* girl.

Back when I was carefree, but not as reckless as I am now. When my days consisted of nothing more than girlish sleepovers and watching scary movies at night.

To a time when Anna and Emma were all that mattered.

## MIA MANDALA | *Dear Anna,*

I take in a deep breath, the sweet smell of Logan filling the air around me. The taste of salt water mixed with alcohol lingers on his lips.

I look up at him and smile.

*I don't think he smiles back.*

"We should probably go back," I tell him, pulling away slightly. He doesn't reply and drops his hands, already walking back to his friends. I stay standing in the hot sand, my feet burning up as I watch him walk farther and farther away from me.

A small tear forms in my eye, threatening to fall. I wipe it away, knowing if one comes, then the rest won't stop.

"Come on!" I snap out of my trance as I hear Harper call me over. I smile, and walk back toward everyone. Every step I take feels like my feet are falling deeper and deeper into the hot sand, and the walk back to my friends feels like it takes an hour rather than a short minute.

Sam walks up to me, handing me another cup that I chug down in a matter of seconds.

I bend down to sit next to Harper, but trip over my feet while doing so. I look up and see Logan and Sam staring down at me, laughing as I lay sprawled out on the sand. Harper stands up and gets close to Sam's face. "Shut up, you guys. And Sam, seriously, stop giving her more. She's had enough." Sam laughs in her face, pours yet another cup, and hands it to me once I'm sitting upright again.

Sam and I go back and forth pouring, drinking, and quickly getting more and more drunk. My whole body feels like it's been lit on fire, but in a strange way it feels almost comforting. Through my blurred vision I see Logan waving for me to come over to him. I give him a big smile and push my hands on the sand underneath me, trying to stand up properly. I take a few steps his way, and instantly begin to feel my insides churning. My head feels like it's in flames, I start to freak out and suddenly feel incredibly sick.

I try to call out to Harper but no sound comes out. Instead, I close my eyes as I throw up all over myself.

*Oh my god.*

*Oh my god. Oh my god.*

I turn around, trying to hide from everyone, but I can't ignore the gawking stares coming from Logan and Sam. I hear them snicker, and desperately try to find Harper. I start to hyperventilate, unable to catch my breath. I've never felt so disgusting in my life, and I pray that this is all just a bad dream.

"Harper!" I yell out, to no one in particular. My brain feels like it's gone to mush and I try to get my breathing under control. I spot Harper a few feet away, but even that feels like miles away. She sees me, and immediately runs over. She freezes in place, her jaw dropping slightly.

"Oh Missy."

I start to cry even harder. "I'm so sorry," I say through my sobs. I watch as Logan walks closer to us, and I'm absolutely terrified of him seeing me like this. I look at Harper, silently asking for her to help me.

*Please, help me.*

"Seriously, Missy?" Logan says as I take a step toward him hoping he'll help me. Instead, he backs away laughing. "You look gross."

Harper looks at him with disgust, and pushes him out of the way, "What the hell is your problem?" He doesn't say anything. "Whatever, I'll help her. Missy, come with me."

She helps me walk, taking one slow step at a time. I look back at Logan, only to see him walking away from me, once again.

We get to the car, and she pops open the trunk. She helps me up, till I'm able to sit with my legs dangling off the back. She leaves for a minute then comes back with a giant blanket pulled from out of the car. "Here." She hands it to me, and I immediately wrap it around myself, still shaking from my breakdown. I wipe my eyes with it, and Harper doesn't seem to care I've now gotten her blanket covered in snot. "Drink some water, I'll find a towel to clean you up." I gladly take her water bottle, enjoying the cool taste of the water going down my throat and taking the opportunity to rinse out my mouth.

She comes back with a towel, and I wipe most of the mess off of me, the smell still lingering. Once I've cleaned myself up and seem more calm, she hands me a clean t-shirt, and leads me back to the sand. I stop for a second, putting my head in my hands as it starts to pound. Harper rubs my back till I'm ready to keep walking.

We find a spot in the sand, far from everyone else and she sets out a blanket for both of us on the ground. I kneel down next to her and cross my legs as I sit. I watch as she plays with the sand next to her, and doesn't look up from the ground.

We sit in silence, too many questions left hanging in the air between us. Finally she looks at me, "Can you *please* tell me what's going on?"

"What do you mean?" I ask.

"You *know* what I mean."

"No I don't, I don't know—"

"Missy, just stop." I look down, fiddling with my hands in my lap. "You can talk to me about anything you want." I look back up at her and can feel tears welling up in my eyes.

*I don't want to cry.*

*I can't cry right now.*

*If I cry I may never stop.*

Harper looks at me and starts to say something, but stops herself. She stares at me for a few seconds, and I wish I could understand what was going through her head. "What is it?" I finally ask. Harper takes in a deep breath, and looks down at something. I follow her eyes and see what she is staring at.

*My arms.*
*And all the cuts that cover them.*
*Shit.*
"Missy—"

I wrap my arms in the blanket, trying to cover myself as much as possible. "It's not what it looks like. I swear, I fell off my bike—"

"We both know that's not true," she says, in almost a whisper.

"I—"

But she cuts me off before I can continue lying. "Look. You don't have to tell me what's going on. But I *really* think you should."

"I don't know what you mean, nothing is wrong. I'm fine—"

"Don't bullshit me." She's still staring straight at the ocean, but it's like I can feel her staring into my soul.

*She sees right through my bullshit.*
*She's really the only one who can.*

"OK, listen Missy," she says seriously. "My life used to be shit. I *let* my life go to shit. Because I didn't care, I didn't care about anything, *not even my own life.* I ignored all my feelings until one day there were just too many to handle." Then she turns to me and says, "That's when I tried to kill myself." She said it so easily, so casually.

"What?!" I started. *What are you supposed to say to that?*

I have no idea.

"Oh my god, I'm so sorry."

"Don't," she stops me mid-sentence. "No need to apologize. It was a long time ago."

"Why—?" I wanted to know more but I was scared to ask.

"It's okay, you can ask," she says, as if she can read my thoughts.

I bite my lip nervously, "Why did you do it?"

Harper takes in a deep breath, "I grew up with a really messy family. Parents were never home, and a lot of the time I was left to take care of my siblings. But that wasn't why I tried to kill myself. I love my siblings, I would *never* mean to leave them."

I look at her confused. "So why did you do it?"

She keeps explaining, "Beginning of middle school I was getting sick of it. Of *all* of it. I wanted my parents, I wanted their attention. I felt"—she searches for the words to continue—"I felt invisible. I wanted someone, *anyone* to notice me. I started trying to make a ton of friends, but then that all went to shit too. I was never really my true self around them." I nod knowingly.

"Anyway, fast forward a few years and I still felt alone. Not many friends, at least not many I would consider actually calling good friends, and still desperately craving my parents' attention. I turned to tearing myself down. I stopped caring about school, and any other responsibilities I had. I started trying to find ways to destroy myself. Inside and out, I wanted to turn my pain into something I could physically feel or see because it just felt like there was all too much of it to handle. I think a part of me thought that if I didn't care about anything I would feel a lot less invisible. That was *really* wrong."

    She takes a moment to finish her story, and I sit there listening intently. It's hard for me to even imagine the Harper she keeps talking about. The Harper I know has lots of friends, and everyone seems to love her so much.

    She's been one of the nicest and most caring people I've ever met.

    She keeps talking.

    "It continued like that throughout freshman year, and one day I was just so done with everything. I didn't find the point in anything, I thought no one would care if I lived or died. So I went home, and shoved handfuls of pills down my throat. I don't remember what happened after that, at some point I just passed out." Harper takes a moment to wipe her eyes, and I realize she has started tearing up. "I found out later that it was my youngest sister who found me. I felt *so* guilty for having her find me like that. I made myself promise that I would never let that happen again. I was done letting my life go to waste."

Harper looks out to the water where Morgan is swimming around with Mark nearby and she smiles looking at them. "The very next day I met Morgan. And we *immediately* became best friends."

She turns back to me, putting her hair behind her ears to stop it from blowing in her face. "If I hadn't met Morgan, I don't know what I would have done."

*Anna was my Morgan.*
*And I lost her.*

"Look, Missy." Harper gives me a serious look. "All I'm trying to say is that I understand what you're going through, and I'm telling you, if you let this continue it will just get worse and worse." She takes a pause, "I would *never* forgive myself if that happened to you." She says it so quietly that I'm not sure if she said it to me or to herself. "You don't have to right now, but just know you can talk to me, okay?"

I nod my head, doing my best to give her a small smile, tears welling up in my eyes. I want to say something, but I'm scared I'll start crying if I do. We both spend the next few minutes in silence, staring at the horizon.

My mind starts running through memories of Anna.
*I wish she were still here.*
*I miss her more than anything.*

I look at Harper for a moment and debate whether I should tell her about everything.
*About Anna.*
  *About my parents.*

MIA MANDALA | *Dear Anna,*

*About my friends.*
*About everything.*

But I don't tell her any of that. I don't even think I could find the words if I tried.

I stare back at the ocean, and a faint memory of Anna pops into my head. It was the summer before sixth grade, and Anna and I were a mess of excitement and being *absolutely terrified* for middle school.

She and I were still in our phase of wearing long matching socks that reached all the way to our knees, and dying our hair with crappy drugstore dye.

I can still picture exactly how we both looked that day.

Anna had taken streaks of her blonde hair and covered it with a chalky pink dye, and I had put blue in mine. Anna had come up with the idea to do it, because she thought everyone would think we were sisters if we did.

She had come over that day for some last minute back to school shopping, and when we arrived back at my house *all* we could do was talk about middle school. All the boys we were going to meet, all the new friends, the new teachers, and of course what we wanted to wear, everything a young girl dreams of when starting sixth grade.

A couple hours later Anna's mom showed up to take her home. I remember so vividly how sad I was that she had to leave, I started crying and begging for her to stay and sleep over. I told everyone it was because I needed her help with packing my backpack for school, but truthfully, it was because I was so nervous for school and she was the only one who could really help me calm down.

    In the end, Laurie still wouldn't let her sleep over, but agreed to take us out of the house and on a little "road trip," as she called it, to help us both calm our nerves.

    The whole car ride, Anna and I blasted music, screaming the lyrics out the car windows. Neither of us could sing to save our lives, but we didn't care. We laughed and sang and talked the whole way. Looking back, I don't know how her mom dealt with us.

    After about an hour of driving, Laurie parked the car, and we ran out to see where we were. "Surprise!" she exclaimed, as we looked out to see that she had taken us to the beach. Neither Anna nor I had been to the beach in months, but had been talking *nonstop* about going for the past week. Her mom grabbed towels and a cooler out of the trunk of the car, and let us run ahead.

    We didn't bring any bathsuits, but we couldn't have cared less.

    We raced toward the water, tearing our shoes off as we ran across the hot sand. I let my hair down out of its braid, and watched as the blue dye slowly faded away as I got deeper in the water.

    The whole day felt like it was out of a movie. We layed out towels to sit and watch the sunset, and stayed until it got dark.

I would do anything to relive that day.

I snap out of my daydream and tears start flowing that I desperately try to wipe away before Harper notices. "Oh Missy ..."

*Too late.*

Harper encloses me in a warm hug, my tears seeping into her sweater.

*I can't stop them.*

I wrap my arms around her and bury my face in her shoulder in an attempt to quiet my sobs. Harper rubs my back and whispers little sayings in my ear, "It's going to be okay... I'm here... You're okay..."

I want the tears to stop, but they just won't.

All I can think about is Anna. How much I wish she were here. She would *love* Harper, but probably *hate* Logan.

My sobs quiet down but Harper continues soothing me. "Do you want to talk about it?" she asks in a whisper. I lift my head up from her shoulder and shake my head. Harper starts to protest, "But are you sure—"

"I *really* don't want to talk about it," I say, cutting her off. She nods her head understandingly, and I wipe the dried tears off my cheeks.

"There's something else I wanted to talk to you about, Missy ..." she begins, slowly pulling back from our hug. "It's about Logan."

"Wait, what?"

"Whatever you have going on with him. It needs to stop."

"What? Isn't Logan your friend?" I don't understand why she is saying this, I only met Harper *because* of Logan.

"He is, but Missy"—she stops, as if searching for the right words to use—"he's not a very good person to you, or even a good person in general."

"If he's that awful, then why are you friends with him?" I say, crossing my arms.

She sighs, "It's more complicated than that, but I'm telling you, he's hurt people really, *really* badly in the past and I can't have that happen to you. So please Missy, you *have* to stop this. You're being completely reckless and you know it. If you continue like this, you're going to end up the same way I did."

I back away from her a little.

How could she comfort me, then say all this? *And about her own friend.*

"I'm not being reckless!" I stand up, towering over her.

"Missy, I'm just saying he might not be as good for you as you think."

"No!" I am screaming now, I don't want to hear any more of what she has to say. I'm so angry I can feel it in my bones. "He *is* good for me. He's *great* to me!"

She tries reaching up to pull my arms back down, but I pull away fast. "Please, I'm only trying to help you."

"I'm not some little kid. I can make my own decisions!"

"I never said you couldn't, I just—"

"No. Logan is the best thing that's happened to me in a long time!" I am trying to stay strong – to keep my voice from breaking, and my knees from buckling underneath me. "I *love* him, Harper!"

She stands up, her face level with mine. "No. You don't."

"*Yes*. I do."

She steps in closer to me. "No, Missy. You don't. And don't let him trick you into thinking that you do."

"And how would you know? You don't know *anything* about me! I'm not your broken mess you get to fix!" I'm screaming now, my voice echoing in the air around us.

"Missy, I—"

"Harper, what is your problem with me?" I don't understand how our conversation has even turned into an argument, but I can feel the anger rising through every inch of my body.

"What are you even saying, Missy? I'm just trying to help you."

"Well, stop. I don't need your help. Just leave me alone!" I give her one last look, and take off running away from her as fast as I can.

And right back to Logan.

# 15

## April 30th, 2017

*Six months ago*

"*A*nd this year's prom queen is ... Emma Marie!" I watched as the biggest smile came over Emma's face, and seeing how happy she looked made the stressful hours of getting ready all that much more worth it.

The anticipation leading up to our eighth grade prom was nothing compared to the actual day of the event itself. I truly thought Anna and Emma were going to *lose* their minds if something went wrong.

We all met up at Anna's house about three hours before we had to leave, and it was *absolute* chaos.

Three hours full of Emma bitching at us, jewelry being tossed around, *and lots and lots of laughing.*

Makeup was being thrown all across the room, clothes were everywhere, and the three of us were trying to squeeze our way in front of the small bathroom mirror, all while sharing makeup tricks and curling each others' hair. Eventually Anna offered to do my makeup, and I was extremely grateful for it. Emma though, was truly starting to freak out. She was in the running for prom queen, but seemed to be taking it with the same level of seriousness as if she were in the hunt for an Oscar.

"Where's my mascara?" she asked us, as Anna applied the final touch of lip gloss to my makeup.

We both looked at her blankly and Anna shrugged, "I don't know Em, but here, you can use mine if you want." Anna offered her mascara to Emma, but she pushed it away.

"Whatever. I'll find it," she said, rolling her eyes and walking away from us.

I *really* hated it when she snapped like that, but *especially* when she did it to Anna.

Luckily, we all finished our makeup and curled or straightened our hair, with few to no issues in the next hour. When we were done, Anna connected her phone to a small speaker I had given her a few years back, and she started blasting a playlist the three of us had made together one night.

We danced around Anna's room, singing at the top of our lungs, until we realized the time and rushed to change into our dresses and shoes. "Girls! Are you almost ready?" Anna's mom yelled from downstairs.

"Almost Mom!" Anna replied, as Emma quickly finished zipping up the back of her dress.

Anna's mom walked in shortly after, gasping happily at the sight of us. "Oh! You girls look beautiful!" she said through a teary-eyed smile.

"Mom! Don't cry. It's just prom!" Anna teased, hugging her mom tightly.

"You girls have just grown up so much."

Looking at Anna and Emma, I had to agree with Laurie. We *had* all grown up so much, and it was crazy to think back to the day we first became a trio, terrified and awkward on our first day of middle school. Now Emma stood before me, her black hair curled so perfectly it bounced right off her shoulders. Her simple makeup highlighted all of her best features, and the deep blue dress she chose for tonight swayed all the way down to her ankles.

It was hard to look at her and remember *that was* the same girl who barely spoke a word the first day we met.

Anna's dad walked in soon after, a bulky camera in his hand. "Quick! Get together for a few photos!" he exclaimed, motioning for us to move in closer. We posed for a few photos, smiling stiffly at first, but as time passed we relaxed and got more and more into them. Anna stood between me and Emma, and we both kissed her on the cheek, receiving a laugh from everyone in the room.

Emma pulled out her own phone, snapping a few selfies with the three of us before running out to get into the Williamses' car. It wasn't easy fitting all of us and our giant dresses into the back of their car, but eventually we found a way to get in comfortably.

"Ready?" Laurie asked from the front seat, and we all cheered in response.

"YES!"

The car ride there didn't feel real, all of us wanted to get there so badly that we spent half of it tracking how much longer till we arrived, and the other half dreaming what it would be like. "Oh, I know I shouldn't say it ... but I really hope I win prom queen!" Emma exclaimed nervously as we were a few minutes away.

The winner was chosen by an anonymous ballot listing every girl in the grade who wanted to run for queen. I knew there was no way I would be doing that, not wanting to embarrass myself in front of everyone. Regardless, I didn't have nearly as many friends as Emma did. Out of the three of us, Emma had come out of her shell the most drastically since we met her. What once was a shy little girl had now turned into one of the most popular and loved girls at the school.

Even I had to admit, she looked beautiful up there. Our principal placed a cheap, plastic tiara on her head, and layed a long "PROM QUEEN 2017" sash over her shoulder. Everyone clapped and cheered, and Anna had the biggest smile on her face.

As embarrassing as everyone found it, our school kept with the tradition of the Prom Queen and King dance. The music started playing again, at first some old love song that made Emma and Jack, her prom king, laugh at as they swayed back and forth. Anna couldn't contain her giggles watching their awkward attempt at a slow dance. Soon after, the music picked back up and more and more people joined in on the dancing.

"Want to dance?" Anna asked, stretching out her hand to me as if we were waltzing in the 1800s. I laughed, "Well, of course!" I intertwined my hand in hers, and let her pull me onto the dance floor.

Anna spun me around with her. She placed one hand on my waist, and kept her other hand clutching mine close. We waltzed around the floor like we were little kids again watching princess movies. I spun Anna out, then back to me, swooping her into a dip as I did. I pulled her back up slowly, admiring how her face lit up as I did. Looking at her just made me want to smile.

"You look beautiful, Anna," I whispered in her ear, and saw her blush in response. It was the truth, she looked *stunning*. Her dress of choice was completely white, and although the design was simple, I knew when she first tried it on that it was the perfect dress for her. With her blonde hair curled softly, and dainty pearl earrings to match, she looked absolutely angelic.

If it were up to me, Anna would have been the one up there with the sash. Showing everyone just how beautiful she looked today, sparkling in her prom queen tiara. I was happy for Emma, of course, but in my eyes, Anna was the perfect prom queen.

We continued to dance around, giggling when we bumped into people. "We should go find Em," she said.

"Yeah, I think she's over there by Mia." Anna left to go find her before I even had a moment to find my balance. Truthfully, I didn't want to go find her. I wanted to stay on that dance floor spinning with Anna forever and ever.

The music was now much louder than before, and almost everyone was dancing around me. It took me some time to make my way toward Anna and Emma, having to push past a sea of people on the way there.

When I found them, Anna was howling with laughter at something Emma had said, and Emma was giggling at her reaction. I walked up to them slowly, unsure if they realized I was there. When they did, Anna's attention turned straight to me, smiling.

"Em! Congrats on prom queen!" I exclaimed, as I squeezed her into a tight hug, while Anna came up behind us and joined in. We all cheered for Emma, for each other, for tonight.

It really was an amazing night. I wished it would never have to end.

"Oh my god!" Anna exclaimed. Some pop song that Anna and Emma *always* insisted on playing in the car, started booming through the speaker.

"C'mon! Let's go dance!" Emma yelped excitedly, pulling me and Anna by the arms and onto the dance floor.

We ran to the center of the floor, and joined in with everybody who had started jumping up and down, singing along. We threw our arms in the air, and danced around like it was just us out there. Emma and Anna had begun to scream the lyrics at each other while I watched and couldn't contain my laughter. The smiles on our faces felt contagious, it felt like we were little girls again with no cares in the world.

At some point, Anna grabbed my hands in hers, and started dancing around again with me. She lifted her arm, and twirled me around a million times till I was so dizzy I almost fell into her arms. We collapsed into a heap on the floor, laughing so hard our eyes started watering. Once my vision felt back to normal, she helped me up to my feet and we continued to dance around. We made our way to the corner of the room where we reenacted an old handshake we used to do as little kids. I went to slap Anna's hand, but missed completely and almost hit her right in the face, causing us both to laugh even harder.

Anna pulled me in for a tight hug, and I wrapped my arms around her neck. I felt like I could feel her smile radiating onto me.

"I love you so much, Missy."

"I love you more."

We stayed in that hug for a few minutes, soaking in each other's happiness. The music started to slow down, and more and more people made their way off the dance floor. Everyone gathered with their friends at different tables, chatting and grabbing food. But Anna and I were lost in our own little world. I hugged my arms even tighter around her neck, and we started to sway gracefully along to the music. Her grip on my waist tightened, and we made no effort to move away from each other.

Suddenly, Anna dropped her arms and began to look around frantically. "Wait, where's Em?" she asked anxiously. I turned around, suddenly realizing Emma wasn't with us anymore.

"Wasn't she just with us a few minutes ago?" We both scanned the room, trying to see where she might have gone. I spotted one of Emma's friends walking by, and motioned to Anna.

"Sophie!" Anna and I shouted in unison, grabbing Sophie's attention from across the floor.

"Hm?" she pushed her way through a few people till she reached us.

"Have you seen Emma? We were just dancing with her but now we don't know where she went."

"She didn't tell you guys?" Anna and I shook our heads, unsure as to what she was referring to. "Pretty sure she went over to Mia's—"

"Wait. She left?"

I looked over at Anna, and watched as her expression dropped.

"Uh ... yeah, I think," Sophie said, looking at us confused. "Do you want me to call her or something?" she asked.

I shook my head. "No, it's fine, don't worry. Thank you." She gave us a small smile, and turned to walk in the opposite direction. I looked at Anna, who hadn't spoken a word since Sophie told us.

I had never seen her look so dejected. She wouldn't look up from the floor, but I could tell she was about to cry. I placed my hand on her back, not knowing what else to do. I rubbed small circles on her lower back till she finally looked up. Her eyes were red and teary-eyed. "Anna, what's wrong?" It was a stupid question to ask, I knew. I just didn't know what else there was to say.

"Why did she leave without us? She didn't even say anything! We had a whole plan, we were all going to leave, then we were going to sleep at your house, and it was going to be so much fun and—" Anna was spiraling, trying to understand what happened, then she broke into small sobs in my arms. I helped her walk to one of the tables, careful not to let anyone see her cry. I pulled out a chair for her, and sat down next to her. She tried wiping away her tears, but they just kept coming.

It felt bizarre to see her like this.

In all the years we had been friends, I had rarely seen her cry. She was always so happy and outgoing, but now she just looked broken. I took her shaky hands in mine and squeezed them tight. "I'm sure there's a reason why she left," I said, trying to reassure her.

She kept shaking her head. "No. No. I know there isn't. She just didn't want to be with us, I guess," she said, trying to make a joke, but her smile just made her crack even more. She buried her head in my hands, trying to catch her breath. She lifted her head back up. "I'm so sorry, Missy."

"For what?"

She wiped away her tears, and tried to look somewhat composed. "For crying like this at prom!"

"Anna, it's okay."

She sighed dejectedly, staring at the floor.

"Do you want me to see if we can go home now?"

She nodded her head sadly. "Okay."

By the time my dad got there to pick us up, Anna had stopped crying. She still looked incredibly sad, but she was much more back to her usual self now. We got in the car, and spent the ride to my house in silence. I occasionally looked over to find her sniffling, or wiping away a few stray tears.

We got to my house, and changed out of our giant dresses. Once we were in more comfortable clothes, and had wiped or cried off most of our makeup, I offered to watch a movie with Anna. "We can even watch that *super* cheesy movie you've been trying to get me to watch," I told her with a wink.

While Anna settled into the couch, I grabbed a few blankets for us, and a glass of water for her. We cuddled up next to each other as Anna turned on the movie. I was happy to see that she seemed to be enjoying the movie, laughing at the funny parts, and of course, adding her commentary throughout it.

By the time the film was over, she didn't seem to be thinking about Emma anymore, and was just about ready to fall asleep.

# 16
## October 2017

"Well, stop. I don't need your help. Just leave me alone!"

I run on the hot sand, away from Harper and over to Logan. He is sitting with his legs out in front of him, talking to Sam and Mark. I straddle my legs on either side of him, pushing my body as close to him as I possibly can. But no matter how close I get to him, it never feels like enough.

I need him.

I need him more than *anything* right now.

I grab his face in my hands, and kiss him hard till we can't breathe. He stops me for a second and I get scared he's going to get upset with me for interrupting his conversation. Instead, he picks me up in his arms, and twirls me around before racing back into the water with me still gripped tightly in his arms.

Once we're in the water I wrap my legs around his body and my arms around his neck. He keeps me from falling from the push of the waves against us. We kiss, and kiss, and I try to forget about the argument with Harper with each one.

With Logan, I can do anything I want. I feel invincible. His hands make their way up my legs, then he stops for a second, and just smiles at me.

His smile reminds me of the first time we met. How little I knew back then, how little I knew that my life was suddenly going to change after meeting him. The sweet, sly smile I go to sleep dreaming about.

The smile that I so desperately *love*.

Morgan and Mark join us in the water, Morgan on Mark's back and him pretending to almost drop her as they run through the water. I watch them with envy, how happy they always seem with each other. The way they look at each other with such joy and light that makes my heart melt.

"So, Missy"—Morgan makes her way over to me—"my birthday's on Halloween and every year I throw this giant party, it's a lot of fun! You should come, if you don't have any other plans." I take no longer than a second to reply, knowing the Halloween I usually would have been spending with Emma will look *very* different this year.

"Of course I'll be there!" I say, as Moran squeals in excitement.

"Okay, perfect! I'll send you the details later. Also, it's a costume party and everyone always goes all out."

"Oh, I don't really have anything to wear."

"Oh my god!" Her face lights up, like she just came to a brilliant revelation.

"You should totally come costume shopping with me and Harper!" I look back to where I can still see Harper sitting alone in the sand. "C'mon, it'll be so much fun!" Morgan grabs my hands, pleading with me to say yes.

"Okay ..." I tell her, hesitant about being around Harper.

"Yay! We're going to have so much fun. Oh my god, I can show you all my favorite stores ..." She continues rambling on and on, but her voice gets drowned out in the back of my mind as I take another look back at Harper.

Her words linger in my mind.

I don't *want* to believe anything she said.

She was wrong. I know Logan is better than that. But still, her words won't leave my thoughts.

"So, I'll pick you up tomorrow?" I turn back around to Morgan, who is still standing behind me, now joined by Mark, his arms wrapped tightly around her waist.

"Yeah, that's fine." I give her a slight smile, then dunk my head under the water.

Wishing I never had to come back up again.

## 17

### October 2017

"*M*issy! Your friends are outside!"

"One sec!" I grab some money off my desk, and run outside to where Morgan is shouting my name from her car. Her window is rolled down, and her head sticks out the side. She has bright pink, heart-shaped sunglasses on her head, and her hair is tied up in a high ponytail.

"What are you waiting for? Get in!" I laugh, and climb in the back of Morgan's jeep. She leans back and embraces me in a tight hug, kissing my cheek and leaving a slight lipstick stain. I look over at Harper, and smile slightly as she turns to look at me.

"Hi, Missy."

"Hi."

Morgan doesn't seem to notice the tension between us, and if she does, then she does a great job at hiding it.

Morgan leans over and turns up the volume, till the whole car is blasting full of music. She plays some upbeat pop songs that I've only heard once or twice before on the radio. She rolls our windows down, speeding in and out of lanes like she is in a race to get somewhere. It is incredibly exhilarating, the feeling of the wind hitting me in the face full force, holding on with all my might as Morgan races around.

"Whoohoo!" she yelps out the window.

We approach a stop sign, and she reapplies a hefty load of bright red lipstick. Instead of dabbing the excess off onto her hand, she opens her sun visor and leans in to leave a kiss on the mirror. I can see tons of other faint kisses along the mirror, all at different stages of fading away.

She turns up the volume of her music *even* louder, and I didn't know a single song could blast through my ears so loudly. She takes off once again, humming along to the song. Slowly I realize I recognize the tune, and join in on her humming. She looks at me surprised when she hears me, and I laugh a little, feeling embarrassed. She bops her head back and forth, tapping along to the rhythm on her steering wheel. She begins singing along in an off-tune, uncaring kind of way. She sings with full confidence, even when she must know that not a single note is even close to being correct.

She doesn't seem to care.

She throws her hands up through her open sunroof, and whistles with the wind. There is something so beautiful about watching the confidence Morgan carries herself with, that I so wish I had even an ounce of.

I've only met one other person in my lifetime who came close to sharing that same type of energy.

"Come on! Sing with me!"

I let my fears wash away, and sing out the car window with the same confidence Morgan seems to have.

We laugh and scream songs out the window the rest of the way there.

*For a moment I have forgotten.*

Forgotten about *everything*.

Including the girl just a few feet away from me in the front seat, who hasn't spoken a word since I got in the car. I actually start wondering if she has somehow fallen asleep. It isn't until we're getting out of the car that I finally hear her speak up.

"So, where should we go first?" she asks so quietly that I think maybe she only meant to say it to Morgan, not to the both of us.

"I know the best place for makeup, we *have* to show Missy!" Harper stays silent, and nods her head. Morgan gives her a confused look, but brushes it off quickly and heads inside.

"So ..." Morgan says, and I spin around, feeling the light tap of her hand on my shoulder. "How's it going with your new boyfriend?"

"Uh ..." There was that word again.

*Boyfriend.*

*I guess that must mean it's true.*

I start to smile, just thinking of him.

"I don't know, it's good ... I think. What about you and Mark?"

She smiles, looking like she just entered some lovesick trance. "He's amazing. He's always been"—she takes a short pause—"I *really* love him."

"Ugh! You guys are absolutely adorable!" I tell her.

I didn't think I'd ever be one to envy the love two people have for each other till I met Mark and Morgan. You can actually see their eyes light up around each other, and Mark is so gentle with her, like she deserves the sun and the moon. They always seem so sure of themselves; I long to have a relationship that I feel that confident about.

Just hearing people call Logan my boyfriend sends a pit down to my stomach that I can't explain.

Harper walks by us quietly, looking at a pair of shoes. She glances over at us, and our eyes meet for a split second. I want to say something.

I want *her* to say something.

Her words ring like bells through my mind. I can't stop thinking about the beach. I can't tell who I'm more mad at.

Her or myself.

"Come with me."

I follow Morgan into a store with a wide wooden door at its opening. We push our way in, and I find that every inch of the shop is covered from floor to ceiling in makeup of every kind. Morgan's smile brightens, and I follow her as she mindlessly wanders around. She stops to look at something almost every second, and picks out different things for me to try.

"Here, let me put a little on your eyes, I promise you this would look *perfect* with your eye color." I close my eyes, and they flutter slightly as Morgan lightly applies a neutral colored eyeshadow to the corners of my eyelids. "Oh! You have to try this lip gloss too." Before I can open my eyes, I feel the sticky taste of gloss running over my lips. "Okay ... and open." She holds up her camera phone so I can see myself. "You look so pretty."

The moment she says that, I start feeling like I just might cry right then and there.

I swallow back tears, confused by my emotional response, and smile at my reflection. I smile at her and sincerely say, "Thank you."

"So how long have you and Mark been together?" I ask.

"Since sophomore year, so almost two years."

"Wow, that's crazy."

"Yeah, it was really fun when we first started dating, we would go on *tons* of double dates, almost every weekend!"

We slowly make our way into an aisle filled entirely with lipsticks.

"Double dates with who?" I ask, as she tests different shades of lipstick on the back of her hand.

"With Harper and Sam, obviously."

"Wait. Sam and Harper are dating?!" This was definitely news to me.

"No, no, no they *used* to be together," she explains.

"Oh, I had no idea."

"It was really fun, they started dating around the same time, and we literally did *everything* together." She links her arm in mine and we continue walking, swerving in and out of the aisles.

"What about you and Logan? When did you guys meet?" I stop dead in my tracks, quickly trying to come up with an explanation that might make any sense at all out of what was actually a totally random encounter.

"Uh … we met at a park a couple weeks ago." She turns to look at me, confused, yet still smiling.

"A park? That seems strange."

I force out a laugh, "Yeah."

"How did you guys start talking, did you kiss the day you met?" She continues pressing me with questions, and all I can muster is a nod yes or no.

I try to steer the conversation away from me and Logan, "Whatever happened with Harper and Sam? I had no idea they were even together at one point."

Morgan stops walking, dropping her arm from mine. She takes a second, looking around as if to make sure no one is listening.

"Honestly, I'm not really sure." I cock my head to the side as she continues. "It all happened so fast, one second they were great and going out on dates with me and Mark. Then they got all weird and distant, but Harper *insisted* everything was fine. Then one day Harper came up to me at school and just told me they had broken up."

"Do you know why they did?" I ask.

Morgan sighs, "Nope. She told me it just wasn't working out, but that they ended on good terms. Honestly though, I always thought it was something more. I don't really know, she always seemed to change the topic whenever I brought it up. So, I just stopped asking."

"Yeah, that's weird," I agree. We don't talk about it after, and I don't consider asking about it anymore.

Morgan turns to me, "Wanna find some costumes?"

"Oh my god, yes!" We giggle, linking our arms back into one another and going to find Harper.

"Where did she go?" Morgan swivels her head around, and I look for Harper in the crowd of people. "Oh! There she is!" Morgan runs ahead of me, pulling Harper out from a group of people all looking intently at a display of fake eyelashes. Morgan turns to her and quietly whispers, "You okay?" Harper nods and smiles. Morgan leans over and gives her a quick kiss on the cheek, brightening Harper's smile. "We were just about to go look for outfits for the party, you coming?"

"Yeah, of course."

Morgan turns to Harper, her face lighting up. "We *have* to take her into *Howie's!*"

"What's *Howie's?*" I ask.

They turn to each other, Morgan's jaw dropping. "You've *never* been to *Howie's?*"

"No ..."

"Well, then we *definitely* have to take you!"

They start walking ahead. "Come on!" They cheer in unison. They take off running, and I speed up to catch them. I watch from afar as Harper's smile returns to her face, running around with Morgan.

I don't think I've ever seen Harper unhappy when she's around Morgan. It's like they bring out the best in each other. Their smiles are always full when they're near each other, and their conversations always seem to be filled with so much laughter and light, it would make anyone want to join in.

I speed up, making sure not to lose them as they make a sudden left turn into a store. "Welcome to *Howie's!*" they both shout as Morgan pulls me inside excitedly.

"Oh my god," I can't contain my laughter as I walk into the store. It looks like Halloween threw up all over itself, and there isn't one inch of the store that isn't covered in Halloween costumes, wigs, and decorations.

"Isn't this place just *amazing*!" Morgan throws her hands up and spins around. I try not to laugh as I feel someone come up behind me.

"She's *obsessed* with anything having to do with Halloween, even something as ridiculous as this is." I look back at Harper standing behind me. I almost didn't know what to do at first, surprised she was even talking to me. I was expecting the silent treatment from her the whole day.

"I can tell, she's been *very* enthusiastic about all this," I say, agreeing.

"Well ... you've never been to one of Morgan's parties. They're all amazing, but her birthday party is always the best. You're going to have so much fun!"

Morgan runs up to us, "Yes you are! I'm *so* excited that you're coming!"

She takes off into one of the aisles, and when she realizes Harper and I aren't behind her anymore, she runs back out. "Why are you guys standing around? Let's go find some costumes!" We follow her down an aisle. The further we walk into the store, the more absurd looking it gets. I must have passed by at least a thousand witch hats and fairy wings of every color, shape, and size.

Harper walks up next to me, "Last year we went as Regina and Cady."

"And we were *adorable*!" Morgan adds.

"Oh yeah. I know you and Mark had *lots* of fun that night," Harper says to her with a wink.

Morgan playfully pushes her. "Shut up! I'm not the only one. You and Sam—"

"Look! This is cute!" Harper cuts her off and picks up an all-white mini skirt from the shelf, showing it to us before Morgan can finish speaking. I watch as both of their smiles slowly fade. Harper's at the mention of her and Sam, and Morgan at the sudden change in mood from Harper.

I try to quickly change the topic, "Do you guys have any ideas for outfits?"

Morgan takes a moment to think. "Not really. Why don't we split up and each grab a bunch of stuff to try on?" We all agree, and go our separate ways.

I make my way to the opposite end of the store, and slowly browse the shelves. I'm walking through and realize I have ended up in a section entirely devoted to decorations, and have to find my way back to the costumes.

If I pass one more version of a pumpkin bucket I think I will go insane.

I just manage to find my way back to the actual costumes, when I hear one of them calling me from afar.

"Missy!"

I turn, trying to find the voice. "Missy! Over here!" I come to a halt when I run into both Morgan and Harper, each one carrying stacks and stacks of Halloween costumes piled high in their arms. I can barely see Morgan's eyes over everything she is holding. I laugh, and offer out my hands to help them hold everything.

They each hand me a couple different costumes to try on, before sending me into a dressing room. I lay the clothes down carefully, and start looking through what they have picked out. Some of the clothes seem absolutely ridiculous to wear, but as I search more, some of it doesn't seem half bad.

"Try on the black dress!" I hear Harper yell from inside another dressing room. I look to find what she is referring to, and pull out a silky black dress from the bottom of the pile. The back of the dress is almost entirely open, and the bottom hem lands just a few inches below my butt. I slip the dress on, and before going out I take a look in the mirror.

"Ready?" Morgan yells. She counts down from three and all at once we walk out of our rooms, ready to check each other out. Morgan and Harper are both wearing similar dresses, but each one has a slightly different style. They both "oooh ..." and "aaah ..." looking at the three of us in the mirror.

"What costume is this for?" I ask. Morgan walks away for a second, and comes back carrying two giant black witch hats and one pink one. She puts a black one on each of our heads, and places the pink one on hers.

Harper looks at her and starts laughing, "I knew we would make such cute witches!"

"Why the pink witch hat though?' I ask.

Morgan rolls her eyes playfully, "Well! *I* thought we should all wear pink hats to change things up a bit, but Harper didn't love the idea," she explains, taking the hat off reluctantly.

I walk up to Harper, and whisper, "Yeah, I have to agree with you on that one."

Morgan turns around sharply and says, "I heard that!" We all laugh, agreeing that we could do better than witch costumes. They tell me to try on the all-white clothes, and to let them know what fits.

I search through the pile and find a small white mini skirt with tulle on the bottom and a white corset top that laces up tightly in the back. I put them on, and turn around to look at myself in the mirror.

*And I look amazing.*

I step out, and so do Morgan and Harper. They are both matching with me, except they have angel wings on their back and fluffy halo headbands on top. They hand me a headband and wings, and I quickly put them on. We walk over to the big full-length mirror on the wall and admire our reflections.

Morgan turns to us. "Okay, this is *definitely* it! We look amazing!" We all nod in agreement.

Harper moves away from the mirror and turns to face us, her eyes lit up with excitement. "I can bring all my face glitter and do our makeup before the party if you guys want!"

"Yes!" Morgan and I exclaim. We all agree to get this outfit, and go back in to change back into our regular clothing. We pay, and Morgan drives us back. This time, the three of us talk the whole way back. I start to forget about the argument Harper and I had at the beach, and I'm hoping she does too. I hug them both before getting out of the car, squeezing Harper tighter than usual.

*I can't wait for this Halloween*, my first one spent outside the comfort of my house in years.

I just *know* it will be the best one yet.

# 18
## October 31st, 2017

"**O**kay, close your eyes, I'm almost done …"

I shut my eyes, and Harper smears sparkly silver glitter along my eyelids. "Open." My eyes flutter open and Harper faces me toward the mirror. She gave me light eye makeup, glitter, and delicate eyeliner along my lash lines.

"I love it!" Morgan squeals.

"I'll do yours now Morgan, if you want," Harper tells her, grabbing her makeup and bringing it onto the bed where Morgan sits. I grab my clothes from my closet, and shut the door behind me to change.

When I walk back out, Harper has finished her and Morgan's makeup and they both start changing into their costumes.

"Morgan, if this is your party, why are you going with us? Shouldn't you be there already?" I ask, realizing the party was scheduled to start almost an hour ago, but Harper wouldn't be driving us over for at least another thirty minutes.

"Don't worry, Harper and I have been showing up *fashionably* late to our own parties for years."

"You're going to have so much fun, Missy! These parties are always the best."

Morgan stands up, and sits on her knees next to me. "Yes!" she exclaims in delight. "Plus, Logan's gonna be there!" she says, poking me in the side. I blush almost instantly, and they both tease me for it.

We finish getting ready in the next thirty minutes, and I watch as they scramble to add the finishing touches to their outfits. Morgan's phone starts to blow up with a flurry of texts and calls asking where she is. We hop into Harper's car, and race to the party.

Her car comes to a stop, and we slowly step out.

I pause as I take in the enormous house we've pulled up to. "Woah! Who's house is this?"

Morgan pulls me up a long set of light-colored marble steps. "Well, one of my close family friends has this house here that her parents rarely use. She's been letting me use it to host my birthdays for the past few years, plus she caters the whole thing."

MIA MANDALA | *Dear Anna,*

She pushes open huge, wooden doors, and I have to stop myself from gasping when I walk in. At first glance, there must be at least a hundred people here. We've barely taken two steps inside, when a swarm of people begin crowding around us, everyone trying to be the first to say, "Happy birthday!" and "Happy Halloween!" to Morgan. Morgan must have hugged and greeted twenty people before we were barely in the door.

Once inside, Morgan leads me around, and everywhere we go we are showered with compliments. "Half the people here, I barely remember their names," Morgan whispers in my ear admittedly, and we both laugh. She drags me up a flight of stairs, where we have to step over a dozen people to get to the top. "Look, I think Logan's over there," she points a couple steps up, where I spot Logan at the edge of a railing. He has a drink in one hand, while the other is draped around a blonde girl's neck. They are both cracking up, and I watch him laugh with her, never having seen him laugh like that with me before. I walk up to him, and for the first time, feel intimidated by him around his friends. I don't know whether I should approach him and kiss him hello, or wait till he notices I am there.

I turn around to find Morgan has left me to go talk to her other friends. Logan notices me standing there, and for a split second our eyes meet. A moment later they are back on the girl to his right. *derek This is Logan,* I remind myself. I have no reason to be scared.

But he doesn't react.

I step closer to him, wondering if maybe he didn't notice me in the crowd. "Oh! Hey ... Missy." He unwraps his arm from the blonde girl to pull me in by the waist for a sloppy kiss, his lips nearly missing mine. I laugh as our lips finally meet, and pull away slowly. "I missed you," he tells me, his words slurring together.

I smile at him. "I missed you more." Suddenly, Morgan comes up behind me, linking her arms around my waist. She spins me around so I'm facing her, and she hands me some sort of drink.

"C'mon, guys!" She pulls me through the crowds, and motions for Logan to follow behind.

"Where are we going?" I shout over the noise of everyone's voices.

"Just follow me!" she shouts back, leading me back down the stairs.

We end up in the middle of what I assume to be the living room, but it looks nothing like it should. Decorations and bottles of booze cover every inch of the place, and there are people lounging on any type of furniture they can find.

Morgan introduces me to what feels like dozens of people, their names and faces blending together as the night goes on. The music starts to turn up, and Morgan hops onto a table, singing off-pitch to the music and dancing with some of her old friends. I follow after her, and she spins me around, catching me just in time so I don't fly off the table. It feels surreal, like I'm living in a movie I've watched before.

"Take a shot!" someone yells from below us, handing us each a small shot glass. I look to Morgan for approval, before taking it. "Let's do it!" she shouts over the music. We count down from three, and on one, we tilt our heads back, letting the vodka pour down our throats so quickly we don't have time to taste it.

We both scream like little girls, and suddenly everyone is passing around shots like they are party favors.

Time seems to fly, and somehow we end up sitting squashed together on a couch between two juniors, who look to be on the verge of throwing up.

Morgan leans over and hugs me so tight, I feel like I might collapse. "I love you, Missy!"

I laugh, "I love you too!"

That's when I realize that Harper is gone.

As if on cue, I hear a voice yelling for me in the distance. "Missy!" "Where's Missy?!" I see Harper pushing past people, her head swiveling around frantically. "Missy!" No one but me seems to notice her, as she pushes her way through another group of people.

I slowly slip out of Morgan's arms and into the crowd of people. I push my way through, till Harper's voice is no longer just in the distance. She looks as if she has just witnessed something awful happen. I don't want to know what. "Oh, Missy—" she says breathlessly. I take her hand

and lead her outside to get some fresh air, as I wait for her to catch her breath.

"What happened?" I ask cautiously, as Harper looks around to make sure we are alone.

"Missy, I need to tell you something."

"Okay. What is it?"

"Logan is cheating on you ... and I don't think it's the first time."

*No.*

"Harper ... what? What do you mean he *cheated* on me."

"Missy, I saw them—"

"Saw who?!"

"Logan and Julia!" she screams a little too loudly, and a few people nearby turn their heads toward us.

"Who's Julia? I've never even heard of her—"

"That blonde girl he was with when we got here." I give her a withering look, starting to understand who she's referring to.

"I mean yeah, they were friendly, but I hardly think that counts as cheating." I laugh a little, sometimes Harper can be overdramatic.

"C'mon, let's go back inside—" I go to grab her arm, and she steps away from me.

"You don't believe me." She genuinely looks hurt and I can't tell if it is for me or herself.

"Harper, what—"

"Did you not just hear anything I said? Logan is *cheating* on you!"

"No, he's not. Look, I saw them at the beginning of the party too, they just look like good friends."

"He's cheating on you!" she screams, stopping me mid-sentence. She looks insane, like she is going to cry.

"Harper. Stop it."

"No, Missy. You stop it!" I yank her arm and lead her as far from the crowd as I can, trying to diffuse the scene she is beginning to make.

"Why are you yelling at me? You're acting insane!" I scream as softly as I can, drowning out her protests as I lead her farther away from the house.

"Why don't you believe me?" Her tone makes it sound like less of a question, and more like she is telling me. I can't help but laugh, out of nervousness or genuine laughter, I don't know.

"What are you even saying, Harper? Seriously, I think you've had too much to drink. Maybe it's time we get you home—"

"You don't believe me?"

I don't say anything in response. "Just drop it, Harper." She shakes her head, keeping her lips tightly pursed. "God, why are you making this such a big deal? Look, I get it, you've never liked Logan and me being together. I *get it*, Harper. But this is taking it too far."

She doesn't move, and for a split second I could swear a tear runs down her face. She wipes it away so fast I can't tell if it had been there or not.

"Come with me then," she says, breaking the silence. "What? You still think I'm lying? *Come. With. Me.*" Before I can respond, she takes my hand in hers and drags me back inside. Her grip on me is harsh and tight, and no matter how hard I try, she won't let go.

I jerk my body back and forth. "Seriously, Harper!" She leads me past Morgan, who stares at us dumbfounded. "Stop it!" She doesn't stop until we have walked up the full two flights of stairs. She drops her arms from mine, and motions warily to the door directly down the hallway from us.

"See for yourself."

I look back to her, unsure of what to do. She crosses her arms and nudges her head in the direction of the door. I stare at her warily, before turning my back to her and walking ahead. As I reach the door, I hear the slight murmur of two people coming from the other side.

I knock once on the door.

*No response.*

I knock again.

*Nothing.*

I begin to doubt myself, wondering if I had even heard anyone on the other side. Just as I'm about to turn back to Harper, and ridicule her for making me even question

Logan's loyalty, the door swings open, and a voice I recognize all too well screams.

"God! Can't you see we're busy here?!"

My body freezes, and by the look on Harper's face, I know.

I know it is *bad,* and I know I don't want to see what is on the other side of that door. I turn around slowly to find Logan standing in the doorway. His shirt is off, and his pants are barely held up by a carelessly put on belt.

"Logan!" a shrill voice screeches. I peer my head inside, and the lights in the room are dim.

Yet not dim enough to hide Julia, laying shirtless under the covers of the bed.

In a split second, I watch as Harper runs toward me. Logan and I lock eyes, and I try so hard to scream. But nothing comes out. My throat is dry, and my head is buzzing. I can hear Harper screaming mindless insults at him, but the words fly up and over my head. I feel like I'm going to throw up, so I squeeze my eyes shut, quickly running out of view from Logan and falling to the floor.

All I can see when I close my eyes is the look on Julia's face when she saw me.

Logan is in the doorway, laughing.

He is *laughing*.

Then he sees me. For a split second our eyes meet. "Logan—" my voice breaks. "Is this—did you—?"

*"Fuck!"* He slams the door so hard it makes a crash when it closes. I run to the door handle, trying to pry it open but it's locked shut. I pull and pull until my arm goes weak and my knees buckle underneath me. Harper runs up behind me, pulling me into a hug on the ground.

"No, Harper. He's going to come back! Just leave me alone!" I shriek. I try throwing her arms off of me, to escape her tight clutch on me, but she won't budge. "Harper, stop it! Get off of me!" I scream and thrash in her arms until she finally lets go.

She grabs me by the face, forcing me to look her in the eyes. "He's not coming back."

"You're lying," I insist.

"Missy—" she starts, but I can't take it anymore.

Every emotion inside of me is riled up, and I just start screaming as loudly as I can, "No, Harper! You have no idea what you're saying! Just leave me alone. God! You keep messing everything up. Just *go*!"

She stares at me. No expression on her face, just a blank stare. "Is this really what you want?" she asks.

It takes all the energy left in me to nod, and choke out a few lasting words, "Please. Just leave me alone." She gets up and leaves without another word.

*I've never felt more alone.*

Only steps away, the party is still raging, the music blaring, and lights flashing. However, the world has never felt so quiet and dark. I give one final try at the door, but nothing changes. It won't open, and he isn't coming back out.

I still wait at the door, *but he never comes out.*

I would have waited all night.

But he *never* comes.

*"OH MY GOD!"* I shriek, almost unintelligibly. I cover my mouth with my hand, trying to muffle the sound of my own sobs. I can hear the party continuing downstairs, and I can't fathom having to walk down there and past everyone. I run to the nearest bathroom I can find, and slam the door behind me. I fall to the ground, unable to keep up with my thoughts. Everything moves through my mind in such a hurry.

I don't know how much time has passed. Every inch of my body burns in pain, and I bury my head in my hands wanting to drown everything out. For a moment, everything feels quiet, and I try to focus only on my breathing and the darkness around me.

When I finally feel like I can breathe again, I slowly push myself off the floor. I look in the mirror, and all of the beautiful makeup Morgan had applied so carefully is now washed away by my tears. Before I have time to process anything, the bathroom door swings open.

"Hey, Missy!" I watch in a confused panic as Sam drunkenly stumbles in. He seems to not notice anything off about me, and walks in like we're continuing an everyday conversation.

"Sam? What are you doing?" He uses one of his feet to push the door shut behind him, and almost trips over his other foot in the process.

"Missy!" he repeats, walking even closer to me. I go to say something, but just as my mouth opens to speak, he grabs my face tightly and kisses me on the lips.

*He kisses me on the lips.*

My entire body goes into shock. He kisses me again, one hand gripped tightly around my waist, the other on my neck. I try jerking my face away, but his hold on me is too strong.

"Sam. Sam! Stop it. You're drunk, and I'm with Logan!" I push him off of me, and he goes tumbling to the floor. Regaining his balance, he takes my hand in his and pulls me down to the floor with him. Sam slowly shakes his head, and leans forward as if to whisper a secret into my lips.

"Missy, Missy …" he slurs, the smell of vodka on his breath lingering in the air. "I know what Logan did."

I pause. "Wait. You do?"

He nods slowly. "You think that's the first time he's done that?" he asks with a small laugh.

I don't respond.

*I don't want to know.*

He shakes his head. "It's not. That's just the first time you caught him."

Before I can react, he's kissing me again. Messy, wet kisses that reek of weed and vodka. He kisses me slowly, smiling as he pulls away gently. "You know, I've always had my eye on you." He pushes a piece of my hair back, and tucks it behind my ear. I stare at him blankly, unable to move or speak a full sentence.

He just stares at me.

I wonder what he thinks when he stares at me.

*Is he looking at me, or what he wants from me?*

More kisses come and I don't have the energy to stop them. I shut my eyes and imagine how Logan would feel if he saw us. I hope he would feel every ounce of pain I feel now.

Then all at once he stops. Swiftly he stands up, pushing himself up with the help of the bathroom sink. And he leaves without another word.

He never comes back.

Ten minutes, then fifteen, almost twenty minutes pass without him returning.

I know only two things then. That he isn't coming back, and that I have just made a horrible mistake.

"Missy? Missy! Are you up here?" I can faintly hear two voices coming down the hall, slowly getting closer to me. "Missy?" They reach the bathroom, and I watch as Morgan pushes open the bathroom door with a slight nudge. Their faces drop when they see me, and they crouch down to the floor beside me.

"Oh, Missy..." Morgan says sympathetically, wiping a stray tear off my cheek. Harper looks unable to speak, and neither can I. "We gotta get you home."

Harper shakes her head in disagreement. "We can't let her go home in this state, Morg," she says, using a nickname for Morgan I've only heard her use once before.

"That's fine, you guys can stay at my house tonight."

I start to protest, "But you can't leave your own party."

"It's not a big deal," Morgan insists.

"No, I'm fine, let's just go back downstairs." I try standing up, but the weight of everything that just happened pulls me back down.

"Really, Missy. It's okay. The party is getting boring anyway." Morgan cracks a smile at the end, and I let out a small laugh, seeing how desperate she is to try to lighten the mood.

"Are you sure?" I say, almost whispering.

"Yes. I promise. Let's get you out of here."

Morgan and Harper share a quick look, one that I can't quite read. They stand up, and each reach out a hand toward me. With their help, I slowly stand back up, my legs wobbling underneath me.

We walk out slowly, making our way down the hall in an awkward silence. I stop as we reach the top of the staircase. "I don't want to see him," I admit, not knowing which "him" I mean.

Morgan rubs my back softly. "It's okay, we will be out super fast."

Harper speaks up, "I haven't seen him since, I don't think he's even here still." I nod my head, and start walking down the stairs carefully. My eyes scan the party, but all I can see are flashes of people dancing around, and so far, no Logan.

Or *Sam*.

Morgan breaks away from us for a second to hug someone goodbye, and Harper continues out the door with me. She leads me to her car, and opens the back door. I climb in, and Harper sits up front. After a moment of silence, I hear her sigh. She turns around to face me. "It's going to be okay." I nod my head and force a sad smile, unable to muster a response.

I close my eyes and lay my head against the window, blocking out anything and everything. I *want* to believe Harper.

I *want* to believe her more than anything.

# 19

## May 1st, 2017
*Six months ago*

"*M*issy! Missy! Misssyyy!"

"What?" I rolled over, adjusting my eyes to the light. Anna hovered over me, whispering my name till I eventually woke up.

"Hi," she said, smiling.

"Anna! Go back to sleep." I rolled back over onto my side.

"But Missy!" she insisted, shaking my body back and forth till I gave in and rolled back to face her.

"Yes?"

"Ugh"—she flopped onto her back—"I can't fall asleep."

"Anna, it's past 1 a.m. Plus, we have school in the morning," I protested. She rolled her eyes, and I curled back into my blanket.

"Missy!" She jolted me wide awake by abruptly pulling the blanket off me.

"Ugh! Let me sleep!" I groaned, yanking the blanket back.

She pulled it back off and whined, "I haven't been able to fall asleep once! Please, Missy, I'm *SO* BORED!" I shot out of bed, clasping my hands over her mouth.

"Shh ... I don't want to wake my parents," I told her.

"Fine, I'll be quiet," she promised, and I layed back down again. "But only if we do something fun."

I sat back up. "What exactly are we supposed to do at one in the morning?" I asked.

"We could sneak out," Anna deadpanned.

I laughed.

Anna didn't.

"You're joking, right?"

"Nope."

"Anna ... we can't. My parents—"

"Are asleep," she said.

"Yeah, but—"

"Missy. Nothing's going to happen. I promise."

***

Next thing I knew, I was tiptoeing out my front door with nothing but a half-charged phone and my best friend.

The door creaked open, and I silently prayed no one would hear anything. Once we were outside, Anna whispered to me, "Grab your bikes." I made my way to the side of my house, grabbing my bike and my mom's bike that Anna liked to borrow.

I wheeled them quickly back toward Anna, and she hopped on hers right away.

"Let's go." And she took off into the distance.

"Anna! Wait up!" I jumped onto my bike, pedaling as fast as I could. I followed behind her, letting her take the lead. For a moment, I took my time to admire how peaceful everything seemed at night. No noisy cars filled the streets, and barely anyone was awake. Just a cool breeze that lightly hit my face.

"Missy! Catch up!" I heard Anna yell from in front.

I laughed, "Not my fault you're so fast!" I did my best to bike up to her, and we biked side by side for a while. "Where are we even going?" I asked, suddenly realizing we never actually made a plan.

Anna looked at me with a sly smile. "Just follow me." I watched as Anna broke out into a huge grin, and the few lamp posts that were working, lit up her face like moonlight.

I followed behind her, keeping closeby, otherwise it was too hard to see her in the darkness. Suddenly she came to a quick stop, and I had to stop myself from almost running into her. We both hopped off our bikes, as I tried to figure out where we were in the dimly lit streets. We leaned our bikes against a bench, and Anna grabbed my hand, leading me up a ramp. "Where are we? Oh ..." I didn't have to finish my question, as the beach came into view.

It was so beautiful this late at night, I wished it looked like this all the time.

The ocean glistened under the moon's light, and it was completely empty except for Anna and me. The only sound that could be heard was the crashing of the ocean waves against the rocks. Out of the corner of my eye, I could see Anna smiling wide at me.

"C'mon, let's go sit down!" Anna took off running, my hand still in hers. We picked a spot in the sand to sit down on, just a few feet away from the water.

"Let's play truth or dare."

"Okay, you go first," I said. "So, Anna, truth or dare?"

She took a moment to think. "Umm ... I'll start off safe ... truth."

"Okay, what's your biggest fear?" But before I could finish my question, I saw her open her mouth to respond. "And *don't* say clowns!" I finished.

"Rude!"

"C'mon, you've had the same biggest fear since you were like nine."

She scoffed jokingly, "What?! Clowns are scary!" she said in protest. "Well, besides clowns ..." she started. "I guess

... my biggest fear is to be unimportant. I don't know, like dying without ever actually accomplishing anything meaningful."

*Oh.*

She looked away, embarrassed by the sudden personal confession. "Anna," I finally said, my voice just merely a whisper.

"Yeah?" she answered, turning back a little.

"*You* could never be meaningless."

*I could have sworn she started blushing.*

Those five words. That was all that she needed to hear, I could tell from the way her demeanor changed after it was said. She started smiling and tried to hide it under her hands.

I changed the topic, sensing she may not want to talk about it anymore. "Well, it's my turn now," I reminded her.

She perked up. "Oh, yeah. Truth or dare?"

"Well ..." I contemplated it. "Truth. You did it, so it seems only fair that I do too."

She pursed her lips, unable to think of a question. "Do you like anyone?" she eventually asked.

"Ugh, so boring!"

"Shut up! You know I'm bad with this stuff!" she protested.

"But, *no*. I don't like anyone. No offense, I know you have your little crushes, but the boys at our school are just so gross! I would rather date *you* than date even the hottest boy at our school!"

*Oh shit.*

*That sounded better in my head.*

"Anyway!" I recovered quickly, trying to take the attention away from my weird comment. "It's your turn now. So, truth or dare?"

"Dare," Anna declared, taking no time to think about it.

"Ooohhh. You *may* regret that once you hear my dare for you ..." I teased.

"C'mon, what is it?" she asked, rolling her eyes at me.

I took one look at the water, then back at her.

"I dare you to jump in the water," I said with a sly smile.

"Missy! It's *freezing* in there!"

"You wanted a dare didn't you?" I laughed.

"Yeah, but—"

"No buts," I said. "You have to do the dare. I don't make the rules," I insisted, shrugging my shoulders.

"Fine!"

"Have fun!" I yelled, and she took off running, stopping right before the shoreline ended.

She gave me one look back, then jumped into the water, falling over. For a moment, I wondered if I should go look for her when I didn't see her come back up to the surface immediately. But right before I got the chance to do that, I saw her head pop up out of the water.

"Missy! I. Am. Going. To. KILL YOU!" I heard her scream as she ran out of the water as fast as she could while dripping wet, running across the sand. I couldn't help but burst into laughter at how ridiculous she looked. She stood over me, water dripping from her body, jaw dropped. "Oh my god, that was SO cold!" I shrugged and laughed, pulling her back down to where she was sitting before.

"Okay, it's your turn now. Truth or dare? Choose wisely ..." she said, lifting up one eyebrow, then the other, and wiggling them like worms along her skin. Something I *still* have not managed to learn how to do.

"Dare," I answered.

"Copycat," Anna teased back. I stuck my tongue out mockingly. Anna took a moment. She scooted closer to me, so we were both sitting, legs crossed, staring directly at each other.

"I dare you to kiss me."

*Woah.*

"What, uh ..." I said, my words becoming a mumbled mess of words and giggles.

*Missy, chill out.*

"Well, neither of us have had our first kiss ... What better way to practice?" Anna explained. I nodded my head, laughing nervously.

"Yeah. Yeah. That makes sense. So uh ..." Anna sat closer to me, so her knees were almost on top of mine.

*And for a moment, we just looked at each other.*

In my opinion, Anna had some of the most beautiful eyes I had ever seen. A green that glowed in the sun, like when sunlight hits a grassy field just right.

I felt as if I were moving in slow motion. The most I knew about kissing was from movies, or kissing my pillows for fun. Anna seemed to have a bit of a better idea of what to do and took the lead, leaning in, and placing her hand softly on my cheek. "Ready?" she asked. I just nodded my head. A million thoughts were going through my mind.

I leaned in.

She leaned in.

*And then our lips met.*

Her lips tasted like vanilla chapstick.

I could smell a hint of the lavender perfume I bought her last Christmas.

It was a kiss that felt like fireworks.

That was the only possible way to describe it. It was unlike anything. Truth be told, I had never kissed anyone else. But I couldn't shake the feeling that it just felt so *perfect*.

It really was nothing special. Barely more than a light, innocent peck, if anything. But everything at the same time was so, so special.

Neither of us said anything, we didn't have to. It was like an invisible spark had been ignited between us.

"Anna—"

"Don't say anything," she said.

And then she kissed me.

And kissed me.

And kissed me *so much more.*

Time flew by, and the only thing that mattered was me and her.

And then she stopped.

Anna opened her mouth as if to say something, but quickly closed it. I sat there dumbfounded, staring at her. She kept looking around, then back to me frantically. Then without warning, she stood up, ran to grab her bike, and pedaled away.

Leaving me alone, on the cold, dark, empty beach. More confused than ever.

That's when I started to cry.

I cried like I never had before. My voice broke into sobs, and I could barely make out what was in front of me because my vision had entirely blurred. I became more aware of the eerie silence that filled the beach. The only sound that surrounded me was the waves and my thoughts.

*What the hell just happened?*

*Why did she run away?*

*I need to get home.*

*I need to go home right now.*

So I wiped away my tears, picked myself up, and grabbed my bike.

MIA MANDALA | *Dear Anna,*

    I biked home along the dark, quiet streets that only a few hours ago were filled with me and Anna, and the sound of our voices and laughter.

    Now a vacant shell of what I once was.

## 20
## October 31st, 2017

"*M*organ, I need to tell you something."

I'm back in the comfort of Morgan's house, wrapped up in her silky smooth bed sheets. I lay my head against her pillow, wishing I could fall asleep and never wake back up again. Harper had just left the room to get me some water, and I waited till the door was fully shut to motion Morgan to sit next to me. "I *really* need to tell you something."

I need to get it off my chest, the weight of what had happened was slowly sinking in. I don't think I can go any longer without telling someone.

"Missy, what is it?"

"Something happened with me and Sam." Her expression drops, confusion painted across her face.

"What? What do you mean?" I start to fidget with the sides of the blanket, recounting the memory of his lips on mine.

"He came into the bathroom, and ... I don't know, I guess he was drunk and ..." I take a deep breath, debating whether or not I should keep going. "He kissed me." I watch as Morgan's eyes widen, her eyebrows shooting upwards.

"Oh my god, Missy." She is so completely taken aback by what I have told her that she is barely able to utter a sentence.

"Morgan, I made out with Sam." I wince at my own words. She goes to speak, but before she can say more, I stop her. "You can't tell Harper," I say sharply.

"What? Why not?"

"Please, Morgan. Just *promise* me you won't tell her."

She starts to protest, "I just don't understand why not." I hear footsteps coming closer to the door, and quickly interrupt her.

"Just promise me." As if on cue, Harper walks through the door, two waters in hand. *"Please,"* I mouth to Morgan. She looks to Harper, then back to me, and nods slightly. "Thank you," I whisper softly so Harper won't hear.

To my luck, Harper doesn't seem to suspect anything out of the ordinary when she walks in. Her concern seems solely focused on me, making sure I am okay.

For a second I thought about telling her, admitting what I had done. But I stop before making yet another rash decision.

"Missy. We need to talk about what happened," Harper says sternly, joining Morgan and me on the bed. I start to panic.

*Oh shit.*

*Does she know about Sam?*

*How does she know?*

"You need you to break up with Logan."

I feel a weight lift off my shoulders, before realizing what it is she actually said. "Wait, what?"

"Missy, he's *awful* to you."

"I can't break up with him though ..."

"What are you talking about? He cheated on you. *At a party*. Everyone will know."

I struggle to find my words. I can't break up with him, it isn't right. I try to talk calmly to them, "Guys. I get that you're worried about me, but just let me talk to him first. I'll figure things out ..."

"Yeah, and when you talk to him, you'll break up with him," Morgan states sternly.

"No, I'm not breaking up with him," I say, with the same tone as Morgan.

They give each other a look. "Missy ..." Harper pleads, "... you have to. He's a horrible boyfriend and you know it."

I look back and forth to them nervously. "He's not horrible!"

"He cheated on you!" As Morgan interrupts me, Harper gives her a look to calm down.

"We don't know the full story anyway, we can't assume the worst in everyone—"

Now it's Harper's turn to interrupt me, "We saw him with that girl! C'mon, Missy, *I know* you're smarter than this."

Morgan adds on, ranting about how awful cheating is and how I deserve better. Nothing they say sticks with me, I let their words simply drown out like bees buzzing in the background.

I know they aren't going to drop it, and that this is an argument I'm not going to win. "Okay, fine," I say, stopping them mid-conversation. They switch their focus back to me, and wait quietly to see what else I will say.

"I'll break up with him."

*That was a lie.*

They let out a sigh of relief, sharing a slight smile with one another.

Morgan leans over to hug me, squeezing every inch of me tightly to her. "Don't worry Missy, there are *so* many men out there who will treat you *amazingly*!" I force a smile, nodding along as I let my lie take root.

"I'm sure there are a bunch of great boys in your grade," Harper suggests.

I shake my head. "I don't really know any ..."

"Well, ask your friends."

"You guys are my friends."

They pause. Morgan inhales deeply, fidgeting with her hands. I can see she is trying to find something to say, her eyes not fully meeting mine. "We're your friends too, *of course*," she says.

"But Missy ..." Harper winces. "We're seniors and we don't want you to be alone after we graduate."

*I hadn't even taken a second to think that far ahead.*

It feels wrong thinking that far into the future, when tomorrow still feels like its own treacherous feat I have to complete. I don't want them to worry, I *hate* when people do that. When they fret over every move I make or word I say, it makes me feel helpless.

"I'll be fine." *That may well be yet another lie.*

"You must have some friends in your grade, right?"

I shrug. "I did, but most of them are super rude anyway," I say, thinking of Emma.

Morgan cocks her head and gives me a suspicious look. "Really? There's *no one* your age you get along with?" she asks with a small laugh, a clear attempt to lighten the mood. My mind starts to wander back to memories I so badly wish I could forget.

"There was this one girl—"

"What's her name?" Harper asks.

"Anna."

I almost gasp out loud at my own response. Her name feels almost foreign to my mouth.

*Anna.*

I can't remember the last time I said her name out loud.

"See? There are other people, you should invite her to hang out with us sometime!" Morgan suggests.

I shake my head, my mind in another place than in Morgan's bedroom. "Yeah, maybe ..."

*Another lie.*

Morgan seems to take the hint and changes the subject, "Hey, why don't we watch a movie? It's still Halloween, you know, we can watch something scary!"

I smile at her attempt to make me feel better. "Yeah, that sounds nice."

We make our way to the living room, and get settled on the couch.

Morgan reaches over and hands me the remote. "Here. Why don't you choose something for us to watch?" I watch as Morgan motions slightly for Harper to come with her. "Harper, can you help me get some snacks?" They walk off into the kitchen, and I see Morgan grab Harper's hand and pull her out of my view.

I can hear them whispering to each other in the hallway. Quick, secretive whispers that I can only hope have nothing to do with me.

*Please, Morgan. Please, don't tell Harper.*

The most I can do is convince myself that Morgan stays true to her word. They come back a few minutes later, snacks in hand. Morgan puts back on the cheery smile that's been plastered on her face all day. It's only now that I realize how much of a mask her smile has become. "What did you choose?" They take seats on either side of me, laying out the food on the coffee table in front of us. I realize I never picked a movie, I was too focused on trying to listen to their conversation.

"Oh, I don't know. It's your birthday Morgan, you should pick." At the word *"birthday"* Morgan's smile drops, but only for a second.

Morgan picks the first movie that comes up on the screen, and I can tell she has no real desire to watch it. For the first half hour or so, Morgan and Harper spend over half the time stealing glances at me.

At one point I catch Harper just staring at me. It's like she is trying to make sure I am still there. Even after I make eye contact with her, she doesn't drop her gaze.

Something about it makes me incredibly uneasy.

I'm relieved to soon find them both fast asleep.

I make my way to the couch across from them, grabbing a blanket along the way. I open my phone and scroll until my eyes start to droop. A collage of photos catches my eye, and I stop to look at them. It's *Emma*. Emma with all her new friends, all dressed as different *Disney* characters. Even I can't deny how beautiful Emma looks in her posts, and how happy. Every photo I scroll through, they are all smiling and laughing, it makes my heart hurt a little. I can't quite tell where the photos were taken, but I can assume they were at Emma's house.

Suddenly I feel a tear roll down my face. I continue scrolling through her posts, and make my way deeper into her account, and onto some of her older posts. I have to stop when I can no longer see anything clearly, my eyes welled up with tears. I shut my phone off, and quietly let the tears roll down my face.

I fall asleep with a passing thought; I've spent so much time missing Anna, I never realized how much I was missing Emma too.

## 21
## November 1st, 2017

"Good morning Missy!" It takes my eyes a second to adjust to the light. My whole body feels stiff from sleeping on the couch, and my face still has the residue of dried tears. I roll back over, groaning about not wanting to get up.

"You should probably check your phone," Harper yells from across the kitchen. "It's been blowing up with calls all morning!" I pick up my phone and realize it's already past 11 a.m. *How have I slept so late?* I find I have dozens of missed calls and texts from my mom and dad, both wondering where I am. I quickly dial my mom's number, and she picks up after the first ring.

I apologize profusely for not texting or calling last night, and tell her I'm at Morgan's. She says she will come over to pick me up right now. I try to protest, but she doesn't budge.

Morgan strides over to the couch I'm on, a plate full of small waffles in one hand. They smell gloriously, each one topped with a small dollop of whipped cream. She places them down in front of me, taking one for herself. Harper comes over, and we all dig in.

A few minutes later, I hear the dreaded sound of knocking at her door, and I know I have to leave. "Ugh, my mom's here," I tell them, gathering my stuff and making my way to the door.

They both pull me in for a hug goodbye, and as I pull away Harper whispers in my ear, "Please text us if you need anything. *Please.*"

I don't know what to say, I just nod quickly and make my way out the door.

My mom is standing there with her arms crossed and a scowl across her face. She doesn't say hi and doesn't ask about the party. Instead, she just turns around and walks to the car. I take the hint to follow her, and do my best to look anywhere but at her.

The car ride home is spent in almost complete silence.

After a few minutes of not speaking, my mom finally makes the first move. "So how was Halloween?"

I stare out the window, my mind too unfocused and my thoughts too hazy to come up with an interesting response. I respond blandly, "It was fun."

"That's good." We both nod our heads at the same time. She doesn't try making any more conversation after that, and neither do I.

My mind and body feel at a halt. I lay my head against the window, never taking my eyes off the horizon in front of me.

When we get home, I don't even take a second to put my stuff down before going straight to my room, wishing I could disintegrate into my bed.

As much as I try to, I can't seem to fall back to sleep. My body feels jacked up on energy from sleeping in so late. I lay awake, staring at my ceiling. If I lay here any longer, I will have memorized every crack and paint chip in the ceiling. My mind races, full of unanswered questions. I reach for my phone, and dial Logan's number almost out of instinct. But I stop the call before it starts to ring. I want to talk to him. I have so many things I want to ask, to understand everything that has happened. But right now isn't the time. I delete the number and throw my phone down in frustration.

As it always does, my mind finds its way back to Anna. Back to simpler, better times. Times before Logan, before Sam, before everything went to shit.

I close my eyes and, for once, I let myself imagine her.

I imagine she's sitting here, right across from me. Her legs crossed, and arms slightly folded as she listens to me. The way she cocks her head ever so slightly to the left when she's deep in thought ... I would tell her everything about last night. She would hug me when I start to cry, and scold me till I break up with Logan, just as Harper and Morgan did.

My mind falls into a trance, and my eyelids grow heavy. I'm not fully sleeping, but not fully conscious either. The memory of Anna swirls around my room, the way a passing thought does. I realize I'm dreaming, but it doesn't quite make sense, as Anna suddenly starts to grow wings.

She waltzes across my bed as large, angel-like wings sprout from her back, growing wider and wider till they almost fill up my entire room. "Anna!" I yell happily, like a little kid. She looks down, her expression shocked, as if she is surprised to see me in my own bedroom. A glowing smile creeps across her face and her arms reach down to me. I stretch one hand out to her, but every time I get close to holding her hand, she flies higher. I stand on my bed, jumping to reach for her but every time I get close, she flies out of reach.

In a blink we are out of my room.

I whip my head around, trying to understand where we have ended up. It's a classroom. *I know* it's a classroom, except it looks nothing *like* a classroom. The walls are made of paper and the roof looks as if it has been blown off. "Missy, sit down!" Before I can move, I am seated at a table, two familiar faces staring back at me.

A dark-haired girl whose eyes speak a million things that go unsaid. Next to her is the most beautiful girl I've ever laid eyes on. I *know* them. I *know* these girls, these girls are my friends.

*But what are their names?*

*Who are they?*

The dark-haired girl stands up, and stretches her hand out to me. She swallows me in a hug so strong it engulfs my whole vision. The girl starts to cry, meaningless apologies fly out of her mouth.

*I wonder if they too have grown wings?*

When she finally pulls away from me, we are not back to where we started. I am alone, nothing but a dark street and single flickering lamppost by my side.

The beautiful girl is gone.

*She's gone.*

*She's gone.*

I remember her name.

"Anna!"

I wake up in a cold sweat.

I have no sense of time, or how long I have been asleep for. My chest heaves up and down, tears flowing freely down my face. My heart aches with pain.

The worst pain of all, *missing someone just out of reach.*

"Anna. Anna. Anna. Anna." I whisper her name like a chant to no one other than myself. "Anna. Anna. Anna. Anna." I do this until I've calmed down and can go back to sleep.

## MIA MANDALA | *Dear Anna,*

*Anna.*

    *Anna.*

        *Anna.*

            *Anna.*

                *Anna.*

# 22

## May 2nd, 2017

*Six months ago*

*I* don't think there is anywhere I'd want to be less right now.

My parents didn't seem to think too much about the fact that Anna wasn't here this morning. So I lied and said she felt sick, and her parents had picked her up early this morning.

Now I was on my way to my own personal hell.

It may sound dramatic and all, but it was truly what I felt going to school that day. I didn't know how I could bear to see Anna. I racked my brain trying to find an answer all night. I wanted to understand her, to understand all of it.

*Why did she run away?*
*Why did she kiss me like that?*
*Why did I kiss her back like that?*
*I think I love her.*

The last was less of a question. But nothing made sense. I needed to talk to her, I craved her presence all night long. I stayed up hoping it was all just a bad dream, but when I awoke that morning to an unending pit growing in my stomach, I understood that it was all *very* real.

On any other day I would have been carpooling to school with Anna. Today was not like any other day. My parents made me take the bus instead, and I hated it. I spent every second of that awful, ten-minute long ride trying to figure out what to say to her. I wanted to scream. To scream right in her face for leaving me like she did. But I could never scream at her.

The bus came to a stop.

*Just breathe, Missy*, I kept reminding myself.

*Breathe and don't say or do anything you will regret.*

I stepped off the bus, walking out of the way of all the other students. Off to my right I found Anna, Emma, and Kaylee standing and chatting in a small group.

*Deep breaths, Missy.*

I slowly made my way closer, stalling for as much time as I could. Anna and I locked eyes almost immediately. Her usually perfect golden locks seemed disheveled and out of place, quickly thrown into two messy braids. She stared at me like I was a ghost, and for a second it felt as if she were looking straight through me. She turned back quickly to her friends as I walked up to everyone.

I exchanged hugs and hellos with Emma and Kaylee. As I did, I could still feel Anna's gaze on me. I turned to her, unsure of what to do. Despite everything, my whole body felt drawn to her, and at that moment all I wanted to do was hug her.

"Um—I gotta get to class," she said in a flash, as she grabbed her bag and ran off. Kaylee and Emma exchanged confused looks, but followed behind her quickly.

The rest of the day was absolute torture.

I had four out of my five classes with Anna, all of them with her sitting right next to me. All of them without speaking a word to her.

At lunch, I sat at my usual spot along with Emma, Kaylee, and a few other girls. Anna was nowhere to be seen, the seat next to me typically left for her was empty all lunch, and I could feel the weight of her absence like a boulder on my back.

By our last class I was starting to get annoyed. She couldn't ignore me forever, and she couldn't just keep running away. As much as I loved her, I couldn't get the ache in my heart when she left me at the beach to go away.

Making sure no one could see me, I ripped a small piece of paper out of my notebook.

*Can we talk?*

I scribbled it down quickly, in small letters. Folding the paper and sliding it ever so quietly onto Anna's desk, I tapped my foot against hers till she noticed. She looked up confused until she noticed the paper. With a sigh, she opened it. She looked at me, then back to the note and picked up a pencil. She started to write something down, but stopped.

Anna tapped the pencil on the table, looking out at the teacher, pretending to pay attention to the lesson. I sat anxiously waiting for her to reply.

She started to write again. She stopped, went to pass it back to me, then stopped herself again.

Whatever she had written before, she quickly scratched out. I tried to peer over and see what she was writing now, but it was no use. After going back and forth from writing and scratching out her response, Anna read it over once more and finally handed it back to me.

I read over her response:

*I don't know what there is to say.*

That was it? I looked up at her, trying to ask for more than that but she was busy scribbling down her notes from the newest lesson. I flipped over the paper, thinking maybe she wrote more. But no. It was empty.

"Anna," I whispered softly under my breath.

No response.

"Anna!" I whispered a little louder. Maybe a little too loud, as our teacher sharply turned around and walked toward our desks.

"Missy! No talking in class. If Anna is going to become a distraction to you, then I'll have to separate you two." I nodded my head, and pretended to look at the "notes" in my notebook.

We didn't talk for the rest of the class. Anna barely even looked my way the whole hour and a half we had left.

When the final bell rang, Anna practically ran out of class. I tried to catch up to her, but by the time I had packed everything away in my backpack, she was already gone.

## 23

## November 2nd, 2017

"Oh my god, Missy! Where the *hell* have you been?" I turn around to find Emma walking up to me, arms crossed, with a scowl on her face. I scoff as she gets closer to me, and promptly turn the other direction.

*I cannot deal with her right now.*

I feel something tug on my arm, and find Emma grabbing onto me. She pulls me around till I'm turned to face her. "What the hell is your problem?" I try walking away but she doesn't let go.

"What the hell is MY problem?!" she screams. "Missy, *what* is going on?!" She looks me dead in the eyes, and I don't know how to react.

I've never seen her like this.

I've barely even seen her angry before.

"What are you talking about?" I fight against her grasp till she finally lets go of me. She steps closer to me, so close I can feel her breath on mine.

"You know *exactly* what I'm talking about."

I step closer, and see the crazed look in her eyes. "No, I don't. *Please* tell me," I say as sarcastically as possible. She breaks her death stare, struggling to find the words.

"I just don't understand what's gotten into you!" she finally says, throwing up her arms in frustration. "I mean, you never show up to class, and you look like a *mess*, Missy!" I back up a little, knowing there is no way *Emma* out of all people is going to yell at me right now. "And then I find you've been skipping class with a bunch of seniors?!" I glance over to where I know Harper and Logan will be soon. Emma looks at me, waiting for a response. "Hello?" she asks.

I just shrug. I can see her getting more and more angry. I'm having fun with this.

I look the other way, but she blocks my view by stepping in front of me once again. "Oh, and that boy you've been all over? He's eighteen! It's illegal!"

I stay completely silent.

Emma walks closer to me, lowering her voice. "Has he— is he doing anything to you? Because if he is—"

I cut her off, shocked that she could even accuse Logan of something that awful. "No. He's a good guy, Em." I start to back away from her. "He treats me well, and we have a good connection with each other. He would never do *anything* to hurt me."

"Oh my god." Emma's face is full of disgust, and it makes me want to slap it right off of her. "Listen to yourself. I mean *c'mon*, you're supposed to be the sensible, responsible one out of us," she says with a little laugh. I don't laugh back.

It isn't funny.

"Look, I understand things haven't been easy lately ... But you can't start doing all this crazy shit and just throw your life away—"

Now it's my turn to get angry.

"So *that's* what you think I'm doing? Just throwing my life away? Well, that's just perfect because I don't even care anymore!" I scream in her face, almost gasping from my own words. I take a step even closer to her so she can feel every inch of what I'm about to say.

"Go fuck yourself."

She stays frozen in place, but I can tell she is in shock.

I keep going, all my pent-up anger finally being let out. So many things I've wanted to say, and I finally have the chance to. "You don't care about *anyone* but yourself. Except for when it's convenient and you think you can just swoop in and save people, and *everyone* will just love you. Isn't that right? Because it seems that only *now* are you even *slightly* concerned with how I am."

She opens her mouth to talk but before she can do that, I turn around and run off in the opposite direction.

"FINE! Then go fuck it up! And don't expect me to be here when you realize it's all crumbled to pieces!" I hear Emma yell back.

I flip her off from behind, before practically running right into Logan.

"Woooah!" Logan puts his arm in front of me, literally stopping me in my tracks. "Where are you going in such a hurry?" he asks, sliding his arm slyly around my waist like a snake. I look back at Emma, who has now begun to cry silently, still standing where I left her.

I turn my attention back to Logan. "Let's get out of here." I don't have to say anything else. Logan knows what I want. In a matter of seconds, he is grabbing my arm and pulling me away from the school, away from Emma, away from my problems, away from Anna, away from everything.

And into *him*.

I take his hand in mine and we take off running. Laughing like little kids, he picks me up and spins me around. We don't stop till we come across a dingy alleyway tucked behind a gas station. Logan kisses my head and leaves me to wait outside for him. Minutes later he comes waltzing out of the store, waving a bottle of vodka in one hand.

He runs to me, a giddy look on his face as he pops open the bottle and takes a long sip of it. We go back and forth, passing it to each other and taking turns drinking. The taste slowly numbs my mind, while tingling all my senses. We drink every last sip of it till we can't take anymore, he throws it to the ground, and lets it roll to wherever.

Logan pushes me up against the concrete wall. One of his hands rests on the wall above my head, and the other is on the left side of my waist. I can smell the alcohol on his breath, and I'm sure mine smells the same. We stay like that for a moment. Just staring at each other. I stare at his eyes.

*I love his eyes.*

They are brown, but not the ugly brown eyes that have no real life behind them. His are like honey, and in the sun they look prettier than a thousand green or blue eyes.

I wonder what his favorite thing about me is. I look at him, and realize he isn't staring back at me.

He's staring at my body.

His eyes are wide, like a wolf stalking its prey. For once, I truly understand what it is he wants so bad. What the girl at the party gave him that I won't. And for once, I'm going to give it to him.

*Whatever he wants.*

I close the space between us, practically throwing myself at him. Our kisses quicken, and so do our breaths. He pins me up against the wall, and holds the back of my head with his hands, grasping onto my hair. His hand makes its way back to my waist, and continues to creep up my side. He lifts the bottom of my shirt a little, and the feathery touch of his fingers against my skin makes me want to laugh.

He pulls my waist closer to him, our bodies as close as possible to each other. I leave little love bites all over his neck, and he does the same. We take a moment to stop, and both take shots of the vodka, alternating between kissing and drinking.

His hands go further up my shirt, stroking the sides of my rib cage. Everything is happening too fast, my mind and body can't keep up. I'm too caught up in the kisses to even notice when he first touches my bra.

He rubs his hands over my bra, and holds onto it as he continues kissing me. I stop for a second, as the feeling of his hands on me start to feel more and more like a weight on my chest.

Then I keep kissing him, snapping out of it. My hand goes around his waist and I try to forget about everything.

*I want to lose myself in him.*
*Forget about everything and everyone.*
*Everything in this messed up world.*
*Because right now all that matters is me and him.*
*All the matters right now, is us.*

We don't stop. We are only getting started.

The alcohol quickly kicks in and I can feel everything. Every sound he makes, every sharp movement, I can feel everything all the way to the depths of my bones.

He makes his way under my bra. His palms feel gross and clammy against my skin, and his grasp on me is way too hard. It's all I can do not to yank his hands off me that instant.

With each kiss, he gets more and more intense.

Time seems to have stopped, while simultaneously speeding up around me. Maybe we are the ones moving slowly? I imagine everyone else around us hurrying on with their lives, while we stay against this wall, stuck here forever.

But we *are* still there, stuck in this moment. I never want it to stop.

*But, at the same time, I absolutely hate this.*

I hate this so, *so* much more than any words can explain. But it's better than anything I would be facing at home, or worse, with Emma.

I grasp onto the back of his head, my hands entangled in his long, silky hair. I am so closely pushed up against the wall, I feel like if he pushed me even more, the wall would shatter into bits.

I become more aware of his left hand, as I feel the slight tingle of his fingers move down my torso and out from under my bra and down to my hip bone. His fingertips are cold against my skin and it makes me jump a little. His hips push against mine, his lips against mine, our hands are roughly holding each other's faces.

I never want to be anywhere else. I want to live in this moment.

Because for once, I'm not thinking about everyone else. My mind isn't scattered into a million separate thoughts, with the majority of those being about Anna. I'm finally not drowning over the sound of her voice, and for a moment, everything feels okay.

*For a moment, I'm okay.*

His hand makes its way to the top of my jeans, and without having to look down at them, he finds the zipper. He slowly starts undoing it, and reaches his hand farther and farther down.

*But a moment can't last forever.*

"Wait—"

But he doesn't stop.

"Ugh. Logan, stop—" I try to pry his hands out from under my pants, but he won't budge. I start to panic. He grabs onto the bottom of my shirt, slowly pulling it up.

*I don't want to take off my shirt.*

My mind screams at me to do something, but my body won't react quickly enough. I hold my shirt down, but he continues to try to take it off. I attempt to say his name but my voice is muffled by him sloppily kissing me. "Logan!"

He keeps going.

I'm able to quickly lift my arms up and out from his grasp, and I push on his chest, making him stumble backwards. "What the fuck was that for?!" he shouts, as he storms back up to me. I zip my jeans back up as fast as I can before looking him in the eye.

"I wanted to stop," I say, my voice slowly breaking.

I've never seen him like this. He doesn't just look angry, he looks like he wants to *kill* someone.

I stand there, against the wall, with him towering over me. My hands are shaking, but I try to hide them behind my back. He doesn't say anything at first. Just keeps staring at me with that nasty look, a vacant expression in his eyes.

The silence is even more terrifying.

I can feel my eyes welling up with tears. I take in a shaky breath as a single tear falls down my cheek. I go to wipe it away, but Logan grabs my wrist before I can. "Oh, don't fucking cry." I try to pull away from his hold on my wrist, but it's so strong it burns. He yanks me over, causing me to fall to the ground in front of him. I try to get up, but he just pushes me back down.

"Mmm—Mi—Missy ..."

He can barely form a sentence. He is *so* drunk, I can even see it in his eyes. The way they look at me as if he's not completely there. He stands over me, while I stay kneeling on the ground. Paralyzed by fear, I couldn't get up if I tried. *"Logan. Please,"* I plead, as he kneels down to my level.

"What?" he says so viciously his spit flies in my face. "What is your deal? Huh, Missy?" He slyly places his fingers under my chin, and slowly inches my face closer to his.

I try as hard as I can to not look him in the eyes, but his hand forces my head back to his gaze.

And then he kisses me. And I've never felt more disgusted to kiss someone.

But he won't stop. He keeps a tight hold onto my face, forcing my lips onto his. I can feel my tears getting stronger, but he doesn't even seem to notice.

*Or even care.*

It dawns on me how little he cares about me, even as he kisses me.

I try to stand up, but his grasp has taken full control over me. I feel as if my whole body is shaking, and the mix of vodka and absolute fear causes my vision to go completely blurry.

Logan is busy kissing the sides of my neck, and has finally stopped gripping my face with his hands.

I try to push him off me, and just barely do so enough for me to be able to stand up. But it's too late.

Logan stands back up, meeting me at my level, holding tightly onto my arm. I try to scream but all that comes out is a shaky whisper of a sob, "Logan. *Please stop!*"

"Oh my god, could you shut up!?" he yells back, stepping closer to me, as I try to catch my breath. "What is your problem?" He looks absolutely crazy. He keeps going, talking over my sobs. "You drag me *all* the way here, get me drunk and all excited, and then back out when I want to have some fun?!"

"Logan what—"

He pulls my arm down hard, and that shuts me up fast. "God, stop acting like a little kid, you're such a tease sometimes."

I feel as if my heart has been shattered into bits.

I don't know what to say. I stand there gawking at him like a deer in headlights.

"But Logan ... I love you."

I don't know what else to say. It isn't a lie, I really *do* love him. I love him more than myself at times. I think maybe if I told him how I really feel then he would stop acting like this. But instead, he looks me dead in the eyes.

And slaps me across the face.

Time stops moving for a second. We both stand there completely still, the sting of where his hand had once been still burning.

"Oh my god—" I'm so in shock. I feel that my body might start crumbling to the ground right then and there.

And then he grabs my hands. "Oh my god, I—I'm so sorry, Missy." He kneels down and starts kissing my hands.

Each kiss feels like poison against my skin.

Standing back up, he kisses my cheek, muttering small apologies. My whole body is shaking, and my mind feels so foggy I can barely understand what is happening. Logan then places a hand against my cheek, and goes in for a kiss on my lips.

And another kiss.

And another. And more.

More. More. Again, he won't stop.

I start to panic, and try desperately to think of a way to get him off of me.

"No. No. NO. GET OFF OF ME!" I scream louder than I knew I could, and kick him in the knee as hard as I possibly can. He falls over backwards, groaning in pain.

*I've never ran faster.*

I can hear Logan faintly screaming my name in the distance, but I don't bother to turn around and look.

"Look before you cross the road!" I spin around, to find an old woman yelling at me out her car window. I hadn't even realized it, but cars were still crossing as I ran into the middle of the street. One of them nearly runs me over. I make my way across the street, and run to the closest bench. My head is on fire, and I can barely keep my breathing at a normal pace. I feel so dizzy and lightheaded, it's hard to make sense of where I am.

All I know is I have to get out of here.

My initial thought is to go home. But I know I can't go home reeking of vodka. One person pops into my mind.

*Emma.*

*She must hate me now.*

*But where else can I go?*

As stupid as it is, it's probably the most logical decision I could make right now.

\*\*\*

*This is a mistake.*

I find myself standing outside the door to Emma's house, still shaking, with the memory of how I got here blurry in my mind. I go to knock, but freeze before I can do so.

*What am I doing here?*

*What am I doing?*

Under any other circumstance I would have been thrilled to have been at Emma's. Visions rush through my mind of me and Anna tackling Emma with hugs, when we would come over on the weekends. I can almost feel them next to me.

*Knock. Knock.*

I regret it immediately.

At first no one answers, and I start to think she might not even be home. I'm about to turn around when I hear, "Missy?" I slowly turn around, to find Emma standing in the doorway.

"Hi," I say, unsure of exactly what to say. Unsure of why I even came here. I face her fully, and watch as her eyes widen.

"I'm sorry, I—I shouldn't have come here, I don't know what I was thinking—"

"What the hell, Missy."

"What—"

She grabs my arm forcefully and pulls me inside. Without saying anything she leads me to her bedroom, still holding tightly onto my forearm. She opens the door to her room, and I realize how long it's been since I was here last, and how much has changed.

The formerly light pink walls now match the rest of her house in a plain off-white. I look at her desk, and almost cry at the sight of it. Emma used to have a bulletin board hanging above it, where she would hang photos of her and her friends, most of them with me and Anna.

All those photos are gone now.

In place of the board, is a large poster of some band I've never even heard of.

It's like she erased every memory of Anna and me. *Nothing* is as it was before, even her curtains are a different color.

Emma looks at me and inhales sharply, dragging out the chair from her desk and motioning toward it. "Sit here. Don't leave. I'll be right back."

I want to protest, to just tell her I should go, but my body collapses into the chair. She leaves the room before I can say anything. I bring my knees up to my chest, and let my head fall against them. Realizing how incredibly exhausted I am, I feel my eyes start to droop.

I'm about to drift off to sleep when I hear the door to her room open. Emma reappears with a small bag in her hand. She kneels down in front of me, and motions for me to put my legs down.

"What are you doing?" I ask.

"Cleaning you up," she answers.

"What—What do you mean?"

"I mean you look like a fucking mess.," she says bluntly, then unzips the little bag. Emma looks back up to me, seeing the confused look on my face. She rolls her eyes and stands up. "Come here." I stand up and follow her to the full-length mirror in her room.

*Oh my god.*

I am shocked by my own reflection. I really do look like a mess. But even worse than that, I am unrecognizable to myself. I *feel* unrecognizable, as if I were a stranger that had walked into Emma's house. My hair had started the day in two braids, but is now completely disheveled and tangled. I have mascara and eyeliner streaks smudged across my face.

I hadn't even realized I was still crying.

I just stand there in shock. Unable to say anything.

Or do anything.

I look at Emma, and feel an immense amount of guilt that she has to deal with my mess now. Her expression hasn't changed. She stands a few feet away, lips pursed, with her arms crossed in front of her. "Can you please sit down now so I can help you?" I nod my head, and sit back down on the desk chair.

She pulls out a few band-aids and some wipes from the small bag. She starts wiping away the dirt and dried blood from where my knees are all busted, then places a few small band-aids over them. She does this all in complete silence.

*I wish I knew what she was thinking.*

I can't understand why she is doing this for me.
*I don't deserve this.*
She should hate me for what I've said.
I'm still mad though. *Is she?*

There's something part calming, yet part eerie, about the silence of her doing this. She looks at my face, and grabs a makeup wipe from her desk. She puts the wipe to my face, softly wiping away my smudged makeup. She stops and tosses the makeup wipe into a small trash can under her desk.

"Done," she says. "Now what the hell happened to you?"

"Why are you helping me?" I ask, ignoring her question.

"Because no matter how much you push me away, I'm still your friend. I didn't have to let you in and help you, but I did. Now answer my question, what happened?"

*She's right.*
*She didn't need to help me.*
I may never understand why she did.

I feel panic start to rise in me again, and I begin to anxiously tap my hand against her desk. "Okay"—I exhale sharply—"after our fight ... I went with Logan somewhere. Some parking lot or something ... I can't really remember." I put my hands to my face, my brain feeling so foggy that it's hard to remember exactly what had happened. She pulls my arms back down gently, and holds my hands in hers to stop them from fidgeting. "It was all such a blur. We started drinking, and kissing, and messing around, and"—my voice hitches, tears start to fall slowly—"he wanted more." Emma looks at me knowingly.

"And then he kept grabbing me, and I said no! I *told* him no! But he didn't listen, and he got mad and—" I can't even finish my sentence before I break down again. My eyes are so filled with tears that I can barely see straight. I try to keep talking, but my crying has stopped me from doing that. "I'm sorry—" I manage to say, and attempt to wipe away my tears.

"Why are you apologizing? There's no need to apologize."

"Okay," I choke out softly.

"Look, what happened today between you and me—it's because I'm *worried* about you. I mean, I see you skipping school with these seniors, dating one of them ... You're never around any more, and you think I don't see what you've done to your arms? You are *completely destroying* yourself. You don't even look like yourself anymore."

My heart drops with her every word. "Well, if you noticed all that, why didn't you say anything?" Emma opens her mouth to speak, but the familiar anger inside me starts rising, and I have more to say. I throw down her hands, unable to control myself. "No. No. I'm not done. I don't want to hear you rip me apart, I've *needed* you! And you haven't been there! No one has been! And you sit here acting all high and mighty because you're somehow holding your life together while I'm struggling. Well, just stop it. Stop trying to help me. The damage has already been done. There's no saving me." I motion to myself. "I'm already fucked up as it is, I can't handle having another person think of me as a dissapointment. I've already lost one of the only people who actually cared for me. But now I realize I've actually lost two, and now it's too late to change that. I don't know what I was thinking, coming here in the first place."

    I stand up, ready to run out of her house. I think I may be sick if I have to be here for another minute. This room is entirely filled with memories and traces of Anna.

    *I can't take it anymore.*

    I barely make it a few steps, my body dizzy from exhaustion and the leftover effects of the vodka. Emma has to practically catch me from falling over. I accept defeat and sit back down in her chair.

    "I'm not going to sit here and listen to you yell at me," Emma says, breaking her silence. Her calm expression doesn't change, but I know she's angry.

    "I *know* I was a bad friend. I *know* I should have done more, but I lost a best friend too. And now I'm trying to be a better friend to you, and—" I am crying so hard at this point it almost drowns out the sound of her voice. She keeps talking, "And I know everything has been so hard, but I don't think you've ever let yourself be sad. I mean Missy—I can't remember the last time you even said her name out loud! You refuse to talk about her, you won't even admit to yourself what happened!" Emma stands up, her emotions finally overtaking her. "You're in *such* denial that I think sometimes you even believe it never happened. But here's the truth, Missy. The cold, awful, *horrible* truth ... Anna's dead."

# 24
## May 2nd, 2017
*Six months ago*

*F*or the first time in a while, I felt completely relieved to be home and by myself. My head was spinning in confusion, and I don't think I fully comprehended a single word my mom said to me the whole car ride home.

 I must have opened and closed my phone a hundred times just waiting for Anna to text me. All I wanted to do was talk to her, to hear her voice again. I didn't care what had happened, and I was sick of being mad at her.

 I just wanted her back.

 Eventually I gave up, realizing she wasn't going to call me any time soon and I drifted off to sleep.

 I woke up to my mom screaming my name, "Missy!"

MIA MANDALA | *Dear Anna,*

A bloodcurdling scream that caused me to bolt straight out of bed. In a panic, I ran out of my room. As I got closer, I could hear my mom crying in the distance, and I prayed nothing terrible had happened. I entered the living room to find my parents in a state I had never seen before. My dad was sitting on the couch, jaw dropped, completely frozen. In his arms, my mother sobbed profusely.

I had never seen my parents like this.

I had never seen my mom cry.

It took every ounce of strength in me to approach them. I walked up slowly, worried that one of them might break. "Oh my god. What happened?" I asked, but inside I wished I never had. My mom peeled her head up from my dad's arm, her tears still streaming. "Anna, she—" But before she could finish her sentence I knew. I already knew what she was going to say, "—she died."

*No.*

*No.*

*No.*

*This couldn't be real.*

*I must have been dreaming.*

*But I wasn't.*

*I know I wasn't.*

*Because no dream could hurt this bad.*

My mom stood up, reaching her arms out toward me to try to give me a hug. I pushed her away, my body unable to move.

"How?" is all I could manage to ask.

My mom looked to my dad sadly. "We don't know much"—he choked—"they said she was biking. Some guy was drunk, and speeding, and—and he hit her. She was already dead by the time the ambulance got there."

My mom spoke up, "We only found out minutes ago. Her parents called and told us. They said they found something Anna wanted to give to you. They're going to come by later to drop it off."

I didn't say anything, I couldn't. My entire body was paralyzed by shock. I felt as if I moved too fast I would faint.

I couldn't believe this happened.

*I didn't believe it.*

Because there was no way that she died. No way that the sweetest, most caring person I know died.

There was simply *no way* that Anna was dead.

I had a million questions, I needed answers.

"Where did it happen?"

"A few minutes from our house," my mom told me. Then it all started to click, and it all sunk in.

A. Few. Minutes. From. Our. House.

She was on her way here.

*Oh my god.*

"OH MY GOD!" I shrieked, my body finally catching up to my emotions. I collapsed onto the floor in a pit of sobs. "Oh my god, oh my god, oh my god!" I could barely talk without it turning into screams. My parents moved down from the couch, and attempted to comfort me. My mom tried to place her hand on me and it sent me into panic mode. My voice turned into a shriek, and I raced to my room, slamming the door behind me.

I threw myself to the floor, my bed feeling miles away.

I was crying so hard, I started gagging and had to hide my head in between my legs to stop myself from throwing up.

"Missy, please. Please come out," my dad said, knocking lightly on the door. I heard my mom whisper to him, "Let her be, she'll come out when she's ready." I didn't hear them for a while after that.

I sobbed into my pillow until my tears ran out and my head felt like it was on fire.

Later, I heard a faint knock on my door, but didn't have the energy to get up and open it. "What?" I asked.

"Here"—I heard my mom say through light sniffles—"her mom brought this. I really think you should read it." She slid a small envelope under the door. Curious, I forced myself out of bed and crawled to the envelope. It looked like any normal, white envelope and I was about to push it off to the side before I flipped it over and found writing on the back. In Anna's neat handwriting it read:

*To: Missy*

*From: Anna*

A small heart was drawn next to her name.

My hands shook so badly I almost dropped it. I went to open it but stopped myself before I could.

It was like my body *wouldn't* let me open it.

I couldn't. I wouldn't. I didn't want to see what was in there. She was dead.

*Dead.*

*Dead.*

*Dead.*

And *nothing* in this envelope would change that.

I made my way back to the bed, stuffing the envelope into a drawer in my desk. I couldn't feel anything. I didn't want to. I didn't want to accept any of this. It all felt as if it happened so fast, but at the same time, so painfully slow. This couldn't be happening, my mind refused to admit it.

We were supposed to spend our lives together, live together during college, and go to each other's weddings. We had it all planned out ... down to what kind of floor plan we wanted in our post-college apartment. No. We *were* going to spend our lives together. That's how it was always supposed to be.

*Nothing* was how it was supposed to be.

Because my best friend in the entire world could not just be gone.

But she was—she was dead.

# 25
# November 2nd, 2017

"*A*nna's dead." The words ring through my head like a siren going off.

"Don't look at me like that, Missy," Emma jeers, and I stare at her in utter shock. "Anna. Is. Dead! She has been for the past six months"—now Emma is crying too—"and I don't like to talk about it any more than you do, but you know what? This may be the only way you can get better. You have to admit to yourself what happened! Let yourself be sad Missy!" She is down on her knees, her voice pleading for me to listen.

"NO! NO! NO!" I start screaming uncontrollably. "If I do that, it means she's really DEAD!" My words come out a shriek. Not realizing I said that all out loud, I jump back in shock. Emma and I both have tears streaming down our faces, she wipes hers away with her sleeve, and clutches my hands in hers so tightly that I think she might squeeze the life out of me.

"Missy. She *is* dead. You can't live your life hoping she'll come back."

I break into a sob because as much as I want to tell her that she and everyone else is wrong, deep down I know.

I know she's not coming back.

I fall to the floor, overwhelmed with emotions and tears. Emma kneels down to my level. "I don't think you've ever actually said it …" I nod, suddenly understanding her. "Say it."

I shake my head, sobbing so hard my whole body hurts. "I CAN'T!"

Emma shakes her head. "You can."

I sit there in my sadness, my tears running down faster than I can keep up with. Emma just sits there and watches. For once I'm glad she doesn't try to comfort me, as I feel the need for some space. My cries slow down, and I wipe some of the tears off my face.

I bring my head up, facing Emma. I take in a shaky, deep breath, before finally saying it.

"Anna's dead."

*She is.*

*She really is dead.*

But this time no tears came to my eyes. I slowly look up at Emma, as two stray tears fall down her face. She nods her head softly, a slight smile appearing on her face.

"Thank you," I whisper.

"I have to go. I'm *so* sorry." I stand up slowly and leave her house without another word.

Then I start to run.

The thought of Anna rings through my head, and this time I can't shut it off.

She's

    Dead.

She's

    Dead

        Dead

            Dead.

Anna.

I miss her. I need her.

*She's dead.*

My body moves faster than my brain can keep up with, and my mind spirals into a deep pit. I don't realize where I have run to till I have stopped at the entrance of a cemetery.

I stand there, trying to catch my breath as I debate what to do. My whole body is shaking, but no matter how hard I try, it doesn't seem to stop.

I take a cautious step in. Then another. Once I'm actually inside, and I can see the rows and rows of graves, I can't seem to stop. I walk carefully, taking the time to look at each and every headstone I pass. Some of them stand out to me, with death dates being from many, many years ago, while some are from just a few months ago. Some graves seem more loved than others, covered head to toe in flowers, while others are left barren, collecting dust and dirt.

In the end, I guess it doesn't matter much, they've all ended up in the same place.

One headstone makes me come to a halt. I know it's hers before I can even check for the last name.

Anna Williams<br>
*April 12th, 2003 - May 2nd, 2017*<br>
*"Loved by many, gone too soon from this world."*

I can't take my eyes away from it.

Somehow, even months after her death, there are days when it feels as if she's still here. Like maybe this is all just a terrible dream I'm having, and I'm just seconds away from waking up. Seeing her grave today though, is like the confirmation I never knew I needed.

All that surrounds her grave is a small bouquet of white lilies. They look new and fresh, meaning someone must have put them here recently, but I have no idea who.

I sit down beside it, my knees tucked under me. I let my fingertips graze the headstone, tracing her name with my fingers, letting them dance over the engraved words.

"Hi, Anna," I whisper, and a single tear falls down my face. I drop my hand, letting it fall against the tote bag still hooked onto my arm.

*The letter.*

The day I had gotten it, I swore I would never read it. I didn't ever want to know what was in it.

But now I have never wanted to do something more.

Every day since school started, I have kept the letter in my school bag, not wanting my parents to read it before I did, if I ever chose to do so. I rummage my hand through the bag, and find it stuffed inside a small side pocket.

I go to open it, but freeze before I do.

*Do I really want to see what's in there?*

*Do I really want to know what she was coming to my house to tell me?*

*To know what killed her?*

It won't change anything if I do know, I think to myself. But that's *exactly* it. It *won't* change anything. It can't. Because she's *gone*. And this time I *know* she's not coming back.

I can't go my whole life not knowing.

In a split second, I tear open the envelope. The paper inside looks like it had been ripped from one of her school notebooks, and is folded multiple times on itself. I take in a deep breath, and unfold it slowly.

Dear Missy,

Where to begin ...

I've been writing, and re-writing this letter for hours now in hopes of being able to find the right way to put everything I feel into words. I still don't know how to, but I can try my best. Before I say anything though, I know I owe you an apology. A HUGE one. I shouldn't have run off like that, it was a jerk thing to do and I'm sorry. I shouldn't have ignored your texts, or you at school. I know I was being a total bitch to you and I'm so sorry. I really hope you can forgive me.

I know this is no excuse, but after the kiss I just felt so scared ... and I was scared because it felt so right. Every moment felt almost perfect. Like it really was meant to be.

And that terrified me.

It was scary to think of what people may say, what my parents may think, scary that this is all happening with you because you're my best friend and I don't want anything to ever change that.

But even after just one day of barely talking to you, I realize that I'm miserable without you. I need you Missy. I need you every moment you're not with me.

And I love you.

God, it feels so nice to even just write that out. I do. I really, really do love you. And what happened at the beach was one of the best nights of my life. And yes, this is all so scary, and I'm terrified even writing this but, I love you too much to live in fear. I don't want to throw away this opportunity just because I'm scared.

You make me feel brave, Missy. Like I can do anything.

And we don't have to do anything right away, maybe just go on a date or something?

I really, really hope you feel the same way.

Love, Anna

xoxo

*Oh my god.* I sink my hands into the ground, shutting my eyes, in fear that I may throw up.

She *loved* me. I feel my whole body shaking, and I think I may pass out.

*She died trying to tell me that she loved me.*

I loved her. *I still love her.*

She's dead.

And then I let out the most heart-wrenching scream. I scream more, and then I completely break down. I break down like never before.

My whole body is racked with sobs, and I cling to the gravestone. My tears wet the stone, but I'm unable to stop them. The same thought keeps ringing through my head.

*She's dead.*

*She's dead.*

*She's dead.*

"I just miss you so much," I whisper my words onto the gravestone, my voice barely able to speak. "We were supposed to spend the rest of our lives together. There was so much we could have done. I *loved* you so, so much. I loved the way you always knew what to say. I loved the way your eyes lit up when you talked about something you loved. I loved how we could sit in silence for hours, and never get bored of each other. I loved every part of you."

I look around, reminiscing on what could have been, all the things we never got to do together. "And we were going to go to college together. Remember? We had it all planned out. We would split the cost and rent some shitty old apartment somewhere in New York"—I force out a laugh—"but we wouldn't have cared because we would have had each other."

I look down at the letter still in my hand. My tears fall onto it, completely wetting the paper. I think about everything said in the letter, and I smile. "And yeah, I would have gone on a date with you. I would have gone on many, many dates with you. And I would have kissed you. Kissed you so, so many more times. And I—I—" There is so much more I want to say, but I start to break down again.

"I just wish you weren't dead," I say, my voice a meek whisper. "The day you died, a part of me died with you. I don't even recognize the girl I used to be."

Flashbacks of the day she died, and the days after, run through my mind. The days, weeks, that I spent locked up in my room. Refusing to talk to anyone, refusing to do anything. I couldn't do anything. How could I, when the only person I truly loved was dead? I let myself wallow in my sadness, and after a few days everyone around me stopped trying. As if they needed to catch up on their own grief in order to care about mine.

I locked myself away in my room for hours at a time. I stopped showing up at school, not having enough energy to get myself ready and out the door. But one day, that all stopped. It was the beginning of summer, and each day was filled with endless sunshine and the heat was becoming unbearable. For the first time in a while, I got out of bed, put on clean clothes, and went about my day like normal. My parents didn't question it, didn't ask me anything.

They have never been the type of people to talk about their feelings. If someone doesn't seem noticeably sad, then they don't push to talk about it. But I guess in reality, I was the one pushing away my feelings. I realized it was easier to live in bliss, pretending like nothing was wrong. But the second I stopped, the reality of what happened was always right there at the front of my mind.

Somewhere along the road though, I started to slip again. I just felt so numb. Like the world outside my head was existing in technicolor, but inside I was living in shades of gray.

"Em's right. I can't believe I'm saying that," I say with a small laugh. "I never truly admitted to myself what happened to you. It was like, if I just carried on with my life as if it never happened—then it never happened. But that's all bullshit. Because you did die! But I'm still alive." I look around and truly realize how lonely I am. The trees around me blowing in the wind are the closest signs of life I have near me. My voice shakes, and it takes all my strength not to break down screaming again.

"Anna, I don't want to be alive without you."

Tears fall down my cheeks like snowflakes onto the ground, and I lean closer to the gravestone. "I don't want to be alive," I admit, my voice breaking with sobs.

"I don't know how much longer I can take this. I'm not myself anymore. You would be so disappointed in me." I realize that now, knowing that if Anna met me now she wouldn't even recognize me.

I am everything I never thought I would become, and everything she wouldn't have wanted me to be.

I sit there in the dead silence, with death surrounding me at every turn.

In a weird way, it's the most peaceful I've felt in months. I gather my stuff, putting the letter gently back in my bag. With a few shaky breaths, I find the strength to stand up. I give a final look at Anna's headstone. I put my palm to my lips and give it a small kiss, planting my hand softly against the grave. "I love you, Anna. I'll see you soon," I whisper so quietly, I barely hear my own voice say it.

Then for what feels like the millionth time today, I start to run.

***

I arrive home just moments later, never realizing how close it was to the cemetery. I think about all the times I could have done this before, how long I could have spent sitting at her grave, but refused to do so.

*I can't quite decide if I'm glad I never did.*

I walk up to my front door, and realize that neither one of my parents' cars is out front. I slowly walk up to find the door was left unlocked. My parents hate leaving me home by myself, so it's rare that I now find myself completely alone.

An eerie feeling creeps over me as I take my first step inside. I feel like I'm walking into a stranger's house.

*I am my own stranger.*

*I have no idea who I am.*

*Who is Missy anymore?*

I walk into the stranger's bedroom. Everything seems familiar, yet, I recognize none of it as mine. The only trace of Anna left in my room is a flipped down picture frame of me and her when we were little.

*How can a place be so filled with endless memories of someone, yet not a single physical trace of them remains?*

I grab the picture frame, and a marker off my desk. I slide the picture out of the frame, and take a moment to look at it.

The smiles on our faces were so pure, I can't remember the last time I felt like that. We had our arms linked around each other, and both our mouths were stained blue from candy we had been eating.

I flip the photo so the back is facing me, and I start to write. At this point, my body is moving on autopilot and I'm not even crying. I write a note on the back of the picture:

> Dear Anna,
> I finally read it. Six months later, and I finally know what you wanted to tell me.

I stop writing, and look at the front of the photo again. I trace Anna's face with my thumb. I take in a shaky breath as I continue to write.

> I love you. More than you could ever imagine, and I wish there was some way I could still tell you. I'd like to imagine what would have happened, if you'd been able to deliver your letter. But as I know, that's all that can be now—just my imagination. But Anna, this isn't a goodbye, because I promise I will see you soon.
> Love,
> Missy

I sign it with a small heart next to my name.

With a sigh, I fold the photo in half, and tuck it in my front pocket. I make my way into the bathroom, slowly tiptoeing around as if trying to not make any noise, even though I'm still home alone. I stand in front of the mirror, my arms resting on the vanity, and stare into my reflection.

Slowly my reflection morphs more and more into a person I can't make sense of. I begin to feel even more like a stranger than before. Not an inch of me is recognizable anymore, even though I'm actually staring at my own reflection.

I'm so entranced by the mirror, I feel completely numb when the tears start flowing down my cheeks. My hands wander downwards, to the drawers below the sink. I pull open the first one, revealing an array of pills. I start grabbing the ones closest to me, not bothering to read what they are. I unscrew various bottles, emptying out what seems like dozens of pills from each. I throw them in my mouth, forcing them down with a big gulp of water from the bathroom sink.

I lean down, and turn on the water for the bath. I sit on the floor beside it, and wait till it's filled up a few inches from the top before I turn off the water.

My body grows weaker and weaker as I watch the water rise higher and higher. It takes me a great effort just to raise my arm to the counter, and I start to feel around till I find more pills that have fallen out of the bottles.

This time I don't even bother getting water, and just dry swallow them.

I'm unsure how many I have taken, but it must be several dozen. However many there were, it is enough to make me feel like my mind and body are shutting down. I am dying.

Every inch of my body is racked with chills, while simultaneously sweating. I try to get to the toilet or the trash can, but my body feels too weak to move. I am now on my hands and knees, gagging violently, but nothing comes up.

It is at this moment when Harper's words finally make sense to me: *"A part of me thinks that if I don't care about anything I would feel a lot less invisible."*

She was right. That was *really* wrong.

But it's too late.

I somehow manage to crawl off the floor and practically collapse into the bath. Right before I do though, I pull out the photo of Anna and me from my pocket, laying it on the tile floor.

My feet rest near the faucet, and my head slumps heavily at the other end. I can feel myself slipping in and out of consciousness, my vision slowly deteriorating.

Flashes of my life run through my mind.

*Anna.*
*The beach.*
*Logan.*
*Harper.*
*Oh my god, Harper.*
*I love you, Anna.*
*My parents.*
*Em.*

*Anna. Anna ...*

My mind travels back to old memories—memories from so long ago I had almost forgotten they ever even happened. But they always lead back to Anna.

The first time we met, the first day of school, our first kiss, our last kiss. So many firsts. But the lasts came too fast.

I start feeling like I'm going to throw up again, but my exhaustion is too great. My breathing slows down, and my body slips deeper and deeper into the tub. My vision narrows down, and the only thing that's not blurry is the water that will soon overtake my face.

The water rises up to my neck, and my legs bend as the water reaches my knees. Slowly, I watch as the water engulfes first my mouth, then my nose, then finally my eyes as it reaches the top of my face.

The last thing I hear before everything fades to black is my mother screaming my name.

MIA MANDALA | *Dear Anna,*

# PART TWO

MIA MANDALA | *Dear Anna,*

# 26

## Harper
November 3rd, 2017
*One day after*

The first thing I do after hearing that Missy has died, is go for a car ride.

I hop in my car and turn the music up so loud it drowns out my thoughts completely. This may seem like a strange way to react, but at this moment I find it perfectly rational. I don't stop driving till my eyes are blurred from tears and my hands are shaking so intensely that I feel I'm going to lose control completely.

I stop my car right at the edge of a cliff. The truth is, in that moment I would have driven off it.

*Yeah, I think I drove here to kill myself too.*

But instead of continuing to drive, I get out of the car and just stand there. I stand there and yell, "FUCK YOU!!" as loudly as I possibly can. Then I give the sky a great big middle finger, cursing whatever "higher power" has decided that Missy's life should end like this. Because if there is someone up there, then seriously ...

*Fuck. You.*

# 27

## Emma
November 6th, 2017
*Four days after*

*I* don't find out that Missy died until *four days after*. My best friend has been dead for four days and no one told me.

Today starts off like any other day. My mom drags me out of bed, I put on a small touch of makeup, and have a quick snack before leaving the house. We pick up Nicolle on the way to school, and spend the whole ride gossiping.

Everything is normal, not *a hair out* of place. *Everything is just as it should be.*

I take one final glance in my compact mirror before climbing out of the car. My under eyes are slightly darker than I would like, but that's likely the result of me staying up all night studying. It doesn't bother me though, because I know it will all pay off after I pass the two grueling tests I have today. Nicolle grabs my arm and drags me closer to her, just as we spot Kaylee waiting by herself a couple yards away.

From this far away, when I squint my eyes enough, Kaylee almost looks like a slightly older version of Anna, with her bright blonde hair and long, thin legs.

"Ugh. Kaylee has been annoying me *so much!*" Nicolle's snarky comment snaps me out of my thoughts and I turn to look at her. She pulls me aside, and her voice lowers to a whisper as it's clear Kaylee just may have heard her say that.

"What? Why? What did she do?" I ask, not understanding. Nicolle and Kaylee have always been like two peas in a pod, since the day I met them. Sometimes it feels like there is a glue between them, preventing me from getting in between them.

Nicolle rolls her eyes so far back they might just fall right out of her skull. "She's just so annoying sometimes. I *literally* can't." I still don't understand what Kaylee has done to warrant such anger.

"But did she do something?" I whisper as quietly as possible, sending a quick glance toward Kaylee, who is now nervously waiting for us to reach her.

"Oh my god, Em! Can't you just be on my side for once?" I don't know how to react, because for all I know, Kaylee hasn't actually done anything wrong.

I don't want Nicolle to get mad at me though, so I just nod my head slightly and mutter, "Yeah, sorry," under my breath. Nicolle rolls her eyes again and strides off away from me, walking right toward Kaylee.

I rack my brain trying to think of what Kaylee could have done to make Nicolle so upset, but the only logical thought I have is that Nicolle might just be kind of a bitch sometimes for no reason. For a while now I've thought this, but have always kept it in the back of my mind. But with every rude comment she throws at one of us, and every hidden insult she whispers about her other "friends" when they aren't listening, that little thought in the back of my mind only grows. No one ever seems to do anything to deserve her snotty, judgemental comments. She can just be really mean without any warning, and I keep letting her get away with it.

Nicolle was the first person to treat me like a normal human after Anna died. I'd rarely spoken to her before then, and was having a hard time fitting in at school. With the relationship between me and Missy growing more tense every day, and my best friend gone forever, I began to realize how lonely I was without them.

Nicolle and I started becoming close the first day of the new school year, when we were seated next to each other in our history class.

She was the first person who didn't start off conversations by asking, "How are you holding up?" or "How are you coping with her death?" I was never one to hide talking about Anna, sometimes the only thing that helped me make sense of her death was reminiscing about how great her life was. But it was nice to talk to Nicolle and not be reminded of Anna's death every second of the day.

Nicolle didn't ask me about it then, and in fact, she never really has.

Our conversations have always focused on normal things like school, boys, and makeup—the type of fun, gossipy talks I had been missing out on since starting high school. She wasn't always so cold-spirited though, and we *had* shared a lot of great times together. The closer and closer we got though, the more her true colors started to shine through.

I met Kaylee almost immediately after meeting Nicolle. I followed Nicolle to lunch and, seated right next to her, was a girl I had never seen before. Nicolle took the lead in introducing us, explaining they had been best friends since kindergarten, and how they did absolutely everything together.

I can still hear the way Kaylee chimed in, saying, "Yeah, so being friends with her pretty much means you're instantly friends with me too! And if you're *not* her friend then I probably won't ever speak to you." They both laughed, but I found it more of an eerie threat than a playful joke.

I always envied their friendship, the way they had known each other for so long and still managed to stay so close. It's just one of those things that makes me hate having moved around so much as a kid.

We reach the spot where Kaylee is standing, and I wait awkwardly for one of them to speak up. I watch as Kaylee bites her lip nervously, and makes the decision to pull us both in for a semi-sweet hug. Nicolle reaches into the hug, and exclaims, "Aww! I missed you! This weekend was *so* boring without you!" I give Nicolle the side-eye, reminding her that just a few seconds ago she was going on and on about how annoying Kaylee has been.

I can tell Nicolle's demeanor has softened, and in a matter of minutes they go right back to their usual buddy-buddy state. I sigh, wondering how they can switch things up so fast. While I feel bad for Kaylee, I feel incredibly confused about Nicolle. They take off, walking into school the moment they hear the bell ring, not bothering to turn around to check and see if I'm following behind.

School continues as usual, and I step into my second period English class that I share with Missy and Nicolle. It isn't any surprise when I walk in to find Missy's seat cold and empty. I simply figure Missy is skipping again with her boyfriend or her new group of senior girl friends.

The seat on the other side is empty as well, and I sit, waiting patiently for Nicolle to come and sit down. Moments later she comes running in, frantically approaching me at my desk. She throws her stuff down, and plants her hands directly in front of me on top of my desk. "Did you hear?" I give her a confused look. Knowing Nicolle, she could be talking about anything from the biggest celebrity scandal to some couple I've never met having just broken up.

I laugh a little, "No, what is it?" It immediately scares me how her expression isn't matching mine, as her face quickly gets dark and her brows furrow.

"I don't know how to tell you—" She seems to struggle to find her words, and I'm suddenly getting a very, very bad feeling about whatever it is she has to say.

"Just say it—" I say, quickly cutting her off.

"Em, Missy's dead."

## 28

## Harper
November 6th 2017
*Four days after*

*"I* heard she *killed* herself."

From the moment I walk into school things feel different. Everywhere I go, whispers flood the halls. By second period everyone seems to be talking about *"the girl who killed herself"*. I bet half of them don't even bother to say her name.

*Missy.*

The girl who, in the few months we knew each other, felt like a little sister to me. The girl who seemed to have so many bad things going on but fought her hardest everyday, and felt like no one noticed.

*But I always noticed.*

Since the first day she and I truly talked, I knew we were similar in more ways than I would have wished.

I feel my legs weaken, and the halls feel like they are about to cave in on me. I start to hyperventilate and suddenly feel as if the weight of everyone's whispers around me will crush me into the floor.

I panic, needing to find a way out. I run to the closest door, and the moment I'm hit with fresh air, I feel like I can breathe again. That is, until I turn around to find Logan and Sam hovering a few feet away from me.

*Just when I thought this couldn't get any worse.*

I can't control myself, and race up to Logan, getting right in his face. I start yelling, no filter to my words, as I let my thoughts and emotions run unchecked. "What the hell did you do to her, Logan?" He takes a step back, caught by surprise.

"Woah, woah. What are you talking about?"

"Don't play dumb with me!" I push against his chest, but I barely move him. "You had to have been the last person with her, what did you do to her?!" My screams are turning into shrieks and I notice how many people are watching. From far away I spot Mark and Morgan, their attention immediately on me. I pray they don't come over here, not wanting them to stop me.

Logan says nothing, so I pound my fists harder against his chest. "Did you say something to her? I bet you did, just *enough* to push her over the edge!"

"What the hell are you talking about?" he pauses. "Oh god, is this about Missy?"

"Of course, it's about her! How do you just continue to be so insensitive and so awful and—" I scream back.

Logan makes his way up to me, with Sam following closely behind. He scoffs, "I'm done with that *bitch*. She was so rude to me the other day. I'm done dealing with her drama, and I'm done with yours, too." He goes to walk away, but I get in front of him before he gets a chance to.

"Logan, what are you talking about?" Then it hits me. *He doesn't know.* He doesn't know *at all. None* of them do. "You two don't know, do you?" The only responses I get are their dumbfounded faces staring back at me. "I had assumed Mark would have told you by now—" I pause, before finishing my sentence. It *doesn't* get any easier the more I talk about it. "But I guess he thought you would know by now that your girlfriend killed herself." He did *not* expect that. Sam turns to look at him and we both stand there unsure of what to do next. In all the years I've known him, I've never seen Logan cry or even get upset. I keep staring at him, desperately trying to find an ounce of sympathy for him. *He did just find out his girlfriend is dead.* But all I can see when I look at him, is the same smug look on his face as when I caught him cheating.

And then he starts to laugh.

*What a dick.*

Suddenly, any semblance of empathy I had for him has been completely wiped away. "Are you kidding me? Did you two idiots hear anything I just said?" Logan turns back to me, walking right up to my face. So close I can feel his breath on mine, he takes a step forward then whispers, "Like I said. I'm done with that bitch."

*I could kill him.*

Suddenly everything after that seems to move in slow motion. I watch as he turns his back to me and walks away with Sam. I run around to face him and get as close as possible before smacking him across the face as hard as I can.

All the anger I had built up for these two idiotic boys all comes out at once. Sam tries to put his hands in front of mine, but Logan pushes him away, "What the hell, Harper?"

I start screaming at him, louder than I thought my voice would have been capable of, "You're a horrible person, Logan! How could you care so little about her? She loved you! She *loved* you, Logan! And you treated her like shit every day." His face never changes, there isn't even an ounce of regret in his body, and he can tell how mad it's making me. I lunge at him, wishing I could punch him until he falls to the ground, but I am stopped by two arms pulling me back. I turn around in confusion to find Mark holding me back by my arms, with Morgan close behind him. Mark lets go of me, and Morgan runs over to stand with me while Mark turns and leads Logan away.

Her face is a mask of anguish. She looks so sad for me, and instead of making me feel better, it just makes me feel like complete shit. "Stop looking at me like that."

MIA MANDALA | *Dear Anna,*

She takes a step closer. "Morgan, stop it." She opens her arms and wraps me in a hug. In an instant, I crumble into her arms, crying so hard I can't seem to catch my breath. She rubs my back so gently, as if not wanting to break me. She whispers softly in my ear, "Let's get you home, Harper. It's going to be okay."

## 29

### Emma
November 6th, 2017
*Four days after*

"You're lying."

"I'm not, Em, I swear."

"Cut it out, Nicolle." I shake my head, I *can't believe* Nicolle would think saying something like this would be even remotely funny.

"Listen to me. It happened on Thursday. I just overheard a teacher telling her students." I slam my hands down hard on my desk.

"No. No. No, she would never do something like that. She's fine, she's fine!" I scream at her, catching the class's attention. I watch as everyone whips their heads around to face me. Blank expressions are painted across their faces, and I wonder how many of them already knew.

*How many of them knew before I did?*

"She's fine," I whisper. Meanwhile, all I can think of is the last time I saw Missy. And how she was definitely *not fine*. All I can see is the absolutely broken look she had at my house. I've never seen someone look more lost than when we sat there in silence while I cleaned her up. Then she left, without barely saying another word.

Oh my god.

It all makes sense.

"Emma—" Nicolle tries to reach out for me, but she feels miles away, despite being right in front of me.

"No. This can't be happening. It's not—she's not—" Everything around me slowly fades in on itself, and my vision starts to blacken around the edges.

I focus on my breathing ... I can at least do *that*. But yet, I still can't seem to catch my breath. Flashes of black and white fill my vision, and I fear I might pass out. I don't know how, but I find the strength to stand up and run out of the classroom, holding my head in my hands. Out in the hallway, I fall to the floor, my back sliding down the wall. I bury my head deep into my knees, my heart beating a hundred miles a minute.

"Oh god, Emma." Slowly, I raise my head up to find Nicolle standing over me. I can't quite read her face, but she doesn't seem to feel bad for me. Instead, she almost seems more surprised that I am this sad.

She stretches out her hands toward me. "C'mon. Let me help you up," she says, and I shakily grab her hands with mine. My vision goes blurry again from standing up too fast, and I barely have a second to regain my balance before Nicolle is pulling me down the hallway.

"Where are we going?" I ask, choking through my sobs. She comes to a stop right in front of the counselor's office. It's not new for me to be here. I still remember the countless times I had to step out of class and sit in this office, too overwhelmed after Anna died to focus on anything.

Nicolle opens the door, and tells me to sit down. I can't hear her quietly talking to the counselor, but I assume she has explained what happened, and they both tell me to just stay calm and sit while they call my parents.

This all feels like a dream. I try making sense of it, but it doesn't feel real.

When Anna died, I felt like my whole world had ended. I never imagined I would have to feel like that again. I start to feel nauseous and my stomach starts to heave, so I grab the closest trash can and hold it under my head just in case.

The counselor walks over to Nicolle, and I can faintly hear her say, "It's just so sad, suicide rates have gone up so much in girls your age."

Hearing that is enough to make me throw up right in front of them.

Nicolle looks at me with such disgust, and I wish I could disappear. I've never felt so embarrassed and humiliated in my life. She doesn't run over to hold back my hair, or make sure I'm okay. Instead, her eyebrows furrow, and her nose turns up in revulsion. I stare at her, catching my breath and wiping the vomit off my lips. I don't say it, but my eyes beg for her to come to me. To comfort me the way a friend *should*.

To do *anything* but just stare at me like I'm some freak.

Nicolle pinches her nose with her fingers to hide the smell, and walks out of the room.

The moment she closes the door behind her, I can't help but burst out sobbing again. The counselor turns to me with a look of pity that makes me feel even sicker. She walks to her desk and hands me a cup of water, awkwardly rubbing my back as my cries become uncontrollable.

*I can't seem to stop them.*

A few minutes pass, and she gets a call. As she walks away, I curl up into myself, trying to become as small as possible. She taps me on my shoulder, and I jolt my head up. "It's okay, sweetheart. Come on, your parents just got here."

## 30

## Emma

July 4th, 2016
*One year and four months before*

"WOAH! Look at that!"

I looked up in amazement at the giant roller coaster towering over the three of us. My eyes widened, and all I could think was how fun it looked. "Oh my god, let's go!"

I turned around to Anna and Missy, expecting them to be matching my excitement. Instead, I found Anna slowly backing up, fear painted across her face.

Missy and I spun her around. "C'mon, Anna! It looks so fun!" we begged, trying to convince her to go with us, but she wouldn't budge.

"It's fine, let's just go on something else," Missy finally said, both of us realizing there was no changing Anna's mind. Anna shook her head, telling us to go on without her and she would wait for us here. We both hesitated, not wanting to go without her.

"Go! You guys will have fun, and I'll be right here when you're done," Anna said with a smile, motioning for us to go toward the coaster. I looked at Missy, and we both nodded in agreement. We took off running and laughing, trying to get a good spot in line.

Despite our efforts, by the time we got in line there was still a 15 minute wait ahead of us. We both sighed, but decided not to turn around.

We spent the first few minutes in silence.

Once our excitement to go on the ride died down, we both struggled to find something to talk about next. I was about to say something, but second-guessed myself and stopped. My foot tapped anxiously on the ground, as I looked ahead at all the people in front of us. Anytime either of us made eye contact with the other, it only lasted a split second before we looked the other way.

I never realized how hard it was to talk to Missy when we didn't have Anna to help lead us. Out of the three of us, Missy and I had always been the least close, our bond came from both being close with Anna. It was sort of an unspoken thing throughout our friendship, but I never realized how little we actually talked one-on-one.

Thankfully, Missy spoke up and suggested we play a game to pass the time. We played a juicy game of *Never Have I Ever*, both revealing things that the other had no idea about ourselves. I burst out laughing when Missy put her finger down for my last question. "No way! You've gone *skinny dipping*?" I exclaimed. She nodded her head, unable to control her laughing. "Oh my god! When? I need to know every detail!" She could barely talk through her laughter, and tried to regain her composure several times. Her laughing made me laugh even harder, and we both struggled to stop for what felt like minutes.

When she finally calmed down, she just looked at me and shrugged. "Hey, you didn't tell me who you've kissed, so I don't have to tell you this." My jaw dropped, but I couldn't argue with that.

"Okay, it's your turn, you ask the next question." I said, resuming the game. Talking with Missy now felt so easy and natural, and I wondered why we hadn't done this more often. I made a decision right then and there that going forward I would make more of an effort to talk to her. I wanted this stupid, unspoken fight over who was better friends with Anna to officially end, as it just made things more tense, and I really did care for Missy.

I think the closer I got to her and Anna, the more she started to resent me for being close with Anna.

I didn't blame her. She had never had someone enter their friendship since they had become friends, but she always seemed like she wanted to pick a fight with me.

Over time I grew to resent her, not liking her attitude toward me, and not liking how much Anna liked her. It didn't make things enjoyable when we were always bickering about small, useless things, and I thought of how much time we wasted when we could have been getting to know each other.

I decided that after today, that would all change.

We got fastened into our seats on the coaster, and gave each other one last look before we took off, screaming and laughing the whole ride.

We got off the ride and sprinted to find Anna and tell her how awesome it was. "THAT WAS SO COOL!" I gasped. We jumped up and down, recalling every loop and turn we could remember.

On our walk out of the fair, we found a big grassy field full of running sprinklers. In an instant, Anna ran through them, spinning around with the widest smile I'd ever seen.

Her smile could always light up my day—when Anna was happy it made everyone around her feel the same.

I stood back for a moment, admiring how lucky I was to have these two girls in my life.

How happy I was to call them my best friends.

*I was still in amazement that I had someone to call a best friend.*

Growing up, I was so scared I would never experience something like this. Everywhere I lived, I was in fear we would move again. When I met Anna and Missy, it felt like something clicked in me, and every second I spent with them

I never wanted to end. They looked back to me and waved me over. "C'mon, Em!" Anna yelled to me.

My *best* friend, Anna. She was so special to me, I never imagined I would ever lose her.

I took off running toward them, and Anna snuck up behind me. "Tag! You're it!" She ran off into the sprinklers and I chased after her. We didn't care that we were getting soaked. We didn't care about *anything* at that moment. Only each other, on the most perfect day, the way things should have always been.

## 31

### Harper

August 28th, 2014
*Three years and two months before*

"Harper?"

*This was a stupid idea,* I thought to myself.

Here I was, standing at the foot of Morgan's doorway, showing up completely unannounced. With tears running down my face.

"Harper, what are you doing here? I didn't know you were coming over today ..." Morgan said kindly, as I lifted my head up slowly, revealing my tear-stained face.

"Oh no, what happened?" I bit my lip to stop it from quivering. She quickly understood that I wasn't in any state to explain myself, and instead took my hand, leading me inside.

Her dad poked his head out of the kitchen doorway, a confused look directed at Morgan. She mouthed something I couldn't understand, and he nodded in return, sharply turning the other way.

In silence, she led the way up the stairs, and I followed her into her bedroom.

Gently, she took a seat at the edge of her bed. I stood there, unsure of what to do. She gave me a reassuring smile and said, "Here," patting an empty space on the bed in front of her, motioning for me to sit. I faced her, but she gently put her hands on either side of me and turned me around. I didn't know what she was doing until I felt her grab all my hair in her hands. She moved it all behind my shoulders, and grabbed a small hairbrush off the desk next to her.

Slowly, she started carding her fingers through my hair. Gingerly, with a touch so soft I almost didn't think it could be real, she worked her way through every small knot she found. Once she was done, she began brushing softly through my hair. My hair had gotten so long, it was almost touching my waist, and I couldn't remember the last time anyone had taken this much care of it.

She separated my hair into three sections, and slowly began braiding it all the way down. "My mom used to do this whenever I was upset," she said, and I could hear the faint sadness in her voice. That small hint of heartbreak came out whenever she talked about her mom.

I didn't know much about Morgan's mom, as she rarely talked about her, but whenever she did, it was always to tell me about the very best parts of her.

"Done. Here, look." Morgan handed me a small, silver mirror and I took a look.

Growing up, my mom never taught me how to take care of my hair. It always seemed like something I was stuck dealing with, rather than something that made me beautiful.

But looking in the mirror, I felt *so pretty*.

I broke out into a smile, my eyes starting to water. For a second it seemed like I might start crying again, and Morgan leaned over to hug me. "No! What's wrong?" she exclaimed, rubbing my back. I couldn't help but laugh so hard my eyes started welling up even more.

I gathered myself together, and looked back at Morgan. Taking in a deep breath, all I could do was smile.

"Are you okay?' she asked.

I nodded and said, "I love you so much, Morgan."

She smiled, taking my hands in hers. "Aww, Harper, I love you too!" We hugged again and her arms wrapped tightly around mine, pulling me in close.

I zoned out, staring at the walls behind her. Stacks and stacks of books covered her walls, surrounded by posters of all her favorite singers and bands. I felt Morgan tapping lightly on my knee, grabbing my attention. "What are you thinking about?" she asked.

I looked at her, wondering how I could sum up all the love I had for this girl in a few simple words.

"You're my first best friend. I don't think I've ever had a friend like you before," I admitted, as if confessing a deep secret. In a way it was a secret, one that I had pushed so far down I almost forgot how long I had spent without any real close friends.

How long I had spent feeling *so alone.*

And now I *finally* had *someone.*

A friend to share secrets with, to spill all the stories to that no one else cared to hear.

She *always* cared.

Ever since the day Morgan and I became friends, I knew she was the one person I could truly be my most honest self around. All my life, I thought I needed to put up a tough facade in order to get by. But the authenticity of Morgan's friendship brought that wall down.

"Look. I'm not going to push you to tell me if you really don't want to. But Harper—what happened?"

I sighed, for a second I had forgotten everything going on.

My only focus was on how nice my hair looked in its braid.

*I wished my thoughts could always stay that simple.*

"I got in a really big fight with my mom," I started to explain, and she gave me a knowing look. I hadn't told her many details, but Morgan knew I had lots of family issues.

She was always so open to listening to me, it was nice to just be able to talk and not feel judged or wrong.

I looked her in the eye, "I'm really sorry I showed up like this—"

"It's fine," she started to say.

"No, really, I should have at least told you—"

"Harper"—she stopped me mid-sentence— *"really,* it's fine. I want you to know that whenever you have something going on, or you just need to get away from everything at home, you can always come here, okay?"

I nodded my head, a loose tear slowly escaping one eye. "Thank you," I whispered, as she tackled me into a hug.

# 32

## Harper

November 6th, 2017
*Four days after*

*W*e spend the car ride in silence.

Well, it would have been silent if it weren't for the occasional sound of sniffles, and the light hum of Morgan's music in the background. Eyes kept sharply focused on the road, Morgan doesn't notice I've put my head down and drifted off into a deep sleep until we are stopped in front of my driveway.

She nudges me gently. "Harper ..."

"Sorry." I lift my head up slowly, wiping the tears and sleep out of my eyes.

Morgan lovingly rubs my back. "C'mon, let's get you home."

She leads me into my bedroom, taking a seat up against the headboard of my bed. "Turn around," she tells me quietly. I give her a confused look, but all she does is motion for me to turn. I move my legs to the other side, so my back is facing her. For a moment she does nothing, grabbing something I can't see on the other side of her room.

I feel her gather my hair in her hands, and feel a light pull on the ends. I begin to realize she's brushing my hair. A wave of calmness washes over my body. It's brief, but it's there.

"Remember when we used to do this as kids?" she asks, taking pieces of my hair and combing her way through them. I nod, careful not to move my head too much. "It's gotten so long." I smile and know she's trying to cheer me up, but it's so hard to feel good at a time like this.

We sit quietly while Morgan brushes through my hair smoothly. Minutes pass, and while my brain screams at me so many unanswered questions, complete silence fills the air around us.

I take a deep breath, breaking the silence.

"Do you ever feel like it's our fault?" I feel her stop brushing and drop her hands beside her.

"Why would you think that?" she asks, turning me to face her. I pause, searching for the words.

"She shouldn't have been our friend," I say.

"What—"

I cut her off, "She shouldn't have been our *best* friend, and she shouldn't have been with Logan. We knew how bad he was—"

"Of course she shouldn't have been, but that's not our fault. We just always wanted to include her, and—"

"But it *is* our fault!" I look away, unable to look her in the eye. "We *knew* how shitty Logan was, but we excused it, because what? He was fun to hangout with?" She opens her mouth to retaliate, but I stop her. "We *could* have stopped it. We could have told him to leave her alone, and let her be a kid. She was still a kid, Morgan!" Now it seems like nothing can stop my anguish. I look up to Morgan and find her eyes watering, but she's not saying a word. I want to reach out to her, to say something that could fix all of this, but I feel frozen.

We stare at each other, and just cry.

I hide my face in the sleeve of my sweater, wishing I could stay here forever.

But then I manage to stand up, carefully taking small steps away from the bed. My whole body feels so shaky, I'm scared I might fall.

"I'm sorry, Morgan, you—you should go."

"What, why?" She reaches out for me, but I turn away. Everywhere I turn, my heart aches. I see photos of Morgan and me from when we were younger up to the present, plastered all over my walls. I wish I could look at them and smile, the way we were in those photos, but all I can think of is all the things Missy won't get to experience.

A certain photograph sticks out to me, Morgan and Mark standing with their hands interlocked, staring at each other like they hold the world in each other's hands. To the left is me and Sam.

We all looked *so* happy.

I can't remember the last time things were that good.

The pictures scream at me, times of good memories and laughs that Missy will never experience. Before I know what I'm doing, I'm ripping them all down off the walls. Any semblance of how things used to be gets stripped away. Because *nothing* is how it used to be.

*A girl is dead.*

She is dead and will never get to laugh the way I did, smile until her cheeks hurt, or just spend time with her best friends. *Ever again.*

*So how is it fair if I still do?*

I want to tear them all down, till every inch of my walls is bare. I claw at them, ripping them off the walls, till Morgan lunges at me.

"Harper, STOP IT! What the hell is going on with you?"

As if things couldn't get worse, my mother waltzes through the door.

"God! Could you stop screaming?" She storms up to me, unaware that Morgan is standing frozen by my side. She looks at the torn pictures and yells, "What are you doing? You're crazy!" She turns and notices Morgan, and rolls her eyes. "And what is *she* doing here? You gotta get down there and watch your sisters!" she shrieks at me, stumbling her way out of my room. "I've dealt with enough shit for today!" And with that, she slams the door behind her.

    I face Morgan. She stands there, and for a moment she almost looks scared. Whether she's scared of me or my mom, I'm not sure.

    Without a word, she slowly moves to the floor, scrambling to pick up the photos I threw down. I bend down to her level, grabbing her hands to stop her. "You should go, I don't want her to get upset."

    She nods, without meeting my eye. In a flash, she is gone, and I'm left more alone than ever.

    "Harper!" a small voice yells from outside my door. I pull myself together, and put on a smile for my sisters.

# 33

## Emma
November 20th, 2017
*Eighteen days after*

*T*wo weeks have passed since I heard the news about Missy.

The first week, I felt nothing but despair. I rotted away in my bed, not even getting up for food. I tried going to school, but couldn't make it through my first class before feeling so sick with grief that I had to call home.

The second week, I felt angry. I was angry at the world, and I couldn't make any sense of it. I acted erratically, yelling at anyone who tried to talk to me. It wasn't their fault, they didn't do anything wrong, but I was just so angry that I had to take it out on someone.

After the first week passed, my parents stopped trying to send me to school, as I would just scream in retaliation when they tried. Another two weeks have gone by now, and my parents finally convinced me to go back.

My parents keep trying to ask me how I feel, but they don't understand that no words can explain it. Everything makes me so mad, and I feel so guilty for it all the time. It's like all the feelings I worked so hard to bury when Anna died, are all just coming back up and I don't know where to put them. Back then, my days were spent in countless therapy sessions and support groups, as well as any new or novel treatment they could find to "fix my issues."

But now I'm right back to where I started. I'm filled with all of this pent-up anger, and no one seems to understand me, *I* don't even understand myself. A part of me *hates* them both for being dead. For leaving me so alone, with no one else who understands how I feel.

When Anna died, all I wanted to do was sit by her grave and talk for hours. But a part of me feels unsure when it comes to visiting Missy. Our friendship was always so complicated, and it only grew worse in the past months.

It's not as simple as everyone makes it seem, my grief isn't just sadness or depression. It's a million different emotions, and feelings, and thoughts all piled together, and *it's making me crazy.*

I just pray no one talks to me about it in school.

***

## MIA MANDALA | *Dear Anna,*

I'm walking to my first class when I hear a shrill voice from behind me yell, "Oh my god, Em, I've been worried *sick* about you!" I turn to find none other than Kaylee and Nicolle standing side by side, calling me over. I look around, walking up to them slowly.

Since I threw up in front of her, Nicolle and I have barely texted. I've hardly spoken to *anyone* since I found out about Missy.

I approach them, and they immediately crowd around me like I'm some zoo animal on display. They pester me with stupid questions, asking "Where were you?" and "Why'd you miss so much school?" and "Are you okay with everything going on?" Their words start to blend together, and I can't focus on any of them.

My body starts to shut down, and I find myself unable to form words that would even be remotely appropriate. They don't stop prodding me with questions, until I finally shout, "I'M FINE!"

They both jump back in surprise, and I take a deep breath, trying to calm myself down. "I'm fine, I just—I need some space, please." I watch as they give each other a look.

This happens a lot, especially when I'm the one talking. People don't like my answers, so they throw each other an unspoken look, thinking I won't notice.

*But I always notice.*

Nicolle rolls her eyes slightly, but enough for me to see. I want to scream at her. To yell and ask how she could have left me in the state I was in, so vulnerable and sad, how she could just walk out on me without a word. But I hold my tongue, not having the energy for a fight right now and instead, continue walking to class.

***

I spend the rest of the day dodging Kaylee and Nicolle, walking away from them in the hallway when I can, and trying to keep to myself during classes.

They don't seem to care, as they're always too engrossed in their own conversations to pay me any more attention than a backwards glance as we pass in the halls.

Being back at school is so tiring already, and the day is barely halfway through.

*I don't know how I'm supposed to keep doing this.*

Everywhere I go, I think of Missy, and I have to push my thoughts so far to the back of my head, just to get through the rest of the day.

The lunch bell rings, and I hesitate walking up the stairs. I can't decide where I'm going to eat. I spot Kaylee and Nicolle at our regular lunch table. They are surrounded by other girls, half of whom I don't know their names. I don't spot an empty seat anywhere near them, and take that as my cue to sit elsewhere.

I find a spot at an empty table and sit down. I lay my head down on the table, my entire body feeling exhausted. I barely have enough energy to go to my next class, and I contemplate calling my parents to pick me up.

I look around at the empty seats surrounding me, feeling out of place. Under normal circumstances, sitting alone would have been torture for me, as I'm usually the most social of my friends.

Today though, it is a blessing to finally have some quiet.

I look up to find a boy I've never seen before, walking around awkwardly. I stare at him, trying to figure out who he is, but no one comes to mind.

He has dirty blonde hair, and even from all the way over here I can see he has bright green eyes like sea glass. He paces back and forth, his entire body looking stressed. It's not often our school has anyone new, but from the looks of it he doesn't know anyone.

I can imagine the awkward scrutiny he must be feeling, and I flash back to the times I was the out-of-place new kid. Despite my lack of energy to talk to anyone, I call him over to my table.

"Hey!" He whips his head toward me, but immediately goes to turn back around. I motion for him to look over at me, and nod when he looks unsure. He takes a few slow steps toward me, and I have to smile at how nervous he looks.

"Sorry, I don't know if you're waiting on someone, but if you want, you can sit here." I give him a genuine smile, wanting him to feel safe. In an instant, a wave of relaxation washes over him, and his demeanor softens.

"Yeah, that would be great. Thank you." He exhales, looking like he can finally calm down, and pulls out a chair.

"I'm Blake," the new boy says.

# 34

## Harper
### November 20th, 2017
*Eighteen days after*

"**W**ooohooo!" The wind hits my face like a giant fan, causing my hair to fly in every direction. I turn the volume up until the music can't possibly get any louder, until the only sound I hear is the roar of drums and bass guitar. I roll down every window in my car, and I hope everyone on the road can hear my music.

I push my foot heavily on the gas, my car speeding along the highway faster than I am used to. Everything passes by me in a blur—people, cars, trees—all of it whirls by before I can even blink.

On my lap, my phone buzzes every second. A string of text messages and incoming calls blows up my phone, so I toss it onto the other seat and completely ignore all of it. My car speeds along the road, faster and faster every second. I don't know where I'm going, and I don't care to know.

I get off the highway, and start driving along a long beach that stretches as far as I can see. I stare off into the distance, to the ocean waves crashing onto the shore. It takes me back to better times, times when I would come here with Morgan and all our friends. Running through the water, not caring we were missing loads of school, with not a sober thought in our minds.

I stop my car as close to the beach as I can, and before I know it I'm running toward the crashing waves. I sprint across the sand, throwing my arms up in the air. The splash of freezing water as the waves hit me cools my whole body down, and I remember I'm still fully clothed, but all it makes me do is laugh.

I fall back against the sand, letting the small waves roll over my feet.

*It's so relaxing at the shoreline.*

Just for a few seconds, everything becomes quieter. The world moves slowly for a moment.

*But I know it can't last forever.*

I sit up, shaking with cold. I play with the sand beneath me and draw shapes with my fingertips. I turn my head around—the only source of life near me is the group of seagulls occasionally diving into the waves for food.

I push my hands down against the sand, and stand up slowly. My feet sink firmly into the ground, and I let the water crash onto me.

Closing my eyes, *I start to scream.* I yell and yell, as loud as I possibly can, I don't care at all who might hear me.

"Harper." I turn around, recognizing Morgan's voice anywhere.

"Hi." Standing just a few feet away from me is Morgan, her arms crossed and her lips pursed. I walk up to her, needing to make sure she is actually here.

"Morgan, what are you doing out here?"

"I should be asking you the same thing," she snaps back.

"What?" She walks up to me, and grabs my face in her hands. "Morgan, stop that. I'm fine." She takes a step closer, pulling me toward her.

"No, you're not. And you're high as shit! What are you doing driving around like this?"

I brush her off, trying to yank my way out of her reach. "I'm not high, Morgan. Now leave me ALONE!" I push her hands off of mine.

She gives me a condescending look. "Oh, really. You're not?" I watch as she whips out her phone, and for a split second I'm startled by the flash in my eyes. She turns the phone around so I can see, and practically shoves it in my face.

"Look at yourself." The photo almost stares back at me, my face is slightly out of focus, but my eyes are visibly *bright* red. Morgan almost has to laugh, "Yeah, you're not fooling anyone."

I want to argue, but from the look on her face I know it is not a fight I will win. She is right to yell at me, this *is* crazy. The more I think back, I can hardly remember how or why I got here in the first place. I try retracing my steps in my mind, but am taken out of my thoughts by Morgan leading me by the hand to a bench up on the sand.

"What are you doing here?" I ask her, waiting for her to answer before I sit down. She sighs, knowing my stubbornness won't go away.

"Harper, you haven't been to a full day of school in weeks—"

"Who cares! We used to skip school all the time—"

"This is more than that, and you know it."

I get up from the bench, and she follows behind as I try to walk away from her.

I turn, crossing my arms. "How did you know I was here?"

"I saw you get in your car on the way to second period—"

"So, you followed me?"

She shrugs.

"If you wanted to come, you could've just asked me," I say with a laugh, trying to lighten the mood.

*She doesn't seem to think it's funny.*

"Seriously, Harper. I'm really worried about you. You're missing a bunch of classes and—"

I roll my eyes. "Who cares!" I exclaim, throwing my hands up like a toddler. "We're all gonna die anyway."

"Don't talk like that."

"Ugh! Don't act all high and mighty, I'm just trying to have some fun!" I say, while spinning around, sand flying every which way. She grabs me, preventing any movement.

"Harper, listen to me!" she yells.

*She actually yelled*, and Morgan *never* yells unless it is really serious. That shuts me up real quick.

"I know her death is really hard for you. But, *you know* this isn't how you should be coping."

"I don't know what you mean—" I protest.

"Yes, you do." She takes a deep breath, gathering her thoughts.

I nod my head, focusing on my breathing, so tears don't escape my eyes. "I should have protected her better," I say, the words barely escaping my lips.

"Harper it's not your fault—"

"I could have done more though. I knew she was struggling, and I did nothing." I am crying now, faster than I can keep up with. "I *should* have done so much more. We both could have!" Now Morgan is crying too, and I wonder if she thinks the same thing I do. Every time I close my eyes and imagine Logan and Missy kissing, I picture him pressuring her, trying to push her beyond her limits. All those times with her that we could have asked her about it, but we never quite reached the subject. We were all too concerned with where we were going next and who was going to supply more alcohol.

All the times I could have done more.

I *could* have helped more.

I *should* have.

We stand there in silence for just a moment. Our tears flowing as free and salty as the ocean nearby, I close my eyes and try catching my breath, but it is like there is no air to be found.

"Harper, listen to me."

I open my eyes slowly, and try focusing my thoughts solely on Morgan. I try to choke out a response, but nothing comes out except for more sobs.

"I know you feel like you could have done something to change what happened, but you *can't* change the past, and you *can't* live your life in regret."

"I know," I whisper, so softly I doubt she hears it.

She takes a few steps toward me and wraps me in a hug, holding my head in the crook of her neck. "I love you," she murmurs, and it just makes me cry even harder.

# 35

## Emma

November 20th, 2017

*Eighteen days after*

"**I**'m Emma," I tell the boy. "But you can just call me Em."

He smiles, "Em. That's really pretty."

I blush, unsure of how to respond. "So ..." I rack my brain for something to say. "Are you new here?" I regret the question the moment it comes out of my mouth.

*No duh, he's new here.* I think to myself.

He doesn't seem to think my question is stupid, and if he does, he does a good job at hiding it behind his smile. He nods and says, "Yeah, I just moved here a couple days ago actually."

"Where did you move from?" I ask.

He takes a second, like he can't remember the answer. "Illinois. Well I *was* in Florida—*then* Texas, and then Illinois, but I wasn't in any of those places for very long."

"Wow, you've been everywhere!" I exclaim, and he shrugs shyly.

"So, are you new also?" he asks anxiously.

I laugh a little, "No, I've lived here since sixth grade."

"Oh, I just assumed, since you're sitting alone—" He immediately tries walking back his comment, fearing he insulted me. "I didn't mean it like that. I'm so sorry—"

I cut him off, and give him a look of reassurance, "Don't worry, I get it." My eyes wander to where Nicolle and Kaylee are sitting, lost deeply in conversation.

"Are those your friends?"

I nod, still staring at them. "Yeah," I sigh and turn back to him.

"Why aren't you sitting with them instead?" he questions.

"I just—" I pause, searching for the right words. "I just—need a little space right now." I don't explain any further, and he doesn't question it.

We each dive into our lunches, eating in silence. It isn't awkward, and despite not talking to each other it still feels comforting, just having someone nearby to share the silence with.

A few minutes before the lunch bell is going to ring, he speaks up, just as I am about to stand up and throw out my napkin, "Hey, I don't know if you're already busy after school, but do you maybe want to go get pizza later? I drove by this little restaurant that looked good on the way here."

I freeze. "Uh—" I hesitate, unsure of how to respond. He's sweet and all, but I also know nothing about him and I'm not in the space to add more drama to my life.

"Sorry, that was weird, I don't mean it like—"

I stop him mid-apology, "Yeah, let's do it." He smiles softly, and I smile in return.

***

Four grueling hours later, the last bell of the day finally rings. I pack up my stuff quicker than ever, and race out of the classroom, not wanting to miss Blake.

I stand outside the school against a concrete wall and wait nervously, wondering if he will even remember. Groups of students walk every which way around me. I stand on my tiptoes, peering my head around, trying to spot him in the crowd. Crowds of people pass me by, and I start to lose hope, wondering if I should just head home when I hear a voice behind me.

"Hey, do you still want to go get something to eat?" I spin around. Blake stands anxiously behind me, fidgeting with the straps of his backpack, and I notice he is biting his lip just slightly.

I let out a sigh of relief, "Yeah, sounds good." We share a quick smile, and he takes the lead in walking us out.

Around our school, are bustling streets filled with shoppers and tourists. It doesn't take long for us to walk to where we're going, and we spend the walk in comfortable silence. Blake seems focused on getting us to the right place, while my mind wanders far off into my own deep thoughts.

We don't talk the whole walk there.

In a way, it feels like we don't have to, just having someone else nearby is comforting enough for the both of us.

Blake comes to a stop outside a small diner-style restaurant. A big, bright sign that reads *"Jerry's Pizza"* hangs over the awning and he shrugs, suddenly looking embarrassed. His cheeks flush and turn bright red. "Sorry, I know it's nothing special. You probably have better things to do, I'm sorry, I just—"

I cut off his rambling and grab onto his upper arm, pulling him inside. He laughs, and gives in.

"Where do you want to sit?" he asks. I look around, and notice the restaurant is practically vacant. I would have thought they were closed if it weren't for the occasional waiter passing by.

We find a small round table near the window, one side is part of a long red booth and the other has a small wooden chair. I sit in the booth, dropping my school bag beside me, and he sits across from me.

The silence fills the air around us, and uncertainty of what to say next hangs in the air, almost mockingly. To our luck, a waiter comes over quickly, breaking the tension. She takes our order swiftly, a cheese pizza to share, and then promptly leaves us alone. I look at Blake, and it hits me how little I know about him. I have so many questions.

"So how have you liked living here?" I ask, taking the opportunity to start up the conversation.

He takes a moment, like he's trying to figure out the right response. "It's different," he says.

I nod knowingly. "I remember when I first moved here. It felt like being on another planet."

He laughs, "Yeah, it's always weird being new."

I pause, "That's right, you mentioned you've moved around a lot recently."

He nods. "Basically my whole life. What about you?" he asks.

"My dad was always being moved around for work. It wasn't till I started middle school that we finally settled in one place and stopped moving around. Even though it's been a few years now, some days I swear, I still feel like that same girl starting a new school with no idea who she will be friends with, and no clue about the place she lives in. It's the memory of the uncertainty of it all that keeps me up at night."

I pause, suddenly realizing how much I just said. Things I never realized I thought. I look at him shyly, scared he will react strangely, thinking I'm coming off too strong, but instead I see that he almost looks relieved.

We share a glance, a small fleeting moment, and I can tell how my words made him feel. I can tell by the way his mouth turns up just slightly, almost into a genuine smile. The way his whole expression drops, as if letting go of all the tension and stress he's been holding onto.

I smile back.

"Here you two go!" The moment is broken by the sight of a large pizza being set down between us. We thank the waiter and dive right in.

Our conversation picks up easily, like two old friends catching up. Blake tells me stories of his old life, his friends and family. I share all the best and worst places to go when you're new, who's nice at school, and who's not.

All the things I wish someone would have told me when I moved here. We laugh like old friends, sharing funny stories, and if you had seen us from afar, you would never have guessed we had just met.

I hear my phone dinging, and quickly silence it, not caring to check who it is.

Minutes go by, and we've eaten almost the entire pizza, when I feel my phone start to continuously vibrate. I groan, flipping it over to find a load of missed calls and texts from my mom. I scroll all the way to the bottom, wondering what is so important that she had to blow up my phone.

MIA MANDALA | *Dear Anna,*

It hits me then, I'm supposed to be at therapy in less than thirty minutes.

*Fuck.*

"Oh shit," I mutter under my breath. I frantically unlock my phone, scrambling to reply to my mom.

"Is everything okay?" he asks, through a mouthful of pizza.

"Yeah, sorry ..." I decline my mom's call once again, and grab my stuff to leave. I fish out a ten dollar bill, and leave it on my side of the table. "I'm so sorry, I *really* have to go." I rush out the door, without another word.

For a second, I glance back, and watch his face sadden, looking more confused than ever. I curse myself for not getting his number, and texting him an explanation. I pray I'll see him tomorrow at school, and that he's not that mad I left so fast.

"Get in, you're going to be late!" I whip my head around to see my mom, window rolled down, yelling at me to get in. I run up to her car and quickly jump in the front seat, before the cars behind us get too mad.

"Sorry, I was getting pizza with a friend," I explain, rushing into the car. I watch as her eyebrows furrow in confusion at the mention of "a friend." She knows I haven't been talking much to Nicolle or Kaylee, but thankfully doesn't push and ask anything more.

# 36

## Harper

September 2017
*Three months before*

*If only back then I had known. If I had a wish, I would go back in time and slap some sense into myself. How could I have been so blind? So oblivious to how bad things were going to get? The questions haunt me. They keep me up at night. I rack my brain for answers, till the only way I can get the noise to stop, is to force myself back to sleep.*

*M*organ nudged me in the shoulder, discreetly catching my attention. "Who's that girl with Logan?"

I turned, watching as Logan strode up near us. Behind him, a young girl followed like a lost puppy. Part of me wanted to laugh. She looked around cluelessly, like she didn't know how to talk. The other part of me felt a little bad, as I watched her in her bewilderment.

*Only a little bad,* though.

I didn't really notice when Logan first showed up with her, and only bothered to pay her any attention when I saw her sulking against the parking lot wall. She had a frightened look upon her face, and her eyebrows shot up in fear when I approached her.

"Hey, I'm Harper."

She introduced herself. *Missy,* she told me.

In the distance, I could hear the laughter of Sam and Logan as they told jokes to everyone else. "Here, come with me, I'll introduce you to my friends." Without a word, she followed me back out to where everyone else sat against the concrete grounds.

To the casual onlooker, the individuals in our group might have seemed drastically different.

*Sam,* who spent his days playing roles for his parents—amusing his dad with early morning golf games, while faking stellar report cards for his mom.

*Logan,* the newest addition to our group, but undoubtedly the one who held the biggest sway over the rest, despite a vaguely toxic demeanor.

*Mark,* angular, muscular, and working toward a sports scholarship—his greatest joy came from whispering sweet nothings into his girlfriend's ear and making her turn a million delightful shades of red.

And *Morgan*, my best friend and Mark's girlfriend. Physically, we couldn't have been more unalike. Her blonde hair was similar to that of a supermodel's, the way it shone in the sun, and somehow only required a minute or two of brushing before it looked runway-ready. Yet, our hearts seemed to beat at the same tempo, our brains worked in tandem. Even if she was the more rational of our duo, we always worked best together.

I went down the line, introducing Missy to each of them. I watched as she smiled and took a seat next to Logan. His eyes barely glanced in her direction for more than a quick moment. A sign I should have taken as *a warning*.

I could easily see that Missy took those quick glances, and turned them into her wildest, most romantic fantasies. I saw it, in the glimmer in her eyes, in the flush that tinted her cheeks when his eyes went toward her for even a second.

I rummaged through my bag, pulling out the joints Logan insisted I take from my dad. I didn't mind doing it, I just didn't like Logan always asking me to.

I passed them around, and we fell into the flow as we always do. Taking turns, and passing them back and forth. One made its way back to me, and I eagerly inhaled as much smoke as my lungs could take.

I reached it out toward Missy, but she declined faster than I could offer. Logan leaned over to her, whispering softly enough that I couldn't make out his words. Just as I was about to take another hit, Missy grabbed it out of my hand.

She choked a little, coughing as she exhaled, but hid it behind her sleeve.

I laughed it off, ignoring her look of genuine discomfort. It didn't take long for that familiar, sweet feeling to sink in. I *loved* it. My body felt weightless, and every bit of stress rolled off my back. It gave me the feeling of complete relaxation and peace that I never found in my home life, or anywhere else for that matter.

We talked for hours, the topic of conversation changing every few minutes.

Morgan and I stood up, eager to walk around and stretch our legs, as the boys stayed behind, catching up on their lives. She pulled me in close, and whispered in my ear, "Let's invite her, I feel bad."

It took me a second of looking back to realize who she meant. *Missy*, who had barely spoken a word since sitting down, still sat there awkwardly, her knees held tightly against her chest. She focused a blank stare in Logan's direction, who paid her no mind and threw his head back in laughter at Sam's stories.

I gave Morgan a withering look.

"C'mon, she looks miserable."

I sighed, giving in, "Fine."

Morgan beamed, and approached Missy.

I couldn't hear their full conversation, but Missy seemed reluctant to leave. Her eyes wandered constantly toward Logan. Morgan flashed one of her more convincing looks, and with a roll of her eyes Missy laughed as Morgan pulled her to her feet.

"C'mon! A little break from the boys never hurt," Morgan told her, and they shared a laugh.

# 37

## Emma
November 20th, 2017
*Eighteen days after*

*I* race into the therapist's office, with my mom following behind me, still pestering me over how late I'm going to be.

As I step inside, a rush of memories washes over me. All the times I came here unwillingly, only agreeing to come because my parents so desperately wanted to find a way to make me "feel better" about all the things that had gone so horribly wrong.

It's the *last* place I want to be right now.

I can't imagine why a place created specifically for fixing people's problems would be decorated in a way that so closely resembled a hospital room, where so many people could be vividly reminded of some of the worst, most vulnerable moments of their lives.

    Bare, white walls in need of a fresh coat of paint surround me on all sides. A long, brown couch takes up most of the room, while an overstuffed, olive-green chair sits across from it. The couch has small, but noticeable scuffs along the bottom of it, likely from years of people anxiously kicking away at it.

    If I had my way, I'd still be out having pizza with Blake, but I made a deal with my parents. When I finally decided to go back to school, I also agreed to go back to therapy, although begrudgingly. The sessions give me just enough time to sulk, or rather, "to sit with my thoughts", as my parents put it.

    Soon after I arrive, a tall woman with red hair joins me in the office. I quickly recognize her as Rebbeca, the therapist I've been seeing on and off ever since Anna died. She flashes me her best attempt at a reassuring smile, and I immediately wonder how many of these "trust-me" smiles she's given out today. I'm curious how long it took for her to perfect that particular smile, and if she had to practice it in a mirror, forcing her lips into stiff, unnatural shapes until she found just the right one.

    The first time we met, just days after Anna's death, I found her smile to be warm and comforting, like I could tell her anything.

    *But looks can be deceiving.*

"Hi Emma, I'm so glad to see you back again today," she says, as if I'm here for a good reason, instead of a devastating one.

I watch as she grabs a nearby pen and a pad of paper, and I sit cross-legged on the couch across from her. The couch is accented with fuzzy pillows and a fluffy blanket, in an obvious attempt to make her patients feel safe and secure. But hugging a pillow and pretending like this is some great, cheerful thing I get to do, won't make me forget the anguish I feel about what I'm really here to talk about. I've always hated it when people won't face the reality of their situation.

"Well, Emma, your mother and father have already filled me in on quite a lot. I want to start by saying that I am so deeply sorry for your loss."

I just nod, having heard those words more times than I can count.

To me, that flippant phrase "your loss" has always felt so insulting to whoever died. To refer to them as something I *lost* ... It makes my heart tighten, and my mind comes up with a million things I want to scream at her.

What about everything *they* lost?

I didn't just *lose* Anna, *she* lost the experience of going to high school.

I didn't just *lose* Missy, *she* lost the chance to see a world where things could feel better.

I didn't just lose *them*, *they* lost their innocence, their future—*they* lost *everything*. And they lost it in the blink of an eye, and it all makes me so angry.

My two best friends died within six months of each other, and I still don't know the right way to respond to that ridiculous attempt at a condolence: "Sorry for your loss." When it's a bad day, as it often is, I feel on the verge of blurting out: *"My 'loss'? I'm sorry, but I'm confused, because I'm just not sure which one you mean. Are you referring to the first one? That happened in May—that was Anna, she was the blonde—Or maybe you're talking about the second one? The one in November? That was Missy, the brunette— So when you say 'I'm so sorry for your loss', I'm just not sure who you're even referring to! Anna? Missy? The one in May? The one in November? The one who was killed? Or the one who killed herself?"*

But instead, all I manage to choke out is a weak, "Thank you."

"I know it's going to be difficult"—she scratches down words on her notepad intensely—"but I would like to take this time to talk to you about the passing of your friend Missy, if you feel ready?" I nod my head, remembering the first time she said that to me, but it was about Anna. "You two were friends for a while, correct?"

"Yeah, I met her the very same day I met Anna. Anna and I got really close early on in middle school, it didn't take us long at all to click." I smile, thinking back to when we first became friends. It felt like finding a long-lost twin, the way we so quickly fell into a rhythm with each other.

She writes something down.

"How did you react when you heard she passed?" she asks.

I take a moment and say, "I was just really in shock..." I pause, trying to remember everything I felt in the moment. It all felt like a blur, and a big part of me still doesn't believe all of it's real. "After Anna, I didn't think I would ever have to go through this again ... but here I am!" I try to laugh at the end, but it doesn't seem to come across as a good joke.

"And how was your friendship with Missy in particular? Did you guys get along well? I'm sensing some reluctance to discuss her. Were there conflicts between you two?"

I think back, *of course* there were conflicts. All three of us argued, but it was mostly Missy and I. But it all seems so stupid now. Disagreements that I was convinced would lead to the end of the world, now are almost impossible to remember.

"Things were generally good. And anyway, Anna and I almost never argued. I think the worst fight we got into was when I stole her makeup as a prank in seventh grade."

She takes a moment, jotting something down in her notes. With a deep inhale, she confronts me, "Emma, I have an observation to make here."

"What is it?" I ask hesitantly.

"Have you noticed that every time I ask you about Missy, you end up talking about Anna?"

My eyes widen ever so slightly, thinking back to my last few responses. It's as if her name is a curse to my mouth, and I'm too afraid to speak it.

Rebecca speaks up, "Emma, you've been coming to me for a while now. I've heard you talk for hours about Anna. All your memories, the good, the bad. Even from the first time we met, you never were shy to talk about her. Why is it you seem so hesitant to talk about Missy?"

I pause, struggling to find a response. Not knowing the answer myself. "I ..." My eyes wander nervously—I hate not having an answer to things.

To me, there is no worse feeling in the world than uncertainty.

"I don't know," I admit, quietly, almost a whisper.

She takes a deep breath, and nods. "I have an idea ..." she begins. "I want you to tell me about one of your later memories with Missy and Anna. A happy moment you girls shared, that you can look back on and always smile when you remember."

I think back to all the times we shared. It was almost never just Missy and me, or just Anna and me, it was always Anna, Missy and me. The three of us shared countless good memories over the years, more than I can count. But the one that keeps popping up in my brain, for better or worse, is the day of our eighth grade prom.

It's one of the last really good moments we all shared together.

Out of all our memories, the day of prom is one that will forever be engraved in my brain, down to the very last detail.

I start to tell the story, "I remember … There was *so much* laughter that day."

## 38

## Emma
### April 30th, 2017
*Seven months before*

*M*y whole life, I *dreamed* of my first prom. I knew it was silly to be so excited for something as cliché as my eighth grade prom, but the little girl in me was inwardly celebrating all day and night.

I had spent days and days of my childhood playing dress up, with no one but my stuffed animals to watch my fashion shows.

For years, I begged my mom to buy me a proper, "big girl" makeup set, an obsession I had developed from compulsively flipping through every beauty magazine I came across, and spending hours watching cringey, tween movies featuring beautiful, fashionable actresses. So many of my early memories were spent traveling for my parents' work, and I practically became an expert at choosing the best airplane movies by the time I was eight. Every movie I watched, a theme seemed to arise among the teenage girls in the films. A shared love for makeup and beauty brought even the most polar opposites together.

    I would stare out the little airplane window dreaming of the day I got to experience a moment like that. A special event with my girl friends, each one helping the other look and feel their very best, a night full of laughter and smiles.

    My wish came true my first Christmas in New Jersey.

    I still remember how excitedly I unwrapped the small box that laid under the tree that morning. I hoped with everything in me that my wish had finally been granted. I ripped away the wrapping paper, to reveal my first-ever makeup set, complete with a set of bright pink makeup brushes.

    *"For me?"* I whispered, looking at my mom, not believing something I had wanted for so long had finally come true. She nodded her head, and I ran to my room, wanting to try on everything I could.

    Every day after that, I would come home from school and spend hours staring in the mirror, practicing my makeup looks. I knew that one day, my dream of getting ready for a night out with a group of friends might now come true. And when it did, I wanted it to be *perfect*.

MIA MANDALA | *Dear Anna,*

  Flash forward two years, and not a single day went by where I didn't apply at least a hint of blush and some well-practiced, winged eyeliner.

***

The day of prom felt like a scene straight out of one of the movies I had watched as a little girl. Dresses and clothes were thrown all over the bed, and makeup spilled out of our bags and covered the floor. There was constant motion from the three of us, each one alternating between who gets the big mirror in the bathroom, and who ends up stuck with the small, handheld one.
  But in the midst of all the stress and chaos, *there was so much laughter.*
  The stress of wanting to look my best was overwhelming at times, and I felt bad everytime I snapped at either of them. But all the tension disappeared whenever Anna cracked a joke, or when we paused to admire each other's hair.
  Anna started blasting music for us and we all stopped what we were doing to sing and spin around her room, and for a second it felt like nothing could be better. It made me wonder if prom could even amount to the fun I was having at that moment, and if maybe the best part of this event would be the getting-ready.

A song came on that I didn't recognize, but after the very first beat, Anna and Missy jumped to their feet and started dancing around hand in hand. I stepped aside, crouching down at the foot of the bed, mirror in hand. I opened my eyes wide, carefully applying eyeliner along my bottom lash lines, while out of the corner of my eye I watched as Anna and Missy fell to the floor, doubled over in laughter.

Their laughter echoed through the room, and their smiles beamed like a thousand suns.

They would never see it themselves, but the smiles I watched them share in moments like these were always bigger and brighter than when they were with anyone else.

*Even with me.*

Anna's parents came in shortly after, gushing about how beautiful we all looked. They snapped about a million photos, and by the end, we were all goofing around, posing in ridiculous ways, surely creating photos that would not see the light of day by anyone but us.

I took one final look in the mirror, letting the girls walk out ahead of me. I fluffed my hair, smoothed my dress, and tried to soak in every good feeling I could.

"Em! Stop fixing your makeup, c'mon!" I laughed, hearing Anna's teasing from down the hallway.

"I'm coming!" I shouted back, and took one more look, making sure everything looked perfect.

We climbed into her parents' car, making bets on who we thought would get prom king.

MIA MANDALA | *Dear Anna,*

"Oh, I hate to say it, but I really hope I win prom queen!" I gushed. In my heart, I knew it sounded stupid and superficial saying that out loud, but the closer and closer we got to the event, the more I had to admit to myself that I really did want to win. After all those years of moving around, and bouncing from friend group to friend group, I finally felt so welcome here and close to all these special girls. To be perfectly honest, it felt like my heart was going to jump right out of my chest.

# 39

## Emma
### November 20th, 2017
*Eighteen days after*

*I* bite the inside of my lip, and look down to find my leg anxiously tapping up and down without realizing I'm doing it. My hands fidget in my lap, and I do everything to avoid eye contact with my therapist. "Uh ..."

Flashes of prom night wander through my brain.

"We got to prom, and it was really pretty. I don't know, I think getting ready was the best part of the whole night," I blurt out, my anxiety rising higher and higher, my fear of getting sick rising along with it.

She seems to take the hint that I don't want to talk about it anymore, and tries to change her approach in getting me to open up.

"You know, we've spent a lot of time talking about their deaths, but right now I'm interested in just *you*, Emma. How have you felt lately, not about Anna, not about Missy, but about yourself? How do *you feel*?"

I take a deep breath in, "I feel *really* angry. All the time."

It's one of the most honest things I've said in months.

# 40

## Harper
November 21st, 2017
*Nineteen days after*

*I*'m relieved to find Morgan in her usual seat next to mine, in the second to last row of desks in the back of the class.

Behind her are two empty desks, only occasionally filled by Sam and Logan whenever they happen to wake up on time for class.

Morgan's hair is tied tightly in a high ponytail that only she could pull off so effortlessly. She gives me a warm smile, and I know from the quiet sigh she lets out that a big part of her didn't expect to see me back at school today.

With every step I take toward her, I *pray* I don't turn around to find Sam and Logan behind me.

## MIA MANDALA | *Dear Anna,*

It's the only class the four of us have together, but the chances of all of us showing up on the same day are usually slim to none. I thought it was safe to assume that if they weren't here by the first bell, then they wouldn't show up at all.

I take my seat as the high-pitched school bell begins ringing throughout the school.

Our teacher, Mr. Roberts, starts shouting about last week's homework before I even have a chance to say a proper "hello" to Morgan.

As Mr. Roberts goes around collecting everyone's work from the last class, the door opens and in walk the two idiots I've been dreading seeing the most.

They stride into class, laughing obnoxiously, and as usual have no regard for anyone around them. They bump into peoples' bags, almost knock over a girl's water bottle, and generally just make fools of themselves.

The class stays silent, and any regular person would have taken that silence as a cue to stop talking. But not Sam and Logan.

They continue laughing and talking until they finally come to a stop at the back of the class, in the row directly behind Morgan and me, and take their seats.

I feel a rough tug at my shoulders, pulling them back and forth, a playful slap against my back, and hear Logan's voice whispering, "Harperrrr ... Harperrrr ..." till I finally give in and abruptly turn around. He must have been expecting me to spin around with a smile on my face, laughing like nothing is wrong, and forgetting about everything he has done. As if this is all a silly fight I should forget about.

But I don't think I will ever forget the way he laughed when I told him about Missy.

"What?!" I say, exasperated.

Sam and Logan laugh. "Geez ... Someone woke up on the wrong side of the bed," Sam jokes. That wins a dab up from Logan.

I roll my eyes and turn back to face the board. Next to me, Morgan is busy writing down notes from today's lesson, and didn't seem to even notice when the boys walked in. I decide her approach might be the best solution for now, knowing the more attention I give them, the worse their teasing will get.

It takes only about ten minutes till they start up again. First it's Logan, then, predictably, Sam follows his lead.

It's harmless at first, as harmless as getting kicked repeatedly in the back of my leg can be. More annoying than anything, is the insistent tapping against my back and the back of my chair. The sound is enough to drive me absolutely crazy.

It amazes me how easily Morgan tunes it all out, her eyes laser-focused on the board ahead, her pencil as sharp as ever. The difference between Morgan and me is that she *truly* does love school. She's obsessed with learning as much as she can, and seems to find great pleasure in proving everyone wrong who assumes the "dumb blonde" stereotype about her. She can go days without showing up to class, spending them running around with me or Mark, and somehow still has perfect grades by the end of the quarter. I strive to be like her one day, but always manage to fall dreadfully behind.

Class drones on as usual, and almost forty minutes go by without a word from either of the boys, but then:

"Harper... Hhhharper... Harrrrperrrr..."

*I spoke too soon.*

I try to block out their whispers and focus on the board in front of me, but with every second, they grow louder.

"What!?" I yell, a little louder than I mean to, still not turning to face them.

Logan starts kicking the back of my chair again, and then the back of my leg over and over again. He and Sam giggle like small children playing a prank.

It takes everything in me not to turn around and smack them both.

Just when I think they have stopped, that an ounce of common sense and decency has come over them, I feel another kick to the back of my leg.

I hear Logan tear a sheet of paper from his notebook, and he slides it toward me. In messy handwriting that could only belong to him it reads:

<blockquote>how's your friend missy?<br>haven't seen her in a while...</blockquote>

Before I can think about what I'm doing, my fist is clenching, and my arm is moving faster than I can control. I turn around, lean over the back of my desk, and punch Logan *hard* in the face.

*Neither of us speaks a word.*

His hand clamps across his face where the blow has struck, and his eyes widen in shock. It takes *me* by shock knowing how hard I hit him when I was that angry. Slowly he removes his hand, revealing blood trickling steadily from his nose.

"I'm going to *kill you*," he whispers.

I gulp, unable to speak. I look over at Morgan, who looks to be in as much shock as I am. I suddenly become aware of how completely silent the classroom is. Not even our teacher is speaking.

*Oh my god.*

*Our teacher is here.*

I take in a shaky breath before turning around. A tall man towers over me, a scowl on his face, his eyes wide open in disbelief. I never noticed how scary he was till I had a reason to be scared.

He opens his mouth wide and screams, "Harper! To the principal's office, NOW!"

# 41

## Harper
November 21st, 2017
*Nineteen days after*

"*W*hat did they say?" Morgan runs over to me frantically, as I slam the principal's door behind me.

"I'm suspended for two weeks. Maybe more, if Logan's parents try to argue for more time."

Her expression turns shocked. "*Only* two weeks?" she asks.

"What?"

"You got lucky, Harper, you know that?"

I could have laughed. *Lucky?* Lucky is the last thing I am right now. "No. I am definitely *not* lucky. Nothing about this is lucky."

"It could have been so much worse. They could have expelled you!" she says, taking my hand in hers, pulling me close. "Nothing Logan has done is right, but I'm really worried for you."

I scoff, "What are you talking about?"

"You *scared* me."

Her words hurt me like a knife to the back.

"I just miss her," I admit, in a whisper.

"I know you do. But this isn't helping *anything*." I go to speak, but she cuts me off before I can start. "You have so much in store for you. You're kind, smart, and such a special person. I want to go to college, and get a real job that *I love*, and maybe one day start a family. And I want you to be able to do the same. But you have to get it together—"

"That's not fair, don't say that—" I protest. She doesn't know how I feel, how I think. She doesn't know the guilt that haunts my mind, that keeps me up all night. The memories of Missy are so strong, I can hear her laugh in a crowd of thousands, even though she's gone.

"You could have been expelled. Think about that for *a second.*"

"I'm sorry," I say.

"I can't just watch you let your life go to shit."

Her words hang over me like a knife threatening to drop. Silence fills the air, and for the first time with Morgan, I have no idea what to say in return.

She checks her watch, wondering how long this quiet between us might last. When I show no sign of breaking it, she speaks up.

"Can I give you a ride home?" she offers.

"No, it's okay," I say quietly.

"Okay. I love you."

"I love you too." She leaves me with a look of pity and sadness I wish I could wipe away. I turn from her so she doesn't see the tears that have begun to roll down my face. As I walk out of school, I pass a dark-haired girl talking to a boy. I don't approach her, but can tell she tries to make eye contact with me. I don't recognise her, but something seems oddly familiar about her.

I leave school without another thought.

# 42

## Emma

Late November 2017
*Almost a month after*

"**H**ey, Emma!" A smile rushes across my face as Blake comes strolling toward me. Our eyes meet from across the hallway, but I wait for him to approach me first. He has a wide-eyed grin plastered across his face, but walks with a nervous gait, the same nervousness still evident from when we first spoke. He just hides it better now.

He towers over me, but not in a frightening way.

His hands are clasped together, a not-so-hidden attempt to stop them from fidgeting. He stands in front of me, his eyes doing more talking than his mouth.

"Are you okay?" I ask.

"Yeah, yeah, I just wanted to make sure everything with you was okay. You kind of left in a hurry yesterday," he explains, tripping over his words.

I reassure him quickly, "Sorry about that, my mom was totally rushing me. I'm good though." He smiles.

We stare at each other, wondering who will speak next.

"Well, I was wondering," Blake started, as I sighed in relief at the awkward silence being broken. "Do you want to hang out after school today? Do something again like yesterday? I saw a bunch of cafés on my walk here, it could be fun ..."

"Yeah, that sounds great," I tell him.

After that, we fall into a routine of sorts.

Like clockwork, every day after school we meet by the gates. We walk in complete silence and then share stories from our day over a few slices of pizza.

He needed a friend, and I needed a distraction from all the horrible things that had happened to mine.

Slowly, I begin to really care for him, and all I can do is hope he cares for me too.

He's always trying to do sweet things for me, like paying for the full meal or picking me up from my classes so I don't have to walk alone, and allowing me to avoid Nicolle and Kaylee. I admire his kindness and wish I had even an ounce of it.

The closer we grow, I realize we aren't as different as I first assumed.

***

We're at our usual table at the pizza place when Blake nervously says, "Em, I wanted to ask you something."

My attention quickly switches over to him, my gaze previously held by an adorable, elderly couple eating outside.

"Hm?" I ask, shoving a bite of pizza in my mouth.

"This Sunday, my family is having a little outdoor dinner at my house. I know it's random, but they're inviting a bunch of their friends, and I have to help watch all the little kids for a while. I was hoping if you weren't busy, you might want to come? You don't have to stay the whole time if you don't want to ..."

"I'd love to go."

*He smiles.* A sweet smile that makes his eyes crinkle slightly, and his cheeks turn shades of pink.

"Perfect. I'll text you the details," he tells me, and our comfortable silence returns once again.

# 43

## Harper

June 2016

*One year and five months before*

Sam met Logan at a party. I couldn't go because I had gotten food poisoning the night before and instead, spent the entire night trying to keep food down without having to sprint to the bathroom. I always wondered what would have happened if I *hadn't* gotten so incredibly ill.

*Would Sam and Logan still have crossed paths?*

Or maybe, would there have been some alternate life where Logan never barged in and wrecked ours?

I'd later learn how surprising it was that none of us had crossed paths with Logan before that party. We shared at least a dozen mutual friends and all regularly went to the same places. I would be lying if I said I wasn't nervous about

Sam going to a party without me, but it was one of his best friend's birthdays and I wasn't going to be the one to stop him.

He came over beforehand, arriving at my doorstep with a bag full of goodies. I almost cried at the sight. He made sure I was comfortable in bed, and opened the bag to reveal an array of tea bags, medicine, and a soft plush dog. He left me with a kiss on the forehead and reassuring words that nothing would go wrong at the party and that I was sure to feel better soon.

I believed every word, *and so did he.*

About an hour into the party, I got a text from him explaining that everything was going well and that he had just met some new guys. I was relieved to hear he was hanging with a group of guys, and he sent me a selfie with all of them to further support his story.

I went to sleep, knowing my boyfriend was at a party without me, and I could trust him completely.

The next day, Sam told me every little detail he had found out about Logan. He told me the exciting news that Logan would be transferring to the same high school as ours, following his recent expulsion.

For reasons he never shared with us, but were not difficult to gather from outside sources, his expulsion came from a mix of drunk driving in the school parking lot and getting caught smoking cigarettes and weed behind the school more times than one could count.

But, I *was* happy for Sam. Sam didn't have a big group of guy friends, at least not a bunch of close friends, and I naively hoped that Logan would become one of his.

To my blind eye, things seemed great as always, but I soon began to notice that my time with Sam was rapidly dwindling, while the time he spent with Logan was quickly beginning to monopolize every free moment.

Almost a month had passed since the night Sam went to that party, and at school he was visibly beginning to struggle more than ever.

When I asked why he was being so ill-tempered and combative in his classes, he only grew even more irritable and blamed everything on his parents' never-ending divorce. He started missing school more often than not, and before I knew it, even his appearance had started to change. His country club polos were quickly replaced by ratty t-shirts featuring band names that I'm positive he didn't listen to. He was even so heavily influenced by Logan that at one point he spent a whole date night debating whether or not to dye his hair from blonde to brown.

Thankfully, I managed to convince him that was a horrible idea, joking that we would look too much alike if he did.

He was changing rapidly and it was completely passing me by.

To me he was still the same Sam. The Sam that opened every door for me, and greeted me with flowers and clothes on every anniversary. The Sam that never let me pay and refused to let me carry my own stuff.

    The same Sam I had been in love with since sophomore year.

## 44

## Harper

August 2016
*One year and three months before*

Morgan, Mark, Sam and I had all gotten together for our monthly boat day out on the bay on Sam's dad's boat. Our sophomore year we made a pact to go out on the boat at least once a month while the weather was nice, just the four of us, a couple of sandwiches, and a long, chill day out on the water.

Since making that pact years ago, those special days had only gotten better, as Sam had recently gotten his boating license, and we no longer needed his dad to drive the boat.

Mark and Morgan were in their usual spot at the bow of the boat. Mark lounged back with his arm around Morgan, visibly admiring her as she read a book in her lap.

I stood by the captain's seat, waiting for Sam to come back. We had all arrived together in Morgan's car, but Sam left seconds after we were all on the boat to walk over and pick up our order of sandwiches from a local shop. Mark offered to go with him, but Sam abruptly shut down the offer. For some reason, he seemed skittish, like a nervous kid, his eyes never meeting mine. But I brushed it off, knowing that if something was truly wrong he would have come to me by now.

*At least I hoped he would.*

Almost twenty minutes had gone by since Sam left to walk a mere two blocks to the sandwich shop, yet he still hadn't come back. I was getting worried, and every possible worst-case scenario ran through my mind in a flash. I was about to call him again when I turned to see him walking up to the dock.

In one hand, he held a bag of sandwiches. My mouth watered at the thought of the delicious, freshly-baked baguettes. Next to him, walked a boy roughly Sam's age. I watched them walk closer, and closer, and with every step Sam took, I waited for the other boy to turn away and get on one of the nearby boats. But by the time Sam neared our boat slip at the end of the dock, it became obvious that they were talking to each other.

And not just talking, but *laughing*—hard.

The other boy held a bag similar to the one Sam had, but it definitely did not hold more sandwiches. With every step they took toward us, the other boy's bag clanked loudly with the unmistakable sound of glass and metal hitting each other.

Approaching the boat, it became clear that the boys were no strangers to each other, and just before Sam could introduce me to his friend, I recognized that face.

It was a face that I had seen only briefly in a selfie, but one that I had heard about a dozen times.

Mark and Morgan joined us at the back of the boat. Morgan threw me a confused look, trying to secretly direct my attention to the strange boy, but I just shrugged in response. I knew about as much as she did as to why this "stranger" was here.

"I hope you guys don't mind, but I invited him," Sam said, reaching out a hand toward me to pull him onto the boat. We all shook our heads agreeably.

"Of course, it's totally fine!" Morgan reassured him.

The boy approached me, a smirk on his face.

"Hey. I'm Logan."

*Logan.*

*Logan*, with his dark, messy hair and smug smile that seemed worlds apart from the clean-cut Sam that liked to play tennis and golf on the weekends.

Within five minutes of meeting him it dawned on me, *Sam* wasn't changing, he was *being* changed—by Logan.

Since that unfortunate day on the boat, I have spent much, much more time with Logan. Although many of our future outings with him would be uncomfortable, awkward, and sometimes downright toxic; it wasn't *always* bad with him, and I'd be lying if I said I never had fun with him.

But there were many times that I felt he was gaining control over our group, and that I was beginning to be fooled by him, as much as he fooled everyone else.

At one point he may have even been one of my *closest friends*.

He had a way about him that made you forget about all the bad. He was often careless and reckless, but to an outsider he seemed carefree, fearless, and confident. It was no wonder people gravitated toward him so readily.

The boys joined us on the boat and Sam walked up to the captain's seat, with me close behind. Once the boys dropped off all the food and everyone seemed ready to leave, I dragged Sam to the front of the boat, and leaned into his ear ever so slightly. "Sam, is there a reason you didn't tell any of us you were inviting Logan?" I whispered.

I didn't want to argue, or provoke anything close to an argument. I was simply curious.

"Really?" Sam backs away from me, a scowl on his face.

"What's wrong?" I ask, my body leaning back toward him.

"Is there a problem with him being here?"

"No, of course not—"

"If you don't want him here so bad, then you can leave. Feel free to go, Harper, the boat's not moving yet."

*I froze.*

Never in our whole relationship had Sam ever stooped so low.

I saw the words leave his body, but nothing about the person standing in front of me *was Sam.*

"Sam," I said more to myself than to him. A reminder of who was standing before me, of who had just said those cruel words. "I didn't mean anything bad by it, honestly I—"

He cut me off with a scoff. "He's my friend and I thought you'd be happy to meet him."

I nodded my head, forcing my emotions to stay down, and letting the tears subside. "Yeah, yeah. I am happy. Let's just forget I said anything, okay?" He didn't respond, with words that is. Instead he brought me in for a kiss that felt anything but romantic. His breath smelled oddly of fresh mints, as if it were a scent used to mask another. Just like every other warning sign, I ignored it, pushing it far down in my mind.

We continued the day as normally as we could.

Morgan and I layed out on the front of the boat, the sun blazing on us as we sped across the water. Morgan's head was in Mark's lap, and I caught him dotting her forehead with occasional kisses. He combed through her long blonde hair with his hands, his eyes more focused on the girl below him then on the water around him. Logan lingered around Sam at the captain's seat and they blasted music till we had to scream to be heard over it.

Sam came to a quick stop by a sandbar and the boat rocked aggressively as he put the anchor down.

When the boat eventually reached a full stop, Morgan and I stripped down to our bikinis. I felt hands wrap around my waist, and found Sam smirking at me from behind. A small sigh escaped my breath, as I realized I could finally relax.

Sam isn't changing, I told myself.

*Everything's going to be okay.*

"You're beautiful Harper," Sam whispered, his hands moving their way further down my waist. I laughed like a little kid, as his hands brushed over my stomach. "I love you," he whispered again, but something sounded off.

I was about to speak when he drew me in for a passionate kiss.

*Something was really off.*

I pulled away, his lips still wanting more.

"Have you been drinking?"

He laughed, "What?"

I asked again, "Have you been drinking?"

Sam stayed silent, looking like a little kid caught red-handed. Logan strode up next to him, except his confident walk had turned into more of a stumble. He swirled a cup in his hand and went to pass Sam another one. It was then that I noticed the pile of empty bottles that littered the floor around the captain's seat.

Sam took a small bottle from Logan, slowly taking a sip, his eyes still locked on mine. "Want some?" Logan offered, handing me a red cup.

I took a step back. "Were you drinking the whole way here?"

They laughed. "Who cares?" Logan asked.

I ignored Logan, my attention focused solely on snapping Sam back into reality. "We're underage Sam! You've got to be more careful, we drove by about a dozen boats on the way here!" I told him, trying to emphasize just how much trouble he could get in if someone had seen. For a moment he looked at me sadly, like he truly did feel bad. Before he could attempt an apology though, Logan stepped between us once again.

"No one saw. No one's going to see. Just *chill*," he told me, a condescending tone hidden in his voice.

I rolled my eyes at his lack of care. "God, you two need to sober up before we head back. I'm going in the water—" I faced Sam, almost whispering, "Seriously, get your shit together." I turned and made my way to where Morgan and Mark had already jumped in the water.

I decided to keep their little "adventure" to myself, and hope for the best. Morgan could tell I was upset about something, and I wondered if she had witnessed the small fight between Sam and me. If she did, she didn't make it a point to ask. Instead she did what she's best at, distracting me and making me laugh.

Morgan and I found a shallow part where we could stand, and gossiped while Mark swam laps along the shore. We told stories from the summer, and reminisced about our funniest days of freshman year. The water felt incredibly refreshing, and every few minutes I held my breath and dunked my head under. When I came back up, the cool water felt calming as it dripped down my face.

Mark joined us, and I watched as Morgan threw her head back in laughter as he hoisted her onto his shoulders. He spun her around in circles, as she jokingly protested. With a loud splash they both hit the water, still smiling as they came back up. I wanted to laugh with them, but my mind drifted back to Sam. How he should be here with us, not back on the boat with a friend he barely knows.

Despite my annoyance, it hit me at that moment just *how much* I missed my boyfriend.

"You okay Harper?" I snapped out of my thoughts, not having realized how long I was staring off at the boat.

I nodded my head to Morgan. "Yeah, I think I'm going to go back to the boat. See how Sam's doing," I told them.

"We'll come back with you, it's getting a bit cold," Mark offered.

I tried to protest against it, wanting to be the first to see how Sam and Logan had been acting, but they followed me anyway.

We climbed back into the boat, which now had music blasting obnoxiously loud from a speaker. All around lay half-empty red cups, and bottles of booze tipped on their sides. Before I got a chance to see the mortified look on Morgan's face, Logan sauntered over. "Hey!" he exclaimed, swaying even though the boat was still. He approached Morgan slowly. She stood frozen in place as Logan reached out a hand toward her long blonde hair. For a second, he let his fingers run through her hair before Mark smacked his hand away. He looked as if he could have punched him, and for a moment I thought he might.

The next few moments passed by in a blur.

The mood on the boat suddenly erupted with the sounds of everyone yelling and fighting. Mark – always the gentle one, was screaming his face off at Logan and telling him to stay far away from Morgan. Sam seemed to think nothing was wrong, probably because he was nearly passed out on the platform at the back of the boat.

His eyes looked up at me, but he didn't seem fully there.

I reprimanded him harshly, and all he could say was that "everyone drinks a little."

"Except this *wasn't* one little beer or two. You guys are seriously fucked up, it's not safe for you to drive us back like this—" And as if on cue, a loud crash of thunder boomed through the air as storm clouds suddenly gathered overhead.

*Oh shit.*

Then in an instant, the rain came.

It wasn't just a light drizzle, instead the rain was loud and heavy, and the sudden winds made the boat rock back and forth. I tried my best to stay calm and reminded myself that this was nothing we hadn't already dealt with. We had been in storms before—but never with a half-conscious driver taking us back.

It would be a miracle if we made it back safely.

Or without being pulled over by the marine police.

At some point Mark must have scared Logan enough into shutting up, and it was the best thing to happen all day.

Unfortunately for us, no one but Sam knew anything about driving a boat. Morgan and I hoisted Sam to his feet, and prayed he would get us home in one piece.

"You girls, relax. I'll stay here with Sam, and take over when I can," Mark told us.

The ride back was rough and bumpy, and I couldn't tell when it was the storm's fault, or when it was Sam's clumsiness.

When we finally made it back, Morgan looked as though she practically wanted to fly off the boat.

I helped her and Mark onto the dock, lending Morgan a hand with all her bags when I could. We made our way down the dock silently.

"I'm gonna take her home," Mark said, motioning to Morgan, who stood clutching his arm like she might fall over.

She looked incredibly shaken up, and I didn't have to question why.

"I'm so sorry, guys," I told them.

Mark shook his head. "It's not your fault, you don't control him—or *him*," he reassured me, motioning to both Sam and Logan. I couldn't help but feel responsible and *so* horribly guilty for their actions. I stared gratefully up at Mark. "Do you want a ride home?" he asked, and I was about to say yes, when my thoughts drifted back over to Sam and Logan. I turned my head to see both of them laughing obnoxiously and stumbling around. Logan laughed heartily at something stupid Sam had said as Sam immediately downed another can of beer. I sighed, turning back to Mark and Morgan.

"I can't leave them like this. I need to drive Logan's car back to his place. I can't let either of them drive anywhere like this."

Morgan stepped up, shivering slightly. "Harper, are you sure? I think you've dealt with enough for today."

"I'll be okay. You guys should go, I'll handle them." They said their goodbyes and Morgan hugged me tighter than usual before going off with Mark to his car. I watched them walk away, waiting till they had driven off before turning my attention back to Sam.

The boys were still on the boat, while I was on the dock, and either they didn't see me, or just decided not to acknowledge my existence until I was standing directly in front of them. "Put the beer down now, Sam. You've had quite enough. This is getting absolutely ridiculous," I said, motioning to the half-filled cup in his hand.

Logan made his way over to me, "You're not his mother. Let him do what he wants!" He aggressively laughed in my face and immediately turned back to Sam.

"Let's get out of here," Logan said, leading Sam off the boat, and nearly stumbling right into me. I grabbed Sam's hand to steady him but he quickly snatched it right out of my reach. They clumsily staggered down the dock, leaving me no choice but to chase after them.

"Neither of you are in any state to drive." I didn't receive as much as a look back.

My frustration only grew as they made their way further down the dock and closer to Logan's car, all while still ignoring me. "Sam! Sam!" I was yelling now, and he didn't even flinch. I finally reached them, right as Sam swung the passenger door open. "Get out of the car, Sam."

He stared at me, a dazed, blank look in his eye.

"Get out of the car, let me drive you guys home."

He finally acknowledged me, but could barely say anything intelligible. "N—n—noooo," he mumbled.

"What?!" I cried.

"I don't want to go anywhere with you, Harper," he managed to say. Logan stifled a laugh, and I rolled my eyes till I thought they might fall out the back of my head.

"Fine. Sam, go home with Logan, but at least let me drive you both there."

"No way," Logan said firmly, climbing into the driver's seat.

Not a single rational thought went through my mind as I forcefully dragged a barely-conscious Logan out of the driver's seat.

"Geez, Sam. Your girlfriend's fucking *crazy*," Logan said under his breath, as he angrily moved himself into the backseat.

My eyes stung as I squeezed the wheel and gritted my teeth. My knuckles turned bright-white as I waited for Sam to chime in with Logan and say something equally asinine and insulting.

Yet, a part of me desperately hoped Sam just might say something—anything—to defend me.

*But he didn't.*

We sat in silence for the entire ride to Logan's house.

I didn't even bother to turn up the radio. Out of the corner of my eye, I caught Sam falling asleep. He laid his head gently against the car window, his head bobbing up and down as he fell in and out of consciousness. He looked so peaceful.

The last sliver of sun lit up his face, and his blonde hair shone brightly. Even though I was *so* mad at him, I still felt the urge to reach out to him, caress his face, and play with his hair till he was fast asleep.

I already knew how sick he would feel when he woke up tomorrow, and I cringed at the thought of not being there to take care of him.

The same way he had for me so many times.

But reality set back in as soon as I heard Logan's annoying voice from the backseat. "It's that house right there," Logan told me, leaning forward to point to a house with two giant pine trees on each side.

I sighed and pulled into the driveway. Sam woke up when he heard the car door open. His disheveled hair and bewildered look made him look younger than he was, and reminded me of the Sam I've always known and loved.

The three of us exited the car in silence, and Logan was already walking up his driveway when I turned to face Sam.

"Sam." I took a deep breath, willing myself to hold my tongue and not scream at him about the danger he put us in on the boat. Knowing it would just go in one ear, and out the other, I decided now wasn't the time. "We'll talk tomorrow," I told him.

I leaned forward, my hand cupping his face as I went to kiss him. Just as my lips were about to touch his, he turned his face abruptly so that my lips awkwardly brushed his ear. He looked at Logan and the two of them burst into laughter.

It took everything in me not to cry.

"Goodbye—"

MIA MANDALA | *Dear Anna,*

Before I could finish talking, he and Logan were already stumbling up Logan's driveway like two idiots. I stood in the driveway by myself, feeling like a fool, as I waited on an Uber to drive me home.

# 45

## Emma
### Late November 2017
*Almost a month after*

*I* open my phone to find a single text from Blake:

*be there in 5!*

I throw my phone down and scramble to find my lipgloss. Silently cursing myself for not getting ready earlier, I quickly brush through my hair till every small knot is perfectly smooth. My black hair shines as I admire it in the mirror, praying it stays looking this healthy all day.

    My hands shake nervously against my sides and my mind is utterly blank as to why. I smooth my dress, and for the hundredth time wonder if I should change.

"Emma! Your friend is here!" I hear my mom call faintly from the living room. I grab my phone, stuffing it in a small bag, and leave without another look.

A small black car pulls into my driveway, and the driver's side window rolls down slowly. Out the window, Blake flashes me a wide-eyed grin, waving me over toward the car.

I climb into his car, and we lean over to hug each other.

He turns on the radio, playing whatever song comes on, and drives off.

We arrive at his house not long after.

Blake climbs out of the car, and before I can even grab the door handle, he is on my side of the car swinging the door open. "Thank you," I tell him, flustered by the sweet gesture.

I take in a nervous breath and smooth down my dress one last time before we enter his backyard through a side gate. For a November day, the sun shone surprisingly strongly, and I can feel it beating against my skin.

The sounds of children laughing, food crackling on the barbeque, and adults throwing bean bags into cornhole fill the air. There are balloons tied to every chair, and if I hadn't known any better, I would have thought it were someone's birthday. A short brunette woman steps off the grass, in a cheetah print top, and jeans that hug her sides perfectly. She waltzes up to us, red cup in hand, with a slight stagger in her walk.

"Blakey!" The woman hugs him tightly. "Is this the friend you told me so much about?" Blake's cheeks turn a bright shade of poppy red.

"Emma, this is my Aunt Rosie. She's lived in the area her whole life—"

She cuts him off, "I'm just so happy Blake lives here now! My son Asher just adores him!" As if on cue, a little boy with reddish hair comes running over. He practically jumps into Blake's arms, squeezing him tightly. The little boy turns to face me, and I watch as his jaw drops.

"Is this your girlfriend?" he asks Blake, giggling into his small hands.

I watch as Blake's eyes widen, not daring to meet mine. His smile grows from ear to ear, and his cheeks grow almost impossibly redder. I bite my lip to keep from giggling as his embarrassed reaction came totally unexpected, but leaves me wondering.

Without giving a real response, he sets Asher down, the two of them laughing together. Asher clutches my hand and Blake's in his other, and starts to pull us toward him. "C'mon! Let's play!" The small boy drags us down the lawn, hand in hand, stopping when he reaches a large soccer goal, surrounded by loads of children. The kids run after each other, all falling to the ground with laughter. A few kids off to the side pass a soccer ball back and forth, taking turns shooting at the goal.

We join in with them, and all the kids cheer as Blake scores a goal. He passes the ball to me, and I pray I don't make a fool of myself.

Everyone cheers when I score against Blake.

The kids *love* him.

They watch in awe as he teaches them how to juggle the ball with their feet, and laugh like babies when he pretends to fall over. We take turns passing the ball and running after the children in a vicious game of tag. I'm just about ready for a break, when I spot a chair nearby. I make my way to it, wiping the sweat off my forehead, and lay back to watch as Blake chases after a squad of kids. Out of the corner of his eye, I see he spots me sitting down, and tags the first kid near him.

"Hey, you okay?" he asks, his eyebrows furrowed in worry.

I laugh, "Yes, yes. I just got tired." He nods and takes a seat across from me. He looks at me, biting slightly on his lip. I want to ask what he's thinking about.

I want to know *everything* I can about him.

But I decide to not interrupt his gaze, and instead wait for him to speak.

"That dress looks really nice on you."

I can barely contain my beaming smile.

"You're just being nice so I don't leave you alone with all these kids," I tease him.

"Well, you're not completely wrong," he says, laughing. We share a brief smile, the corner of his eyes crinkling softly.

"Do you want to get out of here?" he asks, his voice below a whisper.

"What do you mean?"

He takes my hand in his.

"Come on, we can watch the sunset."

# 46

## Harper

August 2016
*One year and three months before*

**S**am never texted me goodnight.

Never called to apologize, or even check in. Still, I clung to the hope that he'd change and hopped in my car first thing in the morning.

I must have rung his cell about a hundred times, and still no reply.

I couldn't stop shaking on the whole drive to Logan's. A sinking feeling grew deep inside me that things would not turn out as I hoped. I blasted the first rock station I could find on the radio and let it drown out my thoughts. I pulled up to Logan's, and mentally went over what to say to him.

I was about to step out of the car, when I saw Logan's front door swing open. My heart sank as I watched a tall, brunette girl, wearing not much more than a large gray t-shirt, step out of his house.

Behind her, Sam followed.

Everything around me seemed to move in slow motion.

My vision blurred on everything, except for the two people outside. My heart raced, and in that moment I wished so badly I could disappear.

Sam stepped toward the girl, his hand on her back.

He leaned toward her, and *kissed* her on the lips.

*Oh my god.*

I felt like I was going to be sick, and couldn't decide if I wanted to run out of the car and yell at him or put the car in reverse and never speak to him again.

He made the decision for me.

Just as he was about to turn back inside, he caught a glimpse of my car. Our eyes locked for a second, nothing more. But I knew he could feel every bit of my pain.

I managed to hold myself back from crying, despite the ache in my heart.

Logan stepped out, looked at Sam, and high-fived him.

Any ounce of shame that I imagined Sam felt for what he had done, had now been entirely washed away. And once again, Logan seemed to be at the center of it. The pair laughed as Logan slammed the door behind them.

My whole world felt as if it just broke into pieces and I desperately wanted to leave.

Before I did though, I pulled out my phone, and wrote Sam a final text.

*we're over.*

# 47

## Emma
Late November 2017
*Almost a month after*

**O**ur feet dangle off the side of a rickety, wooden boat dock. It must be less than a mile from his house, but it feels as if we are worlds away.

*Just us.*

The sun makes the water glisten in all different shades of blue. As the sun moves down, the wind picks up, and I shift my body slightly toward Blake. I look at Blake, the color on his cheeks is a bright shade of red, and the green in his eyes makes them shine like a million little stars. I hear a splash, and my head turns sharply to find a school of fish swimming nearby. They jump in and out of the water, making their way further and further away from us.

"I didn't know you were such a soccer star," I say as he laughs, his face getting more flustered than before.

"Yeah, I used to play all the time."

"Why did you stop?" I ask, realizing just how little I actually know about him, and how much I suddenly want to know *everything*.

"It's hard to stay on a team when you move as often as I do." I laugh knowingly.

There's a silence between us, but it's anything but awkward. He inches closer to me and I keep my eyes locked on the view. Slowly, the sky turns to shades of orange and pink, the sun now setting.

He moves closer and the tips of his fingers are now just barely brushing mine.

A chill goes up my spine.

"It's so beautiful," I tell him, motioning to the view around us. Out of the corner of my eye I catch him nodding in agreement. Except he's not looking at the sunset.

His eyes are focused on me.

Then he kisses me.

A million thoughts run through my mind, but they are quickly quieted. It only lasts a few seconds, but I take everything in. How soft his lips feel against mine, the gentlest of kisses. Our lips fall right into place, as if they had done this many times before. We soon both pull apart. Our eyes widen, neither of us expecting the spark we both just felt. He clasps his hand over his mouth. "*Oh my god.* I'm so sorry."

"No, don't be sorry—"

"I don't even know how you feel, I mean we haven't known each other that long. Really, I'm sorry—" I cut him off, pulling him in close. My hands go to his face and I draw him toward me.

We kiss again, and it feels so right.

Behind us, I can hear the faint sound of water splashing against the shore, while all around us the glow of the day slowly dims with the sun.

We kiss, and kiss some more, and it feels like magic.

# 48

## Emma

Late November 2017
*Almost a month after*

*I* get back home a few hours later.

My mind feels clear, and my face is permanently stuck in a wide-eyed smile. I feel like nothing could bring me down, the memory of his face near mine engraved deeply in my brain. I stumble into my room, throwing myself across my bed. I sink into the pillows, and wonder when I'll see him next.

I reach my hand into a dresser drawer and search through the mess of clothes for a sweater. Under a pile of shirts, I find a small piece of paper wedged carefully between two pieces of clothing. I flip it over, my mind blank as to what it is.

Suddenly it feels as if my world grows dark.

Staring back at me are three girls I once knew. Now, they seem nothing more than faces in an old photograph. On my right, Anna grips my hand tightly, a smile so bright plastered on her face. On the opposite side, Missy stands with her hair tied tightly in two long braids. I stand in between them, a large ice cream cone about to drip down my hands.

Except it's not me.

Not anymore.

The photo can't be more than a year old, but the girl in the middle is practically unrecognizable to me now. I almost want to laugh. How *little* she knew back then, I think to myself.

How *much* she has had to overcome.

My hands start to shake, and a feeling of dread grows in my chest. I sink to the floor, my knees bending on autopilot. I try to tear myself away from it, but my eyes stay glued to the photo.

I start to feel like I'm going to be sick, but I can't even bring myself to stand up. All the memories from today, with Blake, cause a deep pit in my stomach. The smiles of the girls in the photo haunt me, because it's just not fair that they are only alive in photos.

*They should be here.*

They should be here, and be able to do *everything* I'm doing, and will be able to do.

My mind spirals into a deep, dark hole of guilt.

I think back to today. How could I have spent an entire day *so blissfully happy?* It hits me that at no point today did I think about either one of them. Not once did my mind drift off to an old saying of Anna's, or did the sound of Missy's laugh echo through my mind.

Not once.

Instead, I laughed, and smiled, and kissed a boy.

They can't do any of that. They'll *never* be able to do that. How is it fair that I get to run around and live out my perfect teenage life, while they are buried six feet underground? They lost *everything*, and when I lost them, my world fell apart.

*I don't deserve to get it back.*

My sobs grow louder than my thoughts, till all I can see in front of me is a blurred vision of my bedroom. Out of the corner of my eye, I see an incoming call from Blake. I let it ring out, until my phone turns dark. My head hangs, my tears hitting the floorboards quietly. I pull my knees to my chest, and cry into my hands till I can't anymore.

# 49

## Harper

September 2016

*One year and two months before*

*I*t took everything in me to get up and get ready for our first day of junior year.

In a way, breaking up with Sam still didn't feel real.

I still hadn't told anyone what I had seen Sam do, not even Morgan.

"Are you *sure* you're okay? You've barely texted me since the day on the boat. And where is Sam? He always meets us here ..." Morgan had been asking me all morning if I was fine, and her suspicion only seemed to grow as the day went on. Each time she asked, I got closer to telling her the truth.

It felt strange keeping something so important from her.

We shared *everything* with each other.

The good, the bad, the gross, all of it. I knew her as well as I knew myself, and sometimes I wondered if she knew me better than I did. But this was something I couldn't bring myself to confess.

It would change everything.

I knew it would. No matter how much she, or Mark, would promise me it wouldn't.

Whether I liked it or not, Logan was becoming a part of our group. Soon enough Mark would forgive Logan, and the three boys would become inseparable. I couldn't be the reason all my friends split apart.

So I held my tongue, and kept what I had seen Sam do to myself.

Morgan and I were walking through the halls, about to reach our class, when we ran into Sam and Mark. I froze, and prayed Sam would keep his mouth shut. Mark and Morgan fell into their usual routine, a soft kiss, and a hug around her waist.

Sam and I stood there in silence. Feeling miles apart, despite being only a few feet away.

"Harper, can I talk to you?" Morgan asked, snapping me out of my trance.

She whisked me away to the side of the hallway, pulling me in close.

"Seriously, you've got to tell me. What is going on? You guys didn't even look at each other!" I bit my lip, a million different excuses I could give came to mind.

"We broke up the day after we all went out on the boat."

It was the first time I had said it out loud.

I felt my heart sink as I did. All I wanted to do was cry, and tell her every awful thing he said and did. From across the hall, I heard Sam and Mark laughing and chatting away. A reminder of how long we have all been friends, and how good everything once was.

I can't be the reason it all ends.

"I'm sorry I didn't tell you before Morgan—"

She cut me off, "It's okay, no need to be sorry. Are you okay though? What happened?"

I nodded my head, "Yeah, I'm okay." She looked at me doubtfully, but I brushed it off. "No really, I am. After everything on the boat, we had a long talk, it just wasn't working. We ended on good terms, everything's totally fine."

I wished so badly what I was saying could be true.

We went back and forth for a while, Morgan making me "promise that I'm *actually* okay."

I did.

Before she could ask again, the bell rang and we all headed off to class.

MIA MANDALA | *Dear Anna,*

I watched as Mark dropped Morgan off at class, leaving her with a gentle kiss on the forehead. A tear escaped my eye.

## 50

## Emma

Late November 2017
*Almost a month after*

"*E*mma!" A recognizable voice calls my name from down the hall. I almost want to keep walking, keep my head down, and pretend I don't hear him, but he pulls me to the side before I can.

"You didn't call me back last night," he says. His eyes look sad, the usual glimmer in them seems nowhere to be found.

"I'm sorry, I was so tired. I fell asleep right as I got home."

"Oh, it's okay." We stand there in silence, unsure of what to do next. We speak like strangers would, and standing by him so stiffly feels unnatural. "Did I do something?" he asks, breaking the silence. My face drops, and suddenly I feel horrible for how worried he's been.

"No, no." I reach my hand out for his face, and brush the side of his cheek gently. "You didn't do anything wrong, I promise." He sighs, and I see the tension leave his body. My eyes lower to his lips, and all I want to do is kiss them.

"Why don't we go get food after school?" he suggests.

I want to, I think.

I want to *so badly*, I want to walk around with him hand in hand, and kiss him again, and see where this goes, but the image of Anna and Missy haunts my thoughts. Their smiles now existing only in photographs.

*It's not fair.*

I get to keep living as happily as I want, and they can't.

"I can't, I have to do something with my mom today. Another day?" I tell him. Not technically a lie, as I remember I have another therapy session later today.

He gives me a reassuring smile. "Yeah sure, no worries." He leans forward to give me a kiss, but I instinctively turn my head before his lips can meet mine. He leaves a clumsy kiss on my cheek, and I bolt to class before he can question if anything's wrong.

# 51

## Emma
April 30th, 2017
*Six months before*

"And this year's prom queen is ... Emma Marie!"

It felt as if I was dreaming, as our principal called my name from the stage. I climbed the shaky, metallic stairs, and a plastic tiara was placed upon my head.

Soon after, Jack joined me up on the stage once our principal called out his name. We were dressed with long sashes, sparkling silver, that read "PROM QUEEN/KING 2017." Once the applause died down, the music changed to a slow waltz, and Jack and I made our way down the stairs. He outstretched his hand toward me, making sure I didn't trip.

It made me feel like a princess.

We took one careful step after another, with the occasional spin, then he brought me safely back into his arms.

To save us from any more embarrassment, the music began to pick up the beat, turning into a fun dance for everyone. Suddenly the dance floor went from being almost barren, to being filled with friends and couples all dancing along. I had to crane my neck to find them, but I spotted Anna and Missy whirling around each other in endless circles.

Their smiles beamed, and lit up the whole room.

I could pick out their laughter from miles away, even in a noisy room.

Moments later, I felt a tug at my arm. I turned to find Anna and Missy practically tackling me with hugs. They both showered me with compliments, swearing that I looked *beautiful* up on that stage.

"Oh my god!" Anna shouted, as one of our favorite songs came on.

"C'mon! Let's go dance!" I yelled over the blasting music. We ran out to the center of the floor, hand in hand. Our arms went up like we were reaching for stars, as we jumped and laughed like little kids. I was so caught up in the moment, I didn't notice when Missy and Anna broke away from me. I turned to find them, but instead was met with faces of girls whose names I barely knew.

An overpowering sense of panic began to rise, as I wondered where they would have gone. My mind began to think of the worst.

*Did they leave me on our prom night?*

I left the dance floor, having to push past a few people blocking my view. I wandered the ballroom, checking everywhere they could have gone.

Not by the food.

Not by the tables.

I started to feel sick, wondering if my worst fears had come true. If they had really gone home and not brought me with them.

My stress subsided when I finally saw them in the corner of the room. I let out a sigh, and held back a laugh, as I watched Missy just nearly hit Anna's face instead of her hand. I was about to approach them, when Anna pulled Missy in for a hug. Missy tightly wrapped her arms around Anna's waist, as if she were going to blow away. I watched as Anna buried her head in the crook of Missy's shoulder. It was like they had melded together, like two pieces of a puzzle had finally found their match.

I suddenly felt like I was intruding on something I shouldn't be seeing.

Something I should have noticed much earlier.

The way their smiles were only that big when they were with each other. The absolute look of love they always shared, like a secret only meant for each other.

They didn't break away from their hug.

I backed away, wanting to give them their space, even in a room filled with hundreds of people. My mind moved on autopilot, and I found the closest group of girls I knew. I nudged my way into their conversation, and they all showered me in "congratulations" for winning prom queen. I faked a smile, the tiara on my head being the last thing on my mind. An old friend I hadn't spoken to since seventh grade practically tackled me in a hug, and I had to squirm out of her hold. "Thank you, Sophie!" I told her, while I tried to catch my breath.

"It's getting late, I think I'm going to head out soon," I heard one of the girls say – I thought her name was Mia. "Anyone want to come over?" she added, and I practically jumped at the offer.

"Yes!" I exclaimed. "I'm exhausted, and I *desperately* need to get these heels off!" I added, and all the girls laughed in agreement.

Before I could think about what I was doing, I was climbing into the back of her parents' car, along with three other girls I'd met maybe twice before.

And then we left.

That's when the guilt hit me, the reality of what I had just done.

I left Anna and Missy.

*I left them.*

## 52

## Emma

Late November 2017
*Almost a month after*

"*I* left them."

My words come out so quietly, I wonder if my therapist will ask me to repeat them. I sniffle, and realize how blurry the world around me has become. Before she can say anything about it, I wipe my tears away with the sleeve of my sweater.

"Thank you for sharing that, I know it's not easy," she tells me. I almost want to laugh at how obvious it is.

*It's not easy.*

It's not easy to know that I left them, *and then Anna died.*

A guilt that will stay with me for a lifetime.

"Do you think about that day often?" she asks.

"Yeah. Almost all the time," I tell her honestly.

"What does it make you feel?"

I think for a second. I think about the *guilt*. The sick feeling I get that makes my body tremble, and my eyes not see straight every time I think how life could have been if I had just gone home with them. I think about how every time things start to feel good again, I think of them and how they don't get to experience that.

"Guilty," I tell her.

She sighs, "Emma. I want to help you, but I need you to tell me more if you want me to help." I know where she's coming from, and it's no surprise this isn't the first time she's said that. Since I started sessions with her, it's been unusual for me to give more than a few word responses.

I wonder if she's finally seeing behind the wall I've put up.

Or if that wall is just beginning to crack.

Instead of elaborating, I just nod my head. "Okay."

Because I'll tell her what she wants to hear, but the moment I let my tears escape, is the moment she sees the real me.

## 53

## Harper

December 4th, 2017

*Thirty-two days after*

**M**y suspension is almost over. It's been almost two weeks of doing nothing more than driving my sisters around, and the two times I was able to see Morgan.

Mostly, I did a lot of thinking. Not the deep thinking everyone expected me to do. I haven't worked through my grief, or come to any life-changing revelations. I just thought.

About Missy. The day I met her, the last day I saw her. I think through every interaction with her till they're engraved deeply in my brain. I search through her every word, every text, trying to find every red flag I missed. Every cry for help, but no matter how hard I search, a sinking feeling that she was hiding something, gnaws at me.

MIA MANDALA | *Dear Anna,*

I lay in bed, my chest tightening at the thought of going to school tomorrow. I have no idea what to expect, what Logan might have been saying about me while I was gone. I decide the best I can do is just try to sleep, and forget about it all, even for a few hours.

It doesn't take long before I'm fast asleep.

\*\*\*

I wake up in a panic.

Shooting up straight out of bed, I feel my heart race. I take a second, my eyes still adjusting to the light, and tears falling down for no apparent reason. It takes me a moment to remember, but when I do, I wish I hadn't.

I had been dreaming about Missy, no doubt. Her spirit plagues my thoughts so often, she's beginning to haunt my dreams. Some nights I'm thankful for the dreams, another opportunity to spend time with her. Other nights, they just make the hurting even worse.

I toss and turn, I try shutting my eyes tight, hoping eventually sleep will come.

Nothing works. Her name rings through my mind like a siren.

*Missy.*

*Missy.*

*Missy.*

*Missy.*

*Missy.*

No matter how hard I try, I can't seem to fall back to sleep.

I look at my bedside table. The lamp dimly lights up a single red notebook – a gift from Morgan. She came to my house the other day, and told me she thought it might help. She said when she goes through tough times, sometimes writing down her thoughts makes it just a little easier to manage them.

I laughed it off. I didn't see how journaling could solve anything, but now I wonder if it might.

I lift the notebook off the table, sliding the plastic wrap off of it.

Once I start writing, I can't stop.

Every little thought that passes through my mind, ends up on the page.

I write about my memories with her, how much I saw her change from our first encounter to our last.

I wasn't always the nicest to her, the first time we met I couldn't have found her less interesting. She was just another one of Logan's girlfriends. Either he would toss her aside, or she would grow sick of his shit. It's what *always* happens. But then she did something I hadn't seen before.

She stuck around.

She kept hanging out with us, and as time passed, we became friends.

I would watch her and Logan, the same way I did

with Mark and Morgan. Hoping to get a glance of those sweet romantic moments that went unnoticed. The ones that, even years later, make a part of me miss Sam.

Missy looked at Logan like he held the world in his hands.

He looked at her like she meant nothing more than a kiss to him.

It only got worse.

I watched him push her aside at any chance. It was so clear to everyone that he wasn't good for her.

Clear to everyone but her.

I tried to warn her, but she didn't listen.

My mind drifts back to the day we spent at the beach. The first and only time we argued. I tried *so hard* to get her to listen. But she was already in too deep.

I couldn't save her.

# 54

## Emma
December 5th, 2017
*Thirty-three days after*

*I* race into the stairwell of school, hoping I'm not too late.

My alarm never went off this morning, and it seemed like everyone in my house was moving in slow motion. I open my phone to check the time, and am once again reminded of the missed calls and texts from Blake. About a week has passed since we first kissed, and since then we've shared countless awkward conversations, all in which I avoided kissing him like the plague. On the one occasion we did go out to eat after school, I had to leave early because I felt "sick."

I feel awful for ditching him so often, and so many times without a real, sensible reason. I try calling him some nights, wanting to hear the sound of his voice. But I hang up before the conversation can go anywhere interesting.

As I arrive at the floor my class is on, I reach out my hands to push open the door to the hallway when I hear footsteps coming up the stairs below me. I watch as Blake comes into view, silently deciding whether to approach me or not.

"Em?"

I can't find it in myself to meet his eyes.

"Hi Blake." Silence fills the air. So many unanswered questions linger, and I wish I had an answer for him.

This time, he doesn't avoid it. "Em, what's going on?"

I take in a deep breath, doing everything in my power to put off responding. For once, I answer him honestly, "I don't know."

We stand inches apart, but he couldn't feel further away from me.

"Do you not like me? Just tell me the truth, *please—*"

I cut him off, and pull him into a kiss.

I savor every moment of it. The feeling of him close to me, the way his arms feel as they instinctively wrap around my waist. We pull away slowly, and I feel his breath against mine. I hope that my kiss answered his question. "I'm sorry Blake," I whisper, our faces still pressed against one another's.

I push open the doors to the hallway, and walk to class with my head hung low.

# 55

## Harper
December 5th, 2017
*Thirty-three days after*

*I* hear the late bell ring as I walk up to the steps of school.

I make no rush to get inside, having no reason or desire to. I fiddle with my sweater and rummage through my bag making sure I have everything I need.

As I take a few steps closer, Sam comes into my view. I prepare myself for whatever snarky comment he's about to throw my way. We lock eyes, and for a moment I see a different person before me.

The Sam I once loved.

Not surrounded by the harshness of Logan, his eyes seem to glow a bit more, and he walks with his head a little higher.

"Harper," he says, and for a moment it startles me.

"Whatever you're going to say, I don't want to hear it. Just let me get through the day," I warn him.

"I just wanted to say I'm glad you're back," he tells me, blushing in embarrassment.

"Oh." I stand frozen, unsure of what to say or how to feel. Not a bone in my body trusts him, or his friends. But standing in front of me, I see memories of the boy I once loved with my whole heart.

"I totally thought you were going to be expelled after what happened."

I laugh, "Yeah, so did I." Then I remember what caused me to get in trouble in the first place. "You know that note was really fucked up, right?"

He can't look me in the eyes. He just nods, and says quietly, "I know."

I sigh, snapping out of whatever fake reality I was beginning to imagine. "I should get to class," I tell him, and he agrees. We continue our walk up to the school in silence, but before I can open the door, he says, "I hope you're doing well, Harper. I *really* do."

I push open the doors to school, and walk to class with my head down.

## 56

### Emma
December 8th, 2017
*Thirty-six days after*

"*E*mma!"

I'm walking toward Blake, preparing myself for another lunch filled with small talk. He catches my eye from across the room, and we share a soft smile. I make my way down the lunch room, when a shouting girl blocks my view.

"Nicolle?" I take a step back. She hasn't spoken more than a few words to me since I found out about Missy. Now she stands in front of me, arms crossed, brows furrowed, and her voice even louder than usual.

I see Blake still staring at me from across the room, and try to mouth to him before Nicolle cuts me off. "Where have you been?!" Nicolle demands more than asks.

"What?" I ask, confused as to why she is asking me as if I haven't been at school.

"You haven't sat at lunch with us in weeks!" As Nicolle continues to yell at me, Kaylee joins her.

"Nicolle—" I try to speak, but she doesn't seem to notice.

"You haven't called us! We've been worried sick." My heart tightens with anger.

"Worried sick?" I repeat. Letting each word sink in.

"Yes! We've been *trying* to talk to you, but you've just been ignoring us!" Nicolle tells me, a fake look of worry plastered across her face. It makes me nauseous.

"That's not true."

"What?" Nicolle and Kaylee both say in disbelief.

"You haven't asked me to sit at lunch with you, not once. Not once have you tried to talk to me, or reach out, or make plans with me. Not *once* since I found out my best friend died! You've pretended I don't exist. I see the way you look at me when you think I'm not looking. And it's not with worry, it's with *pity*."

Nicolle's jaw drops, and she looks to Kaylee for help.

"Emma, we just want to help you—"

I shake my head. "No, you don't. If *either* of you really cared you would have said this weeks ago."

"*Of course* we care about you," Kaylee says, stepping closer to me. I back away, my breaths becoming short and harsh. I try to keep myself focused, and hold my ground, but my mind becomes fuzzy.

"Then why haven't you shown it?" I scream, and that's when my tears start to fall.

My entire body feels helpless, and I realize how many people are looking at me. I stare at them, silently pleading for them to respond. They look toward each other slightly, roll their eyes, and walk away without a word.

I watch them, as they lean in closely to whisper in each other's ears. I put my hands to my face, and wipe away the tears that won't stop falling. I try to contain myself, but my hands won't stop shaking.

My balance starts to feel like it may falter if I don't sit down soon, as the room around me begins to spin.

*I need to get out of here.*

I run past the crowds of people, and dash outside, praying no one saw me break down. I find the closest empty hallway, and let my back slide down against the wall. My entire body curls into itself, and I hide my head in between my knees. I try to remember all the ways to ground myself, and follow my breathing as best as I can.

Out of nowhere, I feel the soft touch of hands on my back.

I raise my head up slowly. "Blake?"

"I saw what happened," he tells me softly.

I cry, embarrassed at what a fool I made of myself.

"I'm so sorry," I tell him. Then I can't stop, a stream of apologies pour out of me. "I'm sorry, I'm sorry, I'm *so sorry*."

"You have nothing to be sorry for, why are you apologizing?" He comforts me, encasing me in a tight hug. I sob into his arms, and wish I could stay there forever.

He has no reason to do this, I've treated him horribly.

But he does it anyway.

*I don't understand why.*

He rubs his hand along my back, until my cries have calmed down. I feel his lips press against my head, and he tightens his hold on me.

"Shh, it's okay. I'm here for you, Em," he whispers in my ear. Once I feel myself calming down, I slowly begin to lift up my head.

My eyes don't dare meet his.

"Let's get you to the counselor," he tells me, helping me to my feet. Our hands clasp, and he keeps a watchful eye on me.

"Thank you," I whisper as we reach the counselor's office.

He leads me inside, and finds a place for me to sit. Once he sees I'm comfortable, he takes it upon himself to explain to the counselor what happened.

A few minutes later he comes back, and sits beside me. "They're going to call your parents. I'll stay with you till they come pick you up. Is that okay?" I nod breathlessly.

## MIA MANDALA | *Dear Anna,*

Please, *please* stay, I think to myself.

"Yes. Thank you."

As I lay my head in Blake's arms, the pit in my stomach only grows.

## 57

### Emma
December 21st, 2017
*Forty-nine days after*

**S**ince my fight with Nicolle and Kaylee, I've barely been back to school.

Instead of school, my days have been filled with late-night dinners with my parents and an overload of therapy sessions to fill my time. Blake and I have kept in contact at least. I still don't understand why he has been so good to me after how I acted.

As much as I like him, there's still a part of me holding me back. A part of me that screams Anna's and Missy's names, when I feel myself getting in too deep. A part of me I am beginning to loathe.

Despite it all, every night without fail he calls me. Lets me know anything I missed at school, and constantly checks in to see how I'm doing. Every night I come closer to telling him the truth. About Anna, about Missy. About everything. But I never do.

Not once have Nicolle or Kaylee reached out. Not a text or a phone call, and I sure won't be the first one to pick up the phone.

I sit in my therapist's office, where I feel I have spent more time lately than in my own bedroom. The bare white walls are beginning to make my head hurt, and I've practically memorized every inch of the barren room. My therapist pulls out a pad and paper. It is the same routine every time; she asks me how I'm doing, I respond in a few words, and our awkward back-and-forth continues.

Every session she has me share a memory. Some exciting, or sad time spent with either of the girls. I recount these stories with my eyes glued to the floor, and only meet her eyes when I've finished.

"How do you feel?" she asks me, every time.

I take in a breath, deciding how I might respond today. Every day is generally the same.

*Sad.*

*Upset.*

*Heartbroken.*

Just among a few of what my responses typically are.

But today I feel different. Today my heart burns, and the stories of my friends don't make me well up in tears, instead they made me mad, *so, so* mad.

"I'm angry," I tell her.

"You know Emma, this isn't the first time you've expressed your anger. Why do you think that is?"

"Because they lost their lives, but with them so did I."

"What do you mean by that?" she questions. My hands fiddle in my lap, and for once I let my thoughts flow free.

"I can't do *anything* without being reminded of them. Everywhere I go I see them, I hear their voices in every person I meet. I see them in every crowded room. They are *everywhere*, and it makes me crazy. Everyone wants me to feel better, to go ahead living my life, but *I can't*."

"Why not?" It wasn't a real question, she just doesn't want my train of thought to stop.

"Because *they* can't. I want to have normal crushes again, and gossip with my friends about my day. I want to date the boy I like so much, and not hide my past from him. And I hate it. I *hate* how much anger I feel toward them. I should be crying over their memory, and sharing all my greatest stories about them. But sometimes I just feel so mad at them." I stop myself, shocked that I could say such things.

"That sounds really difficult to understand."

"Yeah, it is," I agree.

"It actually makes a lot of sense. You know, sometimes anger is the easiest emotion for us to access."

I let her words sink in.

She continues, "When bad things happen, it's easy to feel upset at the people who caused it, and it doesn't make you a bad person for feeling those things. You can feel sad *and* angry, it doesn't have to be one or the other, and that's okay. Your feelings actually make a lot more sense than you may realize. You have to accept these feelings, and the moment you do, you will be able to live with them. Does this make sense Emma?"

I sit there, frozen in place.

"Yeah, it really does."

For once it's true. Every word she said went straight to my heart and to my mind.

"Thank you," I tell her.

She smiles and tells me, "You're a smart girl, Emma. You're going to be okay."

The clock strikes 4, and with that our session is over.

I leave with a smile, and the moment the door closes behind me, I pull my phone out. Knowing what I *need* to do, I pull up Blake's number:

*i owe you an apology can we meet saturday night?*

Barely a minute passes before he replies:

*of course*

## 58

## Emma
December 23rd, 2017
*Fifty-one days after*

"Thanks again for meeting me."

I bite my lip, rearrange my scarf, then push my shaking hands deep into my coat pockets. The air around us grows cold as the sun moves further down and snow clouds begin to gather overhead. We walk along a narrow path, and with each step I take, a shiver runs down my spine. I had insisted we meet at a park, only a few minutes from his house. I didn't want him to have to go far, and I definitely didn't want to be anywhere I had already been with Anna.

"It's okay, you don't have to keep thanking me," he tells me, but even I know he doesn't need to be doing this. With the way I've treated him, he shouldn't even be talking to me.

I grab his hand, pulling him closer to me. "Let's sit down," I tell him and bring him over to a nearby park bench. "I owe you an apology. I haven't been treating you well at all, and I haven't been honest with you about my feelings." I pause, looking to see if he's going to say something, but he stays silent. I take in a deep breath, "I think a part of me has been holding myself back. There are all these things from my past I haven't wanted to admit to myself, or even think about. It hasn't been fair to you, though."

"I don't understand. What *things*?"

For a moment, I consider it. I consider telling him *everything*. I'm not sure why I can't. "It's not important anymore. It's in the past," I tell him, putting on my most convincing smile. He nods, and smiles back, but something in his eyes tells me he doesn't fully believe me. I continue, my feelings for him pouring out by the second. "I like you so much Blake, I just want to be with you. I want to *actually* get to know you, and spend time with you. I want to know about your life before moving here—"

He stops me, mid-sentence. "No, you don't," he says, almost laughing in pity. He continues, "My life before this wasn't the most glamorous."

"I don't care! C'mon, just tell me something. I won't judge," I tease, but he doesn't return the smile. He looks around, as if surveying the ground below us. Without a word he motions for me to follow him, as he lays down on a nearby patch of grass. My back touches the grass, and I feel the cool of it against my whole body. I wrap my winter coat around myself tightly, the cool wind sending tingles up and down my spine. My head turns to face his, but his eyes stay locked to the sky.

"You really want to hear about it?" he asks.

"Yes, I do." I nod, even though he isn't looking.

He takes in a deep breath, and squints his eyes ever so slightly.

"My parents are an absolute mess. Remember my aunt you met?"

"Yeah, of course."

"I moved out here to live with her, and her family."

"Oh," my heart sinks, as I listen to the rest of his story.

"Growing up, I always knew my parents weren't normal. They were hardly ever home, and left me completely alone to deal with myself. And when they *were* home, it was chaos. All the time. Just lots of screaming, and fighting, and somehow I always ended up in the middle of it."

I watch as he blinks away tears, and all I want to do is wipe them away for him.

"It got *really* bad. They *said*, and *did* things that were—" he stops himself. "I couldn't keep living like that. They made me not want to at all." He finishes speaking, just barely above a whisper.

He doesn't have to elaborate, as I know exactly what he means, and it only makes me feel more grateful to have met him.

"I'm so sorry. For everything they did to you, and everything *I* did."

For once he doesn't try to blow it off.

"Thank you, Em," he says, his head turning to me. Nothing more needed to be said, the silence was too peaceful.

We lay there, our faces barely inches apart. I stare into his eyes, and they seem to glow. Then with a nervous hand, I pull his face toward mine.

Our lips meet.

We pull apart, and smile into each other's faces. He pulls me back in, his arm holding me tight.

We kiss, and I feel the light fall of snow against my face.

## 59

### Emma
### December 24th, 2017
*Fifty-two days after*

*I*'m sitting at my kitchen table, sharing laughs over a freshly cooked meal with my parents.

Our conversation comes to a pause when a loud knock interrupts us. "I'll get it," I tell my parents, placing my napkin down next to my plate. I open the door without much thought, but my body freezes when I see who's behind it.

"Blake?" I whisper, closing the door behind me and stepping out into the cold. Not that I'm not happy to see him, it's just so unexpected. His clothes are nowhere near appropriate for this weather, yet he looks as though he has been sweating. "Is everything okay? What are you doing here?" I ask.

"I have to talk to you," he says urgently, and it only makes me grow more worried. I wait for him to continue, but he only stands there shivering. "Do you think I could come inside?' he pleads, wrapping his hands around his bare arms.

"Uh—Yeah, sure." I creak open the door slowly, wondering what to tell my parents. I make up a lie, tripping over my words as I tell it. "He's here to bring me homework," I tell them, with a big smile across my face. To my luck, they just smile and nod, quickly introduce themselves, then leave us be.

I lead Blake to my room, the only sound between us is the sound of his boots hitting the floor. Quickly, I close the door behind us. "Blake, what's going on?" I ask again, praying he will give me an answer.

"I know what you were talking about," he says, as if I should understand just from that.

"What?" I ask.

"Yesterday, at the park. You said there were these *things* from your past—"

"Blake—" I try to stop him, but he doesn't.

"I *know*, Em."

I sit down on my bed, trying to hide how hard my body has begun to shake. "What are you talking about? You're not making sense," I tell him. It's a lie. I know what he's going to say, I just can't bear to admit it.

"I know your friends died. And I am so sorry."

*Died.*

He says it with such a calmness in his voice.

I shake my head violently, as if there was something I could do to convince him it isn't true. I have a million things I want to say, but only one question comes to mind. "How do you know that?"

He joins me on the bed, reaching out for my hands. I stay frozen in place. "Yesterday, after you left, I knew there was more than what you were telling me."

"I told you it doesn't matter, it's part of my past—" I try to argue and he sighs.

"It *does* matter, and you matter to me."

I let his words sink in.

He continues, "I went home, and it only took a few searches online. I read all about what happened to those girls. It's awful you had to go through that, but you don't need to hide it from me anymore. I'm here for you." Something inside of me sparks, and all I can feel is a deep anger toward everything he is saying.

"Why are you telling me this?" I pull myself up from the bed, backing away slowly with each word.

"Because I care about you, and I see how much this is affecting you. I just don't want you to think you have to hide this from me anymore."

"You don't understand!" I scream, without meaning to.

Blake's eyebrows furrow and he stands up from the bed. "What? Em, of course I couldn't possibly understand what you've been through, but we can talk about it if you want—"

"I don't want to talk about it!" My voice is growing even louder, and I seem to have no control over it. I shake my head back and forth, willing for all this to end. Blake tries a different approach. He walks up to me slowly, grabbing my hands carefully.

"Can I ask you something?" he says softly, and all I can do is nod. "Why did you hide this from me?"

I deny it, "I didn't hide it."

He looks at me knowingly. "Well, you never mentioned it."

"I didn't hide it!" I say, my voice louder than the last time.

"I know you're hurting. You can yell at me all you want, but you can't keep avoiding this. I'm here for you."

I shake my head, feeling the tears well up in my eyes. "You don't understand," I tell him, before bursting into tears. My legs give out, and I fall to the ground. My hands go over my face, catching my tears as they fall heavily. Blake wraps his arms around me, holding me tight, as if he will never let me go. My body shakes uncontrollably, and the only thing I can focus on is repeating the words: "You don't understand" and "It's all my fault" over and over again. Blake combs his hands through my hair, repeating, "It's okay, you're okay."

"I feel *so* guilty," I say, finally lifting my head up from his shoulder.

He holds my face in his hand, and rubs circles on my cheeks while he talks. "Tell me why."

Defeated, I take in a deep breath and close my eyes for a moment to ground myself.

"Do you know *how* Anna died?"

"There were a few local articles about it, they all said she was hit by a car while biking." I nod my head, swallowing away a sob.

I ask another question, "But they don't mention where she was biking to, do they?"

He shakes his head, "No. Do you know?"

"She was going to our other best friend's house—*Missy's*."

"Oh."

My mind swirls with images of the three of us. Before anything bad happened, all the times we smiled. "And it was my idea. It was my fault!"

"Em, what are you talking about?" he asks again.

Then with a shaky voice I tell him, "It was my idea for her to write Anna a letter."

"What letter?" he asks. "I don't understand."

I pause for a moment, my thoughts racing. Then I tell him *everything*.

# 60

## Emma
## May 2nd, 2017
*Six months before*

*T*he bell for lunch rang, and I made no effort to race out of class.

Somehow, I had gone the whole day without seeing Anna or Missy, but knew I would have to soon. I had no idea how I was supposed to explain to them why I left prom.

I took slow steps through the hall, letting the crowds of people pass me by. I was about to turn a corner, when I stopped dead in my tracks. The sound of sniffles and muffled cries came from a few feet away. I saw a girl with her head down and her body shaking slightly. I approached her slowly.

"Hey, are you okay?" I asked.

The girl raised her head slowly.

*It was Anna.*

Her eyes looked bloodshot, and her hair was a mess of tangles.

"Emma."

"Anna."

We said at the same time, then fell speechless.

I put all my worries from yesterday aside, and immediately knelt down to her level.

"Anna, what happened?"

She took a second, biting her lip. I could see in her eyes how upset with me she was, and I prayed it wasn't why she was crying. "You know I'm really mad at you." It wasn't a question, more of a statement.

"I know," I admitted.

She took in a deep breath. "But I'm going to tell you what's wrong. Because I have absolutely *no idea* what to do." Her voice broke as she spoke. Never in all our years of being friends, had I seen Anna look so helpless.

It scared me.

"What happened?"

"Last night—" she took a pause before continuing. As if she had to debate whether or not to tell me. Then with a whisper she told me, "Missy and I kissed." A tear rolled down her face. Any other day I would have laughed it off, not thought anything of it.

*It must have been a dare,* I would have thought.

But this was more than that, I could tell from the sadness in Anna's eyes.

"What do you mean?" I didn't know what to say, but a small part of me wasn't surprised.

Anna went on to explain everything. From when they first biked to the beach, to every dare and truth they told, to when she ran off.

"I don't know what to do. I'm so confused. I shouldn't have left her, I feel *horrible*." Her cries only got louder, as she turned into a state of panic.

"It's going to be okay—"

"How? I *need* to talk to her, but I don't know what to say."

Then an idea came to me.

"What if you wrote her a letter?" I suggested. It sounded corny out loud, but if Anna was too scared to talk to Missy, it might just be the next best thing.

"What do you mean?" she asked.

"That way you can write down everything you want to say," I explained. She took a moment, letting her tears subside. With a sad smile she nodded, "Yeah, that's actually a really good idea. Thank you, Em."

I smiled, and wrapped her in a tight hug.

## 61

## Emma

December 24th, 2017
*Fifty-two days after*

"If I hadn't given her that *stupid* idea, she would have had *no reason* to be biking!"

I can't bring myself to look Blake in the eye. Not after everything I just told him, it all feels so real now.

"Em, that wasn't—"

I barely comprehend that he tries to talk over me. My mind moves a million miles a minute, and all I can see are those two girls. Those two girls who *were* my best friends.

A girl who brought me in with open arms, who I loved more than words expressed.

And a girl who, despite our differences, always came back to me with smiles and laughter in the end. A girl who had been grieving her best friend.

"I was *so* mean to her."

"To who? Em, talk to me," he pleads, in an attempt to get me to focus on one thing.

"*Missy*. I was so mean to her. Since Anna died, I ignored her, and treated her like we were practically strangers." Every word I say makes me sick, but I can't stop. "I was so angry at her for so long. Some days I still am," I confess, a dark secret I tried so hard to keep to myself. "I blamed her for all of it, because *I* was so guilty. It was *my* idea, and if I hadn't told Anna to write that letter she wouldn't have been biking, and she wouldn't have died!" Every word leaves my mouth in a shriek.

I can't stop.

Then in a whisper I admit, "It was easier to blame *her* for all of it, than to accept what I had done." Sobs take over my body. "Blake, I'm not okay."

"I know, but this feeling won't last forever," he promises.

"How do you know?" My body trembles against his.

"Because you're not a bad person, Em." He says it like he really believes it, despite everything I've told him.

I don't believe him.

*I can't.*

Not when I've been mean and distant to so many people who love me.

Blake strokes my hair gently. "C'mon, let's sit down," he offers, helping me up off the floor. He makes his way to my bed, and it makes me sick. So many memories of Anna and Missy flood my mind. All the late nights spent gossiping on my bed, I can see them as vividly as if it were happening right now. I shake my head anxiously.

"Can we go out there please?"

"Yeah, of course." He flashes me one of his warm smiles I love so much, and takes my hand.

We find a comfortable spot on the couch, pushing the pillows aside to make room for ourselves. My body shivers, as the cold air from outside creeps in. Without me saying anything, Blake grabs a nearby blanket and drapes it around me. He wraps one arm around my shoulder, the other one pulls my head to lay down against his shoulder.

We sit there in silence, mesmerized by the glow from the Christmas tree.

As I finally relax, I start to feel my body get heavier. My eyes droop until I can barely keep them open. I force myself to stay awake, but feel Blake stroke the side of my face. "It's okay," he says softly. "You can sleep, I know you're tired." I smile, and let myself doze off in the comfort of his embrace.

## 62

## Emma

December 25th, 2017
*Fifty-three days after*

*F*rom the moment I wake up, everything about this Christmas feels different.

The usual hint of magic in the air is nowhere to be found. I wake up feeling groggy, and my head not clear. The cold is creeping in, and my whole body down to my feet feels its chill. I pull myself out of bed, and prepare myself for a day I have been dreading so desperately.

Christmas was always Anna's favorite holiday.

From the moment the wind turned cold, and flurries started to fall, Anna's happiest self would come out. One year she surprised Missy and me with matching sweaters, and we wore them every day we could. She loved nothing more than to cuddle under a blanket, with all the best winter movies playing on repeat.

We started a tradition three years ago – Missy, Anna, and I would see each other every Christmas night. After spending the day with our families, everyone knew; the night was reserved for us. We would go to each other's houses, bundled up in giant Christmas sweaters, wearing slippers with snowmen on them, with our arms full of our favorite chocolates and gifts for one another.

Today will be my first Christmas without Anna. Without Missy.

*Without either of them.*

Even my family's tradition will be different this year.

Instead of waking up to a tree filled with presents of all shapes and sizes, waiting to be opened, our Christmas festivities would have to wait till later this afternoon. My parents decided this year we should spend the holiday with my dad's parents, which consists of an hour-long drive to their house, and many more hours listening to them bicker about politics. Any presents we were to give each other had already been sent or brought out to their house, which only added to the sadness of the tree, empty and dark. We didn't even put up any ornaments this year.

Once I make my way into the living room, I find that I'm the only one up. As opposed to past Christmases, where I'd wake up to my parents already up and making breakfast, with the lights on the tree shining through the room, this morning feels just like any other one. An eerie silence fills the room around me, and I stand frozen, eyes fixated on the tree, wishing it *were* any other day.

It doesn't feel right, I think to myself.

It doesn't feel right *without them*.

> i'll be back in time to go to grandma's, took a walk.

I scratch out the words on a flimsy sheet of paper, and slip it onto my parents' bedside table. Careful not to wake them, I tiptoe out of their room and close the door slowly behind me.

I slip a pair of boots on, and wrap myself in my huge winter coat. Bringing nothing but a 20 dollar bill with me, I leave my house.

The first good decision I've made in a while.

I pass countless houses, and wonder what is happening in each of them. All the lives I'll never know a thing about, people who one day I may meet and come to love, or hate. A few of them leave their blinds open, giving me a glimpse into their Christmas mornings.

Some families still have yet to wake up, and some are sprawled out on the living room floor exchanging gifts. Bright lights of white and yellow illuminate their faces, wide-eyed smiles on each of their faces.

\*\*\*

I reach the storefront of our local florist. The door chimes when I push it open, and closes harshly behind me with the cold winter wind. Flowers of every kind surround me, some are wrapped in tight bows and stand in large containers on the floors, while others hang in bunches from the ceiling. The shop feels completely empty, as there appears to be not a soul in sight, until I hear the familiar pitter-patter of the old man who owns the shop. He greets me with a smile that's always the same. One that says that while he's happy to see me, he's sad to see me at the same time.

"Merry Christmas, Emma." he says, the wrinkles around his eyes crinkling. "Shouldn't you be at home?" he asks. I shake my head.

I *should*, I think to myself.

"I have to do something first," I tell him, reaching for a bouquet of flowers.

He nods knowingly, and walks behind the counter. "I had a feeling you might stop in today, so I opened up this morning, just in case."

I go to hand him my money, but he stops me before I can. "No need. Have a nice Christmas." He smiles and wraps my flowers tightly with string before walking me out.

I thank him for everything, and run my hands over the flower petals.

He's the only one who knows why I am always buying flowers, and *always* the same ones.

*White lilies.*

It's a tradition I started the first time I visited Anna at her grave.

I stumbled into that same flower shop, trying to hide how much of a mess I was. My eyes were swollen and red and my mascara was running down my cheeks. I grabbed some tissues off the counter and tried in vain to clean myself up. Out of the corner of my eye, a bouquet of all white flowers caught my attention. I immediately felt drawn to them, and asked the old man what they were.

"Lilies, they're my favorite," he told me, and I smiled, remembering who else's favorite flowers they were.

In a way they reminded me of her. They were just like Anna, beautiful and elegant. Simple, but not boring. I *loved* them.

"I'll take the bouquet," I told the man, and made my way out.

\*\*\*

I'm about to walk up to their graves, when I notice an unfamiliar face nearby. I stay back, and watch as she kneels down to Missy's headstone, Anna's directly next to it.

The stranger doesn't do much else, just kind of stares at it.

As I inch closer, I can see the girl lean forward and mutter something under her breath. I slowly take another step, careful not to interrupt the girl when a twig snaps under my foot. The girl jerks her head toward me, her eyes widening.

Getting a better look at her face, I slowly begin to recognize her.

I clutch the lilies in my hand tightly, and watch as the girl before me looks down to find almost identical ones scattered along the two girl's graves.

She looks back to me, and I can see it in her eyes when she realizes we are here to visit the same person.

"You knew Missy?" I ask, not knowing what else to say.

The girl stands up, and I see the words "*Missy Bell*" engraved in stone. "Yeah," she says quietly, and then it hits me.

*I've seen her at school before,* I quickly realize.

I saw her the first time I watched Missy run off, ditching school.

I saw her too when I confronted Missy, yelling at her in the middle of the hallway.

*She was Missy's friend.*

## 63

## Harper

December 25th, 2017
*Fifty-three days after*

**M**y family stopped celebrating Christmas long before any of my sisters were born. To us, it is just another day. Another reminder of the unconventional family life we've been subject to.

 Still, I can't shake the feeling that today feels different. A certain winter gloominess lingers in the air. It creeps through the cracks under the door, through the drafty windows, and sends a chill up and down my spine.

 I tiptoe out of my room, grateful to see I'm the only one awake.

MIA MANDALA | *Dear Anna,*

I catch sight of my coat, hanging by the doorframe. Before I can understand why, I'm zipping it on, scrambling to find any semblance of gloves, and closing the door behind me.

***

The cemetery is completely quiet when I walk in. Not a soul in sight.

I don't know what I expected, it is Christmas after all, and people are spending it with their families, reminiscing about old times.

Still, I can't shake the sadness that all these people here have to spend today without anyone visiting them.

***

I recognize the girl almost instantly.

I don't know her name, but something inside me tells me she is important. I've seen her pass me at school and we've made brief eye contact in the hall, but I've never stopped to catch her name.

"You knew Missy?" she asks me and I realize, we are here for the same person.

"Yeah," I tell her, slowly making my way toward her.

Then, simultaneously we ask, "You were her friend?"

MIA MANDALA | *Dear Anna,*

We pause, almost laughing at how in sync we spoke. Without a word, we both nod, a mutual understanding that there isn't much more to be said.

Silence takes over, and the girl's eyes stay focused on the flowers in her hand. She carries a gorgeous array of white flowers, all the same. I step away, waiting for her to place one against Missy's grave. Instead, she looks at the grave directly next to hers. With a gloved hand she carefully wipes snow off the engraved letters:

Anna Williams
*April 12th, 2003 - May 2nd, 2017*
*"Loved by many, gone too soon from this world."*

She takes her time, letting the words appear one by one. With each letter, she pauses, her hands tracing them slowly. I try not to stare, but find myself unable to look away from her. Her eyes stay fixated on the grave, and my thoughts wander as I try to understand who it is. She separates the bunch of flowers in half, taking one half in one hand and laying it down gently at the foot of the headstone.

Before I can look away, our eyes meet. I blush nervously. "I'm so sorry, I didn't mean to stare," I apologize, but she just smiles.

"It's okay." She places down the last flower.

My curiosity only grows, and as hard as I try, I can't bite my tongue.

"Who was she?" I ask. "If you don't mind me asking?" I add, an attempt to apologize for my rudeness. Instead of giving me a response, she just looks at me confused.

"You didn't know Anna?"

I shake my head, racking my brain for any memory of who she was. The girl takes a deep breath and sighs, and I see a flood of memories rush over her.

"She and I and Missy were best friends."

That catches my attention quick.

"Tell me more."

She stands up from kneeling, and leads me over to the nearest bench. We sit on opposite ends, careful not to sit to close.

"She passed away six months before Missy did."

# 64

## Emma

December 25th, 2017
*Fifty-three days after*

*I* tell her *everything*.

The words just keep coming, even when I try to stop them. I never wait for a response, and she never tries to cut in.

I tell her about our friendship, the beach, their kiss, everything I can think of.

I tell her *everything*, and I barely know her.

When I finally stop to give myself a moment to breathe, I see tears well up in her eyes, along with a profound look of shock. Her eyes widen, and I can almost feel her mind racing.

I just don't know why.

She finally says something after moments of silence. "Oh my god," she says, her words coming out breathlessly. "It all makes sense," she whispers, almost speaking to herself.

"What? What do you mean?" I ask again, when I get no response.

She shakes her head frantically, and I desperately want to know what's going through her mind.

"It all makes sense," she tells me. "I knew she was keeping something from me, I *knew* there was something deeper going on," she continues, and looks as though she might cry in relief.

"What do you mean?" I ask her again pointedly.

"I was with Missy the night of Halloween."

# 65

## Harper
October 31st, 2017
*Two days before*

*I* saw her in a different light that day.

She looked so *young*. She wasn't a short girl, but everyone seemed to tower over her. The whole night, my brain screamed at me that something was wrong.

Something was *very* wrong, with *all* of this.

"C'mon! Let's get a drink!" My thoughts were pushed aside by the incoming squeals from Morgan and Missy. They grabbed me hand in hand, and whisked me away to the other room.

The night moved by me in a blur.

One moment I was saying hello to tons of people, hugging girls I barely knew the names of, and the next I was downing shots with the birthday girl on one side, and my new, 15 year-old best friend on the other.

*This is all wrong.*

The thoughts in my head grew louder and louder, like a warning siren.

I turned to find Morgan and Missy dancing sloppily on top of a table. They shouted "I love you" to each other and twirled in messy circles, each spin just barely missing the edge of the table.

*This is all so wrong.*

I shut my eyes tightly, and tried to catch my breath.

*Oh god, I need some air.*

I disappeared from their view, pushing my way past the crowds of people. I passed so many faces I knew, and so many I didn't. My mind raced too fast for me to question who they were.

I found a quiet place to catch my thoughts on the second floor of the house. I leaned my head back against a wall, and let myself slide to the floor.

From down the hall I heard squeals of excitement and laughter. I peered my head around the hall, and what I saw, I desperately wished I could erase from my memory.

Logan and some random girl totally making out.

I wiped my eyes.

No. That *couldn't* be.

But then I remembered, this is *Logan*.

I raced down the stairs as fast as I could. Searching high and low for her. "Does anyone know where Missy is?' I yelled to anyone who would listen.

I pushed past swarms of drunk teenagers, trying not to gag at the intense smell of vodka that clung to each person.

Missy and I locked eyes from across the room, I tried to keep myself together but practically raced up to her. I felt out of breath talking to her, and barely got a few words out. Every bone in my body felt for the girl before me, and I couldn't bear to break her more than she already had been.

She pulled me outside, and tried to get me to calm down. The pit in my stomach only grew as I realized how ironic it was that *she* was the one helping me right now.

The words spilled out of me, unable to hide any longer. "Logan is cheating on you and I don't think it is the first time."

***

I didn't take my eyes off her the whole car ride home. Her face was stained with tears, and her makeup was smudged across her face. Her red lipstick was completely gone, and her lips puffed out like a little kid pouting.

She looked so young.

All I wanted to do was reach out to this innocent girl, whose sadness poured out of her, so strong I felt it was contagious.

MIA MANDALA | *Dear Anna,*

The silence in the car was overwhelming, but I left Missy with a final sense of hope before she drifted off to sleep.

"It's going to be okay, Missy."

She nodded, but her eyes told me she believed otherwise.

## 66

## Harper

December 25th, 2017
*Fifty-three days after*

"That night, I tried to talk to her. I told her she needed to find friends in her grade, I just wanted to help her. She seemed so against it, I just always thought there was *something* she was keeping from me."

My heart pours with emotion, for so many reasons.

This girl Anna, a girl Missy *loved*, it was all making sense.

"It makes so much sense," I tell Emma, again. For so long, I've spent nights wide awake, running through everything I could have done, searching for an answer

"I loved her so much, but I knew it wasn't right. I knew I shouldn't have been so close with her, she shouldn't have been at that party. And most of all, she should *never* have been with Logan. I just wish I had realized that all a lot earlier."

A regret I will live with forever.

My voice cracks, and I will myself not to cry in front of this girl I've just met.

"Harper," Emma starts, and I wonder what she must be thinking, seeing this girl years older than her, cry over her dead best friend, who she's never met. "That's not your fault."

The words catch me by surprise.

So simple, but they hold so much meaning.

She continues, "You weren't in charge of her, you couldn't have stopped those things—"

"I wasn't. But I was still her friend. I should've looked out for her better—"

Emma sighs, "Maybe that's true. Maybe there's more I could have done too."

Neither of us speak for a moment after that.

Her eyebrows furrow slowly, and I can't read what is going through her mind. She stands hurriedly. "I'm sorry, there's something I have to do. I have to go." She goes to leave, but turns before she can. "Are you going to be okay?" she asks, placing a hand on my shoulder.

I smile, and nod.

"Yes. I am." For once it just might be true.

Then the girl disappears, just as quickly as we met.

## 67

## Emma

December 25th, 2017
*Fifty-three days after*

*F*or a moment I think he might not open the door.
*Probably busy with his family*, I think, almost forgetting it's Christmas.
I knock again.
*If he doesn't answer again, I'll go home.*
Before I can finish my thought, the door swings open. Blake stands on the other side. His hair looks unbrushed, like he just woke up, and a huge green and red sweater hangs off him. His feet have ridiculous Santa printed socks on, and his face couldn't have looked more confused.
"Emma?"
"Hi." I smile, remembering when *he* was the one showing up at my door unannounced.

How quickly things have changed.

"Are you okay? Shouldn't you be home? It's Christmas." His panic grows, and he moves to me quickly.

I stop him in his tracks. "I'm okay." I pause, collecting my thoughts, "But there's something I need to say."

His face grows worried, but I have a feeling deep down he knows what I'm going to say.

"Emma, it's okay. We've already talked about it—"

"No, it's not. You deserve a *real* apology, and a *real* explanation." He stays silent.

I take one of his hands in mine, and hold it tightly. With each word, I rub a circle against his skin.

"You were right," I finally admit. "I *was* hiding it from you, everything that happened with my friends." I bite my lip, searching for the right words. "Meeting you felt like the first good thing to happen to me in a really long time. It was like I got a fresh slate, after feeling like such shit for *so long*. Soon enough I realized you had no idea what happened to either of them, and I wasn't going to be the one to bring it up." I bring his hand to my lips, and gently kiss the top of his hand before continuing.

"After we kissed it was different though, and I should have told you the moment we started getting serious. Because as much as I try to hide it, it *happened*. And it has *forever* changed who I am." For once, my voice doesn't crack through my words. My eyes don't water, and while they may be cold, my hands don't shake.

I look to Blake, giving him time to process my words fully.

He smiles. A real, genuine smile that makes his cheeks turn rosy.

"Do you think you could come inside?" he asks.

"Yeah, of course." He doesn't drop my hand, but holds it even tighter as he leads me inside.

From the large glass window in his house, I can spot the rest of his family outside by a fire. A group of adults drinking coffee, and kids playing tag, despite the cold. I follow Blake into a large room by the kitchen, filled with couches and throw pillows. Freshly torn-apart wrapping paper covers the floor, and large opened boxes lay stacked atop one another.

"Sorry, it's a bit of a mess," he tells me, and I give him a smile.

"Don't be, I wish my Christmas morning looked this fun," I tease back.

We take a seat on a long white couch. As if our bodies were meant to fit together, his arm wraps around me, and pulls me in tight. "Thank you for saying all that, Em."

I curl my head deeper into his shoulder, until I'm practically laying against him. "Of course."

I close my eyes and listen to his breathing. With enough concentration I'm sure I could get mine to match his.

I lay and wonder if this was how Missy and Anna felt for each other. Like every bone in their body was pulled toward one another, as if every crevice in their brain was meant to be for the other.

Or was it all too short for them to even stop to think. I think Anna and Missy fell in love a long time ago. Long before I knew it, and long before they did.

"I got you something." My thoughts are pulled back to the present, as I feel Blake move from under me.

My eyes begin to widen. "Oh Blake, you didn't have to do that," I tell him, as he hands me a small wrapped box. Carefully I begin to unwrap it, trying my hardest not to mess up the wrapping paper, even though I know it will soon be thrown away. I tear it away to reveal a small black box, no bigger than my palm. I look to Blake, searching for his approval to continue. Despite him having handed me the gift, something inside me still isn't convinced this is happening.

"C'mon, open it," he teases, before leaving a kiss on my cheek.

I open the box to reveal a thin silver chain, at the end of it a silver heart.

"It's beautiful—" I begin.

"Open the heart," he tells me, and looking closer I see the heart is also a locket. With some help from my nails, I peel open the locket, revealing two open sides. One half Blake filled with a tiny, printed version of the two of us. A selfie we took one of our first times hanging out. Big, goofy smiles fixed on our faces, and pizza in hand. It makes my heart feel warm just looking at it. My eyes wander to the other half. I almost stop dead in my tracks when I see it.

Not another photo of Blake and I.

A photo of Anna, Missy, and me.

The photo can't be over a year old. Our faces look mid-laugh, Anna's eyes crinkling the same way they did everytime she smiled, and Missy's cheeks bright red. I stood between them, my arms wrapped around them tightly.

*I wish I had never let go.*

"I hope it's not too much. I found the photo on—"

"It's perfect. Really, I *love* it."

Without another word, he helps me put it on. Pushing my hair to one side, he clasps each end together.

"It looks great on you," he tells me. I smile, and my hand reaches for the locket. I hold it against my chest, and vow to never let go of the memories of them.

I lay back against him, my body sinking into his until I can't tell where my body stops and his starts. His hand caresses my face, tracing circles as if he's tracing its outline.

My hand stays clutching the locket, even as my eyes begin to droop. My vision slowly goes in and out, and I stare off into his backyard. I see the glow of the fire light up the faces of laughing kids.

I take in a deep breath, and when I exhale I don't feel my mind race. It stays still, like a boat floating back to the shore.

And for once I think, I'm *going to be okay.*

# 68

## Anna
### May 2nd, 2017

*E*mma's right.

I can't keep putting this off any longer, it's only making my heart ache more and more.

Sitting in class today, I've never felt further from Missy even when we were only inches apart. How badly I wanted to reach out to her, to grab her hand and run away from everything. The love I have for her makes my heart burn trying to keep myself from talking to her.

It consumes my every being.

Yet somehow I can't find the words to tell her.

I know what I have to do, my mind races with everything I *need* to tell her.

## MIA MANDALA | *Dear Anna,*

I scramble to find a pen and paper. I search through my desk drawers, and in between my backpack pockets. Once I do, I sit myself down gently at my desk.

I pull out the pen and begin to write.

*Dear Missy,*
*Where to begin ...*

# THE END

MIA MANDALA | *Dear Anna,*

If you or someone you know is having thoughts of harming yourself, call or text the Suicide Prevention Lifeline at 988 or reach out through chat by visiting 988lifeline.org/chat

# MIA MANDALA | *Dear Anna,*

Photo credits: Paloma Schiavone

Mia Mandala is a teen author based in Miami, Florida. From a young age she has shared a passion for writing and theatre and plans to pursue both of them. She loves to spend time with her friends, and working on articles for online magazines. Mia dreams to one day write and direct her own play, and to continue publishing her books. You can find her online at @mia_mandalawrites on Instagram and TikTok.

Made in the USA
Columbia, SC
12 July 2025